UNPLEASANT TALES

by

Brendan Connell

Unpleasant Tales
by Brendan Connell

Cover Art by David Rix

Publication Date: July 2010
Second Edition Publication Date: August 2015

All text copyright 2015 Brendan Connell.
Art, layout and design copyright 2015 David Rix

ISBN: 978-0-9562147-3-7

Some of the stories in this volume originally appeared elsewhere, as is noted in the following list:

The Maker of Fine Instruments was originally published in *Strange Tales* (Tartarus Press, 2003)

The Black Tiger was originally published in *Succour Magazine* (2008)

The Putrimaniac was originally published in *Dark Horizons* (2009)

A Dish of Spouse was originally published in *The Earwig Flesh Factory* (2000)

The Girl of Wax was originally published in a French translation in *Le Calepin Jaune* (2008)

The Tongue was originally published in *Polyphony 5* (Wheatland Press, 2005)

The Skin Collector was originally published in *Tabu* (2000)

Mesh of Veins was originally published in *Redsine 7* (Cosmos Books 2002)

The Flatterer was originally published in *The Dream Zone* (2002)

The last Mermaid was originally published in a French translation in *Le Calepin Jaune* (2007), and first appeared in English in *Cern Zoo* (2009)

The Cruelties of Him was originally published in *Darkness Rising 4, Caresses of Nightmare* (Prime Books, 2002)

Wiggles was originally published in *The Dream Zone* (2001)

The Last of the Burroways was originally published in *Escaping Elsewhere* (2005)

Kullulu was originally published in *A Capella Zoo* (2008)

Sirens was originally published in *Nemonymous* (2003)

Virgin Hearts was originally published in *Koleidotrope* (2008)

We Sleep on a Thousand Waves Beneath the Stars was originally published in *Fast Ships, Black Sails* (Nightshade Books, 2008)

CONTENTS

THE MAKER

OF FINE

INSTRUMENTS

I.

A smile appeared on Willi's lean face. He considered his friend's remark to be absurdly naïve.

"Smile if you want," Kurt continued, "but trust me—you really do need to get out into the world more. You are becoming a hermit."

"When I am playing professional concerts I will be out in the world plenty."

"And when you are in a madhouse?" Kurt asked sarcastically. He looked at Willi's small head crowned with longish brown hair and highlighted by a pair of cerulean eyes set in the two dark, gouged out caverns above his cheeks. "Yes, I could see you going mad. You are the type."

"I won't offer you another beer Kurt, you are intoxicated."

Kurt drained the last drops of bitter fluid from the glass in front of him. "I don't want one here," he said rising to his feet. "I'll get one at the club. . . . Still don't want to come?"

"No, thanks. I really do have to practice."

Kurt twisted his lips in obvious disdain. "Okay," he said, waving his hand. "*Auf Wiedersehen.*"

Willi, when finally alone, opened a fresh bottle of Franziskaner for himself and lost no time in setting to work. He took his cello out of its case, stroked its neck and then, sitting down, proceeded to go over his scales. The bow danced easily over the strings and Willi's somewhat cadaverous face took on a beatific look, not unlike that of a martyred saint. He played well, with clean tones, his fingers going down in such a way as to hide their unequal strength. There were no audible string crossings, and the positions changed so quickly that the difference between a finger placed on the string and a change of position could hardly be felt, so the rows were uniform, nearly perfect in intonation, and without disrupting, extraneous noises. He then went through a number of pieces, Bach's *Cello Suite No. 1 in G Major, Le Petit Âne Blanc* of Ibert, Emanuel Moor's *Prelude Op.123*, sipping on beer the whole while and certainly enjoying himself much more spending his time this way alone than if he had been amongst people at a bar or club.

It grew late; his fingers somewhat clumsy; his eyes began to close as he played. He leaned his instrument against the chair, staggered to the couch and lay down, flicking off the light as he did so. Several hours later (it was still totally dark) he awoke, disoriented, his throat parched. He stumbled to his feet and proceeded to make his way to the kitchen. He tripped and fell, feeling his knee crack through something.

"*Verdammt!*" he cried.

When he got up and turned on the light, he saw his violoncello lying on the floor with a great hole through its belly. Blood rushed to his head and his knees became so weak that he had to lean against the wall. He stared at the wounded instrument, which lay before him like the expiring corpse of some woman with whom he had had a deep and intimate, physical, relationship.

It was a genuine disaster. The cello, an excellent old Eugen Gärtner, had been given to Willi for his eighteenth birthday by his grandparents, who had undoubtedly paid an exorbitant sum for the instrument, it being hardly one of those run-of-the-mill items turned out of the factories by the hundreds or even thousands.

II.

The next day found him on the street, the broken cello in its case. He had not slept at all the night before; he had spent the morning on the telephone, calling everyone he knew for advice on where he might get the instrument repaired. A fellow student whom he very much respected suggested that he might try one Charles Martens, who was described to him as 'a complete eccentric, but certainly the best luthier in Zürich.'

Willi thought it was curious that he had never heard of the man.

"It is not really so curious," his friend had said. "He is one of those maverick geniuses who are more or less hostile to public scrutiny; the last thing in the world he would want is to have a reputation."

The place was a large old structure on a small street called Zollikerstrasse, which Willi reached by taking the tram to Dufourplatz and then walking up a steep path in the rain.

He rang the bell and a minute or two later the sound of a gruff voice came through the door:

"Who is it?"

"A customer!"

"What nature of customer?"

"I am a cellist!"

The door was opened by a rather short, broadchested man, around fifty-five or sixty years of age, a semi-circle of iron grey hair wreathing his bald head. He stared acutely at Willi for a moment, glanced at his cello case and then said:

"Fine. Come in and we can talk."

Willi followed the man inside, through a very dark vestibule and into a large spacious apartment. The place was set up more like the residence of some fin-de-siècle poet than a shop. Beautiful antique furniture was tastefully dispersed. Several valuable quadros hung from the walls—a Hayez, an exquisite Lorenzo Lotto, a rather bizarre painting by Bramantino of the Madonna looking very much like a thuggish male. A prayer rug from Ladakh sat in the centre of the room. A beautiful English spinet was set against one wall, an extremely antique looking oboe mounted above it, next to which protruded the head of a reindeer stag, a magnificent twenty-pointer. A stuffed quail and a mole sat atop a fifteenth century Florentine armadio; while on a pedestal of its own was a kingfisher. There was an odd but not unpleasant aroma in the room, as if someone had recently been using turpentine and burning joss sticks—a vague fragrance that carried with it something of the opium den, something of the artist's atelier, a touch of the surgical theatre.

"So how can I help you?" Martens asked, sitting down and motioning for his guest to do the same.

Willi sat uneasily on the edge of an extremely extravagant Venetian rococo chair. "I—I was hoping you could repair my cello," he began. "It—it is damaged, and I understand that you are something of an expert."

"Let me see it," the older man said, pointing to the case on the floor.

Willi rose from his seat and, with trembling hands, took out the damaged cello. Martens investigated the instrument briefly (to Willi it seemed in a very cursory manner), and then said in a rather haughty tone, "I don't have time . . . I simply don't have time for these sorts of ordinary repairs. Generally I only repair and restore beautiful Italian instruments, or exotic items, that are either mine or which I'm very interested in. Your cello here simply does not interest me."

"No?"

"No. And, to be frank, I am not really sure if you will find anyone else really able to do the work adequately. It is one thing to repair the body of an instrument, but it is a very different thing, a very difficult thing, to repair its sound. —If this one even ever had a sound worth preserving."

"It has—It *had* a wonderful sound! To me it is absolutely worth preserving. And I will pay for the work."

"You are young. This is probably your first instrument, which is something like a first lover. You cannot bear to let her go. But in the end, should you follow through with your caprice and have it repaired, you will most likely end up with some patched, regraduated, retrofitted old bass-fiddle, a sort of slatternly whore of a cello. —A cigarette?" he offered, opening a case of Egyptians that sat on the little table before him.

Willi abstractedly accepted a cigarette; he inhaled the rich Nilotic smoke, let it surround him like a curling python. This cello was not his first instrument, but it was his first decent one. He certainly loved it, desired it more than the body of any woman he had come in contact with—the young tender-fleshed ones at school, or those he saw on the street, flanks taut in leather trousers or sometimes draped in sheer skirts. To caress breasts and hips, those scrolls of mortal flesh, to look at some pretty woman's face, could never be the same as the touch of spruce, to gaze at its rich ginger-coloured varnish. The body of his violoncello he found much sexier, he far preferred to have held between his knees.

14

Martens drew Willi to some degree out of his abstraction; he asked him about himself, his musical studies and aspirations. Willi at first responded to the questions somewhat sullenly, but soon grew enthusiastic, as it was impossible for him to be otherwise with a subject that concerned him so deeply. They talked until their cigarettes were smoked down to butts and sat crushed in the ashtray.

"Well," the older man said, "you seem to suffer from audiophilia as I very much do myself. Come, I will show you my workshop."

Willi followed him back, along a hall, and into a vast open room with objects ranged thickly on all sides. A great leather apron hung from a hook. On two workbenches were arranged the usual woodworker's tools—chisels, planes, rasps, awls, etc.—and portions of several instruments in various states of repair. He showed Willi beautiful pieces of Brazilian rosewood, grenadilla, and Caribbean mahogany. He had marvelous pieces of elephant ivory, sea-turtle shell and whalebone; exotic feathers, ungulate horns, coral; and certain reptile and mammal skins used for drum and chordophone membranes.

Instruments were everywhere: English horns, sitars, clarinets, bassoons, a few pianos, trombones, bells, drums, gongs, a balalaika, a glockenspiel—even a Jewish ram's-horn trumpet called a shofar. Dismantled pieces of some huge old organ, the kind found only in the grandest churches, sat dusty in one corner.

Willi looked around with interest. He examined a ngombi, a bow-harp used by the Bakalai tribe of West Africa, constructed of thin wood covered with gazelle-skin; it had eight strings made of dried tree roots; its head was apparently the skull of a human, or possibly an ape, a bizarre and misshapen cranium with bulging glass eyes. . . . Then there was a pair of antique Indian cymbals in massive beaten bronze. . . . And a meijiwiz, a double idioglott reedpipe from Old Palestine made from the wing-bones of an eagle and exquisitely decorated around its finger-holes with concentric circles and insect motifs.

Willi gazed at all this with increasing interest, now examining one item, now another. He tested the tone of a variety of Egyptian violoncello called a kemangeh-a'gouz, tried to make out the inscription on a set of panpipes from the Solomon Islands, caressed the nipple of a Javanese gamelan gong.

"And what is this?" he asked, pointing to an object which hung from the wall, the white and graceful neck of a swan, its open-billed head crowning one end.

"That, my young friend, is a swan's horn," Martens replied, with an obvious note of pride. "It is my own invention—one I made keeping in mind only the most hardened laws of science."

"Is it real?—I mean, it really does look like an actual swan!"

"It is an actual swan. The head and neck and a bit of the breast of an actual swan, preserved, even somewhat beautified, with glass-like enamel." He reached up and took it down from the wall. "The unusual conformation of the wind pipe, or vocal chord, of the bird makes it ideal to be transformed into a horn. These properties were first observed by Aldrovandus, though, due to today's rather lame level of education I cannot expect you to have heard of the man. In any case, the length of the swan's neck far exceeds that of its gullet. It has also in its chest a sinuous revolution; that is, when wind rises from its lungs, it ascends not directly into the throat, but first descends into the capsulary receptacle of the breast bone; by a serpentine recurvation it ascends again into the neck; and so by the length thereof a musical modulation is effected. As you can see, I have had to add a few accoutrements, but what I have added does for the most part follow the birds natural structure, though my creation here is of course better formed for music."

So saying, he put his lips to a mouthpiece fitted to the lower end of the object and began to play. The sound was incredibly strange, superbly sweet. Martens stood with his legs slightly apart, eyes closed, a look of supreme concentration on his face as he blew forth wind into the outlandish instrument he had created. Music filled the room, issued from the bill of that long-necked water-bird, almost melancholic, thoroughly mystical, great cries of angst interwoven with splinters of pitch, exceedingly sharp, as precious as diamonds. Feathery high notes flew up, seemed to melt in the air, were suddenly juxtaposed with resonating bass, klaxons of most thrilling, almost impudent flourish. The hair on the back of Willi's neck stood on end. He felt as if transported into some crepuscular place, a region where things might happen outside the physical laws of the universe. The complex orgy of intonations that poured forth from that twisted white neck thoroughly affected his nature, one which was rather absurdly sensitive to the grace of fine music.

"As you can see," Martens said when he had finished, "it is not your run-of-the-mill wind instrument, but a rare item reserved for the true epicure of melody." He twisted his lips into something resembling a smile. "Of course the 'swan's horn' is not your instrument; you are a player of the cello. . . . You might look at this piece here, it is quite decent, certainly better than the item you brought in for repair."

Willi looked at the cello Martens had produced, though in his abstracted state he knew not from where. The instrument was a beautiful 1701 Stradivari with a two-piece back of maple of medium curl, ascending from the joint. The ribs and scroll were also of maple; the table of an even, medium-grained spruce gently arched overall, with a slight dip at the edge. The varnish was a very handsome reddish-gold. The bow was of striped pernambuco, polished a golden brown, with a pronounced chamfer and an emphatic nose, lined with ebony and with an inlaid face of plain grey pearl. The cello was perfectly in tune, and had obviously been played only a short time before.

"Don't just dabble with the strings, let me hear something!" Martens demanded.

Willi, though unaccountably nervous, proceeded to play a piece by Luigi Boccherini. The instrument itself was precious, delivering a peculiar nectarine-like sound which had the solidity of stone, a rich, powerful bass, yet was full of light and air in its vibrant upper register. Feeling the fine tool respond easily to his touch, the young man was inspired, forgot his discomfort, and executed the piece exceptionally well.

"You play not at all badly," Martens said, though neither his face nor voice betrayed enthusiasm. "Your tone is clean and even and, though I would certainly not call your phrasing impeccable, it is quite decent for a tyro. My opinion is that you hold promise."

"If one day I could play half so well as Rostropovich or Yo-Yo Ma, I would be more than content."

"Rostropovich and Yo-Yo Ma!" Martens growled, showing his teeth. "You might at least have said Feuermann or Casals. But Rostropovich and Yo-Yo Ma! And you speak their names in those hushed, respectful tones, as if they were heroes! They are mediocrities—mere mediocrities—scum an ambitious schoolboy like yourself should easily be able to surpass."

Willi held his breath. He hardly believed what he was hearing. The man before him, though he undoubtedly knew music quite well, was also most certainly a bit of a madman. To insult Yo-Yo Ma and Mstislav Rostropovich, two of the world's greatest virtuosi of the cello! If that was not raging madness Willi did not know what was.

Martens looked at the young man with piercing eyes. "Do you think I am a fool?" he asked.

"I never said anything of the kind!" Willi protested.

"A face like yours is easy enough to read. —Here, give me that instrument!"

So saying he literally yanked the cello out of Willi's hands. A moment later the older man was seated on the edge of a work bench, the cello between his knees, the bow flying over the strings. He played Popper's *Spinning Song*. The lightness of his cross-string bowing at the top of the instrument was genuinely awe-inspiring; his technique was wonderfully fluid, near to arrogant. The man exuded the supreme knowledge and blunt confidence of a master. His style was lean and brilliant; his tone like a ribbon of spun gold. Notes were paraded forth in astonishingly quick succession, yet each one was endowed with an amazing degree of clarity, as distinct and expressive as human speech.

When Martens had finished, Willi stood silent. He really did not know what to say—he had certainly never seen playing of this calibre before, playing so sharp it could very nearly be termed dangerous—and he was in something of a state of shock, as a man might be who takes hold of a rope and suddenly realises it is a viper.

"Your playing is . . ." he murmured, without finishing the sentence.

"My playing is good," Martens said. "It is quite good—actually marvellous—certainly better than those heroes of yours. The only man who ever played the *Spinning Song* as well as myself was Arnold Földesy, Popper's pupil."

"I have recordings of him at home."

"Then, if the mechanism of your ears is in order, you can see that my views are not so extravagant."

"Then your own recordings . . ."

"I have none."

"But . . ."

"Young man, one truly interested in the musical arts has better things to do than imprint their genius on circles of vinyl, or little digital disks, so the parade of maggots that inhabit this earth can have their ears massaged while they go about their mundane little tasks!"

Willi was solemnly silent for a moment; humbled. "Your cello is wonderful," he said, "but I am sure I could not afford to buy it. . . . So, I suppose I should not take up any more of your time."

Martens gave a short laugh. "You shall take up more of my time; I can see quite clearly that that is your destiny. —Come back tomorrow, at two in the afternoon, and I will give you a few pointers on your playing. A lesson. You are obviously in sore need of a bit of proper instruction."

"Tomorrow?"

"Yes. And here, put away this violoncello and take it with you. I desire that you practice on it tonight."

"But—But don't you need it?"

"Need it? Look around you. Does it seem that I lack instruments? —Besides, this is just a loan, for a few weeks, or months, maybe more, I don't know—it all depends on your comportment."

Willi left the place with his head almost whirling. He could not believe the instrument he had in his hands. The whole thing seemed a little surreal. He could not really say that he liked Martens, but he certainly was attracted by him. The man's haughty fervour was undoubtedly not unlike that of other great musicians and composers of the past—like Gluck—like Beethoven—like Schönberg who would smilingly bow to the sounds of ignorant hisses as if he were being applauded.

III.

Willi began to take frequent lessons from Martens, who was a demanding, often even aggressive teacher. Occasionally he hit the student with his bow. Sometimes he burst out into peals of grating laughter at Willi's efforts.

Yet the young man was thoroughly content. It seemed to him that he was passing through a barrier, finally learning the subtle secrets of music that had long escaped him while studying under normal teachers. Martens, with his air of authority and genius, his assertive excellence in any instrument he approached, made all others seem like slothful fools in comparison. He was a true artist, shaping his phrases like clay on a potter's wheel, decorating them with a delicacy of touch equal to the Greek vase painter Exekias, giving them as much firm grace as the sculptures of Lysippos.

Willi asked Martens innumerable questions, and could never get enough of the man's words, which seemed to fall from his lips like those precious silvery and bluish-white formations found inside the shells of oysters. In somewhat vague terms the older man described his life. . . . He had been born in a small town outside of Heidelberg. His father had been a taxidermist and, though he never had any intention to follow that trade, he was always quite fascinated by the art, of which he learned a great deal, helping in the workshop with the stuffing and mounting of all sorts of animals and heads. . . . He received his musical tastes from his mother, for whom the violin was a religion and the works of Mozart and Beethoven, Handel and Haydn, were treated as holy scriptures. She began teaching him the violin at the age of six, and by the age of nine he was also playing the cello and piano. Though his father had him en route for a medical career, his mother convinced the man to let Martens spend his summers alternately in Italy, Amsterdam and France to learn the art of the luthier, for which she had a high respect, and considered it good insurance in case the medical career should not work out. . . . He apprenticed, interned, and was tutored and coached in some of the most revered workshops and ateliers in the world: Ansaldo Poggi in Bologna, Max Möller in Amsterdam, Jean-Jacques Pages in Mirecourt. Meanwhile he practised vigorously, not only on the cello, violin and piano, but on any instrument he could lay his hands on. He had been a child prodigy of sorts, and at the age of sixteen, after being heard by a certain prominent musician, received an invitation to be one of the leading cellists in the Court Orchestra in Mannheim. His father, thinking music a frivolous profession, certainly in comparison to that of physician, had him refuse the offer. . . . Angry, he concentrated more than ever on secret practice, and on the construction of his own instruments, letting his invention have free reign. . . . And then, in the early 60's, just when he was graduating from medical school, and achieving a kind of clandestine renown for his playing, he won the Kassel Gold Medal for the sound of his asymmetrical viola. . . . He became a surgeon and, for a period was apparently much respected. Then there was some sort of debacle, which he glossed over with a few sour words. . . . And Martens from that point on devoted himself full time to a musical career, to dealing in and making fine and unusual instruments and occasionally giving lessons.

He was something of the ideal interpreter, being fully capable of grasping the period, style, taste, and intention of all compositions which he played. He showed Willi much about the necessary relaxation of certain muscles and tendons and at the same time the stretching of others, the balancing of burden to make the most of the physical equipment, the distribution of weight on the bow, the determination of fingering, of crescendo and decrescendo, accelerando and ritardando, of feeling for form.

And gradually the student was shown things, the things Martens valued highly, his most treasured instruments, both those he collected and the items he himself had made. Several back rooms on the ground floor were set up like those of a museum, with everything arranged tidily, many of the smaller objects set in cases. There was a six-key bassoon of the Jeanet school, as well as a fine square piano by Erard Frères. With unsuppressed excitement Martens showed Willi a unique proto-type saxello by the H.N. White Co., and then his collection of exotic instruments which included many strange and valuable pieces. There was a slit drum from the Camaroons, a huge log drum, hollowed out from a massive trunk of black-brown hardwood, and then a rather gruesome specimen, a human thigh-bone trumpet from Tibet, a portion of the bone sawn cleanly through to form embouchure; a rudimentary bell was fashioned by two holes perforated at the knuckle end, and covered by a close-fitting membrane neatly sewn along two seams; the article was painted maroon. . . . Along with all this were the instruments Martens himself had designed and made: a wind instrument he had created from the cured proboscis of an African elephant—a giant blackened S-shaped tube, one end fitted with a mouth piece made from an ivory tusk—and another from the neck of a giraffe.

There was a drum he had made from a camel's hump, and a kind of dulali, a nose flute, he had constructed from a marmot, a funny little item which, when played, sounded not unlike the frail weeping of a human child.

Martens showed Willi a kind of musical box, or rather pouch, made from a gopher, as well as a shepherd's shawm constructed, in part, from the entire body of a duck-billed platypus, and then a most curious stringed instrument made from an Australian bat, a delicate miniature harp which he claimed sounded especially charming when played in the stillness of an evening.

"What in the world is that?" Willi cried, pointing to an intimidating and coarse mass of fur, sharply divided horizontally in two contrasting colours, the top half made up of a broad head with a short and square muzzle, upper neck, and back being silvery-grey whilst the limbs, belly, lower cheeks and muzzle were jet black.

Martens picked the object up and turned it in his hands. "This is my redefinition of a honey-badger, a *Mellivora capensis,*" he said. "It is a large mustelid which I have taken the liberty of converting into a most rare melodic apparatus. Notice the bottom end of the belly, where it widens, enclosing a decorative serpentine panel of mammoth ivory and baleen. And the strings, see how they pass through this moveable piece of bone, which is quite simply the creature's femur,—it is used for altering pitch, very much like a capotasto."

"But who in God's name would want such a thing?"

"The Crown Prince of Kuwait for one. He purchased a piece from me very similar to this some years back—the only other one in existence—and he did pay a pretty sum for it. He was a staple customer of mine for a rather extended period of time—until he altogether quit collecting."

"I never knew that such strange instruments existed," Willi said. "Some of these are truly fantastical."

"Oh—one can make musical instruments out of all sorts of things. The ancients were much more flexible than us moderns and had not such a narrow range. These days however people are hardly interested in music as an art, how much less so the manufacture of the fine apparatuses necessary to produce it as it properly should be. . . . When I was younger, and living in Munich, I made a great drum out of a hippopotamus. The large, thick-skinned African river animal filled an entire side of my studio. In the morning I would beat it, that great piece of parchment, and make the hemisphere within resound most beautifully. But oh, how the neighbours complained!"

IV.

Willi kept his appointments with Martens religiously. There was no question that the man, aside from being a truly great musician himself—certainly the greatest that Willi had ever met—was also endowed with the qualities of a great teacher. He made Willi feel thoroughly dissatisfied with himself, and this in turn made the young man focus all the more, striving after that ideal of which Martens was continually talking, that perfection which he indicated as only accessible to a few select souls.

"If you listen to me," Martens said, "and if you are a truly obedient student, one day you might make music the like of which the world has never heard before—music approximating the collisions of planets and suns, of universes belching out new galaxies where the last tonal frontiers are left behind as sounds issue from you like clusters of stars! There is an alchemy to all this, an alchemy of mind and flesh!"

These words were spoken on the sixth week of their acquaintance. Four days later, after the older man had given Willi some valuable hints on the placement of the bow between the bridge and fingerboard, he asked:

"Would you like to see something of interest?"

Willi said that he would. Martens led his student into a set of chambers on the second floor that he had never been in before.

"I do not even allow the cleaning woman in here," Martens said as he unlocked a door. "This is where my most precious instruments are kept—it is where I conduct the more brilliant of my musical experiments."

Willi became very grave as he followed his teacher. He felt as if he were entering a religious sanctuary and was about to be initiated into the rights of some sort of peculiar cult by its high priest.

The first room they walked through was completely bare. Not a single picture decorated the walls. Not a single rug or piece of furniture sat on the parquet floor over which their footsteps echoed. They entered a second chamber, a room that was almost completely dark, the windows being covered with thick red drapes. Martens flicked a switch and the place became flooded with a soft and powerful luminosity, like that in the workroom of a dentist. One wall was neatly lined with bows and various other utensils, tools of all sorts, scalpels and odd shaped pieces of steel that, while being obviously antique, veritably had the appearance of abstract sculpture, the whole array clean and glittering like jewellery. Toward the back of the room was a great blue curtain that hung from a single rod stretching from wall to wall.

"This is where I give my private concerts," Martens said with a wry smile.

Willi stood silent and anxiously ran his tongue over the texture of his teeth. He thought he heard a faint noise, issuing from behind the curtain.

"Is someone back there?" he asked with unease.

"Not someone," the maestro replied approaching the curtain and pulling it aside. "Not someone, but objects material, articles whose nature should be clear to you from their context." He took a step back and stood with his posterior towards Willi, the surface of his body from there to his neck arched, triumphantly, dramatic, like Caspar David Friedrich's *Wanderer above the Sea of Fog*. "What is it you see? What is it you think you see?"

"I don't know."

Willi perceived several sets of eyes, blinking, staring from behind a framework of metal drawn out into threads. Odd things were there, things which he could almost guess at, but did not dare, because they were animate. Martens stood erect, dominant, like some deity or giant, some being to be worshipped as having control over life-forms and mystical spheres.

"Every item of nature is endowed with its own individual voice. Imagine the infinite songs of the cosmos, of the force controlling all phenomena of the physical world—no more human voices—the cosmos is not especially human—it is often quite as savage as chaos!"

He opened the door of one of the mesh cages and the next moment a great band of distorted flesh rested in his arms.

Willi involuntarily retreated a step.

"You need not be afraid of her," Martens said coolly. "She is quite harmless, very nearly domesticated. Thoroughly de-toothed and de-clawed and simply waiting for skilled hands to caress her strings. You still hesitate? Watch!"

He snatched a great bow from the wall, hooked his foot around the leg of a chair, pulled it towards him, sat down and leaned the strange living apparatus up against one knee. The creature's eyes darted fitfully around the room, thoroughly pathetic. Then the bow touched those fibres which stretched across the gut of that wild dog-like animal, the bweha, *Canis adustus*, that poor scavenger plucked from the savannahs, from its mother's teat for most outlandish musical experiments—the bow touched those fibres, danced over them, rending forth sounds thoroughly peculiar, a piece of music that could very well have been composed in the murky world of the intermediate state. The tone was large, ripe and breathy; grave and patently troubling. The eerie melody seemed as ridges of water curling over, crashing on the remote and desolate shores of the underworld; as clouds of *Fledermäuse*, wings beating, might swirl rapturously upward to feed on other clouds of gnats; a strange, spooky piece it was, intoxicating as opium, violent as a homicide. Dismally dark passages collided with stormy orgasms of sound as Martens ran his fingers over the strings, slashed away with the bow as if he were decapitating some host of helpless enemies; now stabbed solemnly, as if he were sinking it in the breast of a betrayer.

"The ancient Egyptians," he said in a sonorous voice, spacing his words out like a poem. "The ancient Egyptians . . . those most mysterious . . . most brilliant . . . dwellers of the past . . . believed a jackal-headed god . . . Anubis . . . guided the dead . . . to those who judged their souls."

Here his thumb and forefinger pinched the creature violently around the neck. It let out a siren-like wail, something like that of a mad woman as she wrenches the hair from her head; the sound of delicate china shattering into a thousand luminous fragments; a welter of tonalities to make ears bleed, eyes water and the blood go sour in one's veins. . . . And then the tempo changed, became more rapid, the music described a wild chase through a phonically dangerous fairyland; every note sounded with immense importance, as if thousands of lives, destinies rested on the power of Martens' bow, the tips of his dextrous fingers. And then a final disarming breath of lyrical innocence, artfully superficial, imbued with a complete and obvious lack of candour, a sweet but deceitful ambrosia, a strange and concluding strain tempting the listener to balance, to frolic on the lips of this modest melodious nepenthes, this musical monkey cup, only to fall inside and be consumed by its digestive enzymes.

Martens was finished; his eyes glowed, radiant as from some inner inferno.

Willi was shaken to his soul; he remained rooted to the spot, lips parted.

"So you enjoyed it?" Martens asked.

"In,"—Willi's voice cracked—"Yes—in a shocking sort of way."

"Shocking? One of the functions of great music is to shock!"

"But this animal. . . . The cruelty!"

"Cruelty?" the maestro cried, his face growing red. "Did I invite you into my inner sanctum to hear such banalities? I am not some kind of simpleton who makes mice sing by hitting them on the head with a mallet; I am an artist, a man who practices his talent with both skill and good taste. . . . I see you quiver. You think that you know what good taste is, but you do not, you know very nearly nothing, young whelp!" A swollen vein appeared on Martens' forehead. He continued, angry, excited: "You have your choice between being an artist and some kind of worm or insect; you can either reach the stars, or creep on the ground like some gnawing worm my foot should crush!"

Willi felt his head begin to swim. His vision became blurry; he felt humiliated, sickened—upset with Martens, but even more upset with himself, for his own inadequacy. He turned towards the door.

"If you wish to leave, then please do so," Martens said coldly. "I will not stop you. You might return when you feel able to humble yourself, when you feel able to see and hear great things, feel capable of taking instruction."

V.

When Willi reached his own apartment on Eidmattstrasse he could not relax, practice or sit still. His mind was full of the fantastic, of the strange things he had seen and heard, of Martens. There was something so mysteriously exciting about this man, so utterly magnetic. To be pushed out of his presence made Willi feel horribly depressed. He lit a cigarette, took a puff, extinguished it in the ashtray and walked out the door and down the stairs.

Outside it was overcast, late in the afternoon, early in the evening; dark grey clouds smirched the sky; men and women walked with umbrellas. He shambled along the street, oblivious to all around him, his small head sunk to his chest and eyes fastened on the ground. The one thing that was clear was that he had to make a decision. Martens frightened him, but the man also enthralled. Willi wanted very much to learn from him, to be his disciple—but he was uncertain what it would cost, for there was something about the maestro that was unaccountably dark, possibly dangerous, and Willi felt that he was very nearly dug in so deep that he would never be able to withdraw.

He passed the Grossmünster cathedral, with its great dual towers, and then the elegant neo-gothic Fraumünster on Stadhausquai. He walked along the Bahnhofstrasse, and without really thinking what he was doing, entered the Carlton Bar, a place he would normally never go—even if he was up for venturing out into the world. Severe bankers sipped glasses of beer and knots of younger people chatted around tables over cigarettes and coffee. An old man with a great white moustache sat in one corner reading a newspaper; two young women talked with animation over effervescent glasses of mineral water. There was the gentle hum and clatter of civilisation.

Willi sat down at an empty table by the window and ordered a small lager. He took a sip and stared blankly at the table in front of him.

In his mind he still saw those fitful eyes, that wild-dog-like apparatus, and heard its cadences. It was a monstrosity, yet he could not deny that he was enriched for having heard it. The making of such a device was certainly a great accomplishment, yet could he trust to put himself in the hands of the maker?

"So you have ventured out into the world at last!"

Willi looked up. It was Kurt, standing over him, the features of his face touched, ever so slightly warped, with subtle sarcasm.

"I was passing by and saw your face in the window," his friend continued. "At first I thought it couldn't be you."

"It's me. I am drinking a lager."

"Perfect. Then you can buy me one as well."

Kurt sat down and lit a cigarette, exhaling two jets of bluish smoke through flaring nostrils. The waitress came and he ordered a tall lager, 33cl, staring hungrily at the young woman's chest as he spoke. He was a young man self-indulgent in regard to drink, food and sexual enjoyment.

"So," he said, when his beer had arrived and he had wet his lips, "you are taking the day off from practice for once?"

Willi shrugged his shoulders and took a swallow of his own beer.

Kurt laughed shortly. "My God!" he said. "You look even more depressed than usual. So, maybe you have finally lost your mind, just like I said!"

"And you?"

"Me! I am doing what any man under the age of thirty should—looking at the young ladies, drinking, enjoying myself. Even if you are mad you surely know what I mean. That is what sitting here and paying six francs for a beer is all about anyhow, isn't it—to be in the company of humans? . . . Come, drink up; we will go to the Oliver Twist—the women are more in our category there."

"No, I can't," Willi said getting up from his seat, though his glass was still half-full. "I—I have an appointment. Sorry, goodbye."

Without waiting for a reply he rushed up to the counter, paid for the drinks and exited the bar. It was nearly dark outside. He strode towards the lake, Kurt's commonplace words still crawling in his ears. Young ladies, drinking, enjoying oneself—these were surely the occupations of the non-entity. Such a creature truly was an insect in comparison to the sublime Martens.

He passed the Kongresshaus, the concert hall which had been officially opened by Johannes Brahms over a hundred years earlier, and in which Willi himself had sat countless times, then crossed the busy General Guisan-Quai and veered right, towards the Arboretum. It was dark; a small scrap of white paper lay in his path and he picked it up; it was just a shred, but to him it appeared to be in the exact shape of a bass violin. He turned to his left, to the lake which was like a great sheet of glass, the lights of the city reflected in it in long, golden strips that shimmered. He looked into that other, even colder world which sat stretched before him aloof and lugubrious, a world where one needed gills to survive, and fins to move about. And then circles began to grow out of the water, to ripplingly expand. Willi felt the drops upon the skin of his face; one splashed against his hand; he lit a cigarette, turned and walked rapidly away.

"Between the two evils," he thought, "Martens is the lesser—or maybe I should really say the *greater*. If he is evil, at least he is great in his wickedness. Kurt is simply sordid. To lead such a commonplace, physical life as his would make me miserable. It would be impossible; it is much too late for me to turn back."

He walked through the town; people still crowded the main streets, and he dextrously avoided the many prongs of their prehensile umbrellas, some red as blood, others black as tar. He looked at their faces and felt contemptuous pity—for these mortals seemed very stupid to him. He now walked with determined, long strides, his eyes keen and head uplifted. Back at the apartment he practised vigorously, until past two in the morning.

VI.

Willi returned to Martens, thoroughly repentant, thoroughly humbled. He offered his most sincere apologies for his lack of insight, and the teacher haughtily accepted them.

"If you listen to me, follow my every advice, you will one day play like a god. As it is, when I listen to you, I feel as if you were trying to chip frozen notes out of blocks of ice. There is no personality, no individuality; you treat the instrument as an object separate from yourself; you really need to be one with it, your every fibre attuned to that other scene of existence, that of the clef, the minim, quavers, bars and slurs—a parallel universe to that of ordinary man, a universe of most pure mathematical equation, where countless births and deaths happen with the stroke of a bow. —But sometimes I think that maybe you lack sincerity, maybe you do not really care for the music as I do."

"I am prepared to do whatever it takes to be a great player," Willi said with feeling. "Show me the path, and I will follow!"

"Ah, if you only meant it! —You could be far greater than I, if you were only devoted, if you were only able to make the necessary sacrifices. . . . My own aspirations have always been put in check, because of my inability to treat myself as an object. The seer cannot pretend to be the unattached seen. Yet an object is what I sorely need—a human being, a young fellow like yourself to mould."

"But that is what I am here for—to be moulded!"

The disgust Willi initially felt for the strange living instruments of Martens was reversed into a dynamic enthusiasm. He investigated these creatures with interest. There was an instrument made from a living vulture, stripped of feathers, its body covered with a marquetry of ivory and abalone shell, soundholes short and perfunctory hollowed from its chest-cavity, a remarkable piece which, to play, required iron-clad control. . . . Then there was a deer with three legs severed from its body, and the fourth, the right hind, left in place with the meat between the skin and bone extracted, disintegrated with a delicate application of diluted hydrochloric acid; and then the hard substance, that *osso*, hollowed out into a pipe; a musical instrument to be played by blowing in at one end while the wind was directed through the animal's hind quarters and croup, along its back and withers, and then out its mouth, into which a bell was fastened.

Willi himself began to enjoy strumming on a cat, that small, domestic animal shaved of fur and turned into a kind of thumb piano, its back fitted with seven iron tongues decorated with bronze studs at both ends with iron and brass fittings, a portion of its body skilfully hollowed out, yet without mortal consequence, without destroying the inner workings of the organs, a pretty zigzag pattern incised on the creature's flesh; an instrument expertly made, with a sonorous tone.

And then there was a little pot-bellied pig turned into a strange, very distinctive type of zampogna, or bagpipe, tassellated and partially covered in green baize; with three of its limbs acting as pipes, one having five square flap-keys, one with four square flap-keys, one regulator; the mounts in gorgeous silver and ivory. . . . Then a very beautiful specimen, an armadillo, that small burrowing animal of South America, turned into a loaf drum. . . . And a donkey, kept restrained in a shed out back, a true zoophonic masterpiece, the long-eared *Equus asinus* metamorphosed into a virginal which Martens kept tuned one fourth below modern pitch, with keys of boxwood, sharps of ebony, implanted, artfully sunk in the animal from loin to chest; a structurally very sound instrument of extraordinary quality and charm.

Willi's favourite, however, was a flamingo which had been divested of those parts of itself used for walking; its beautiful long neck had been stiffened with strips of pine and then inlaid with a finger-board bearing twenty metal frets; thirteen tuning-pegs were mounted down one side, two large pegs for a pair of *cikari* strings and eleven small pegs for sympathetic strings. It was a gorgeous pink chordophone, graceful in the extreme, with a tone delicate and ornamental as gold filigree. Martens was able to play this with an almost x-ray clarity of articulation and an exceptionally wide range of touch and tone that filled Willi with wonder, and to some degree even envy.

"It is the most beautiful instrument I have ever seen," Willi said.

"Oh, I will make better—you for instance; and then something else for myself."

Willi looked at him inquiringly.

Martens showed him his latest acquisition, the large flightless double-wattled cassowary, *Casuarius casuarius johnsonii*, a colourful creature with a brilliant blue and purple head bearing a kind of keel-shaped helmet, red flesh hanging down from its throat, and a body covered with long black feathers, a mass of thread-like growths, that looked more like coarse hair. The great long-legged brute strutted back and forth along the narrow limitations of the cage, an odd and atrabilious look in its eyes.

"In evolutionary terms," Martens said, "the flightless birds, or ratites, are some of the earliest types to have developed. I am highly interested in this creature's throat, and am quite certain that something really magnificent can be done with it; I will make an instrument the likes of which Ctesibius of Alexandria and Vitruvius would have envied."

VII.

"You of course understand that you will never be the same?"

"I don't want to be the same—I am sick of being the same. You have shown me other worlds, other landscapes, and those are the sorts of places I want to live. I feel that this is the most decisive moment of my life—and I am determined to go forward!"

Martens looked at the young man intently; he lit one of his strong Egyptian cigarettes and proceeded to explain about the first phase:

"Normally the intestines are pulled from the animal immediately after its slaughter, while the gut is still hot. This insures that the blood vessels that run into the casing will be broken off close to the gut wall. To allow the organs to cool is to risk having these veins break off as much as five centimetres away from the casing wall. This creates 'whiskers' that lower the quality of the gut for musical string use, as well as introducing contaminating agents into the muscular membrane. To insure the best quality the gut must be removed immediately, separated from the fat, and put into cool water. Traditionally the string makers were located very close to slaughterhouses, so they could get the guts as hot and fresh as possible. . . . My method is of course a thousand times superior. I do not even have the guts leave their source. By letting them remain, more or less, in their natural setting, I can make strings of truly distinguished excellence . . . instruments thoroughly individual."

"But how will I be able to eat?"

"Oh, you don't need to feel any anxiety regarding that. I am not going to use it in its entirety, just a good bit of the second cut of the intestine, where the muscular fibres are longer, but far less necessary to your anatomy. You will still be able to take foods into the mouth and swallow them. . . . Though of course I would have to recommend you stay away from tough things, red meat and the like. . . . But that is a small sacrifice after all. Soups can be quite nourishing."

"Yes; I have always liked soups."

All the old fashioned equipage appeared,—objects sharp of tooth and edge, a trephine, canulas,—all those outdated tools which served him better than the precision gear of the modern specialist. . . . The air became dense with the smell of carbolic acid and chloroform. An incision was made; Martens immersed Willi's guts, the 'second cut' as he had said, in cold water for several hours to make them pliable, then gave them a nice hot soak for about forty-five minutes before machining; using a metal-bladed scraper he stripped off the outer serosa from the muscle layers, pulling away the long white thread of tissue, while at the same time crushing the inside mucosa membrane, so soft thin and pliable. He worked with vigour until the mucosa was a veritable liquid and could be squeezed down and out the opening he had created in the casing tube. Using a splitting horn, he divided the gut into four ribbons, long, white and beautiful, thoroughly chaste. . . . Continuing his strategy, that of procedure and design, he changed the exterior contours of Willi, gave his back a high and full arch so as to give lateral push to the strings, which ran over the fingerboard of his thorax, and to distribute that push evenly over the plate.

"Done?" Willi murmured, feeling himself drift up from his anaesthetised state.

"Not quite, but we are not too far away. I still have to fit you up—shape the pegs, fingerboard, nut and saddle to match the particular behaviour of your body. . . . That is, of course, after I give you a soul!"

Using a Mennell's patented endo-tracheal apparatus, Martens re-anaesthetised Willi. The maestro felt his creative energy greatly stirred, and determined, while finishing work on his pupil, to begin work on the cassowary. He removed it from its cage, anaesthetised it and, when the creature was fully insensible, dragged it with great effort to a work bench, its weight being a good deal more than he had expected.

Willi's abdomen, divested of some of its interior bulk, was a much changed article; a sound post was inserted to reinforce it on the treble side, to affect the vibrational behaviour of the plates and to counteract the forces acting on it from the strings—and this naturally was to affect the timbre of sound and the playability of Willi considerably. The Italian name for the sound post is '*anima*' or 'soul' because of its changeable influence on the sound of an instrument.

"This is no good at all," Martens said to himself upon examining the quality of his nearly completed work. "The sound post must not be fitting quite properly to the inside surfaces. *Verflixt!* I am going to have to go into him again!"

He turned to his selection of gleaming jewels, blades, and gathered a particularly vicious one into the nimble fingers of his right hand. And then, looking around, he was suddenly confronted by the cassowary. The long legs of the bird whipped up in the air; it thrust them forward, against Martens' chest, and the man was hurled to the floor. It was indeed heavier than he had thought, weighing a good one hundred and forty pounds, far too much for the quantity of anaesthetic he had given it.

"You bastard!" he screamed, and made an attempt to stab at one of the bird's legs with the scalpel in his hand.

The cassowary was obviously frightened, disoriented from the anaesthetic, and angry to begin with. By nature it is a creature easily provoked. The loud human cry, along with a slight prick it received to its leg, made it even more alarmed. It darted its long neck forward; a sixtieth part of a minute later it had the left eyeball of Martens lodged in its sharp beak, having plucked out that organ of sight with a single and swift jerking motion. Martens, enraged and somewhat shocked, called out to Willi, but the young man was still fully anaesthetised and could offer no assistance. The cassowary, having once seen blood, grew tremendously excited and proceeded now to attack in earnest with the sharply pointed nails of its three-toed feet, digging deep into the man's neck with the dagger-like middle claw, which was a good five inches in length and as dangerous as the blade of a stiletto. The carotid artery was ruptured and Martens could do nothing more than gaze on with a single bleary eye while the blood flowed fast and freely from him, with a gurgling sound somewhat reminiscent of the Indian dholak drum when rubbed with certain slight motions of the wrist.

VIII.

It was a beautiful and warm day. The outdoor tables in front of the cafés were practically full. By the lake, wienerschnitzel was sold from open stalls and colourful beds of flowers, of zinnias, scabiosas and daisies touched the air with their perfume. Children played in the streets and rushed down the sidewalks on scooters; young women wore skirts and walked with bare legs.

Kurt had not seen Willi for some time, since the day at the Carlton Bar, and, as he was walking along Eidmattstrasse, decided to drop in and pay him a visit. As he entered the large old building he thought he heard screams, some sort of disturbance coming from above, as if an argument were occurring in one of the flats. A woman with a pinched face drooping with folds of yellowish skin accosted him on his way up. Her eyes were dull and bilious; she opened the grim wound of her mouth and spat out her words:

"You going to see your friend are you—the freak musician up there?"

"If you mean Willi," Kurt replied, "then yes, I am visiting him." He felt very much like insulting this yellow and disgusting creature, speaking a few words that would injure her and show her what a foul thing she was, but he refrained. "What business is it of yours?"

"Oh, he has been up there rocking away pretty much constantly. Playing terrible stuff, much more trying than it used to be. . . . Before I did not mind it so much, but now I feel like I was listening to something nasty—nasty and sinful! . . . If you could tell him to cool it off it would be very much appreciated. If he doesn't, of course I will just have to call the police. Your friend is not the only tenant in the building you know!"

Kurt turned and trudged up the stairs without replying; the woman continued to talk behind him; as her voice receded into the background, the resonance from Willi's apartment became prominent. Kurt stopped at the door and listened, shuddered, bunched his fingers into fists; he felt as if needles were being inserted into his ears, his auditory nerves pierced, as they gathered in those most bizarre accents, a plaintive twanging, like the effects of phrenitis, confused stridor that made him think of brutal torture, of men being whipped with fronds of thorns and couples compelled to sport naked upon beds of shattered glass. In a state of astonishment, he leaned his head forward, so it touched that wooden portal, heard phrases that sobbed, screeched and blasphemed as the belching of demons, and rushing scale passages that carried with them the character of rivers of fire, fast flowing rapids of frothing flame that danced with orange-hot globules and emitted sprays of searing white sparks. Certainly if ever there was a music composed out of the torments of hell, this would be it, the music of the damned soul, of the hungry ghost lost and condemned to wander throughout eternity over dead plains in search of some morsel of food for its great swollen but empty belly; of women plummeting into lakes of pitch, blood and mire and men made to wallow in tubs of gore and filth. This was music rank as the obnoxious odours of an unbearable place of punishment, music without any true melodic or harmonic line, wherein the architecture was destroyed as if with a bomb; music suffused with agony, without even an instant's relief from most excruciating physical and mental pain.

Kurt flung one fist forward and beat against the wood; without waiting for a reply, he gripped the handle and threw the door open.

Willi sat on a wooden chair in the centre of the room, shirtless, wearing nothing but a pair of dark-blue shorts. He strummed away on the thick strings made from his own guts, which were secured below his belly to a ring slotted over a large ivory pin stemming from his single garment. He was a phonocidal maniac, no longer quite human but rather a variety of strange monster, the quasi-quintessential dark fantasy instrument; his back was perforated with charismatically flame-shaped soundholes, his abdomen inlaid with graceful ebony fleur-de-lis and pierced with carved Gothic rosettes, and his neck stretched out grossly, into a kind of cylindrical rod, with four ebony pegs set with lozenges of pearl. Yet the sound he gave forth, soulless, was offensively off-kilter, searing the ears in its shrieking intensity as if living beings were being lowered into pits of boiling fire, hung by their tongues, skewered with white hot irons, made to commit obscene acts with reptilian devils and then tenderised, pounded to pulp with blunt mallets.

Kurt stood transfixed in horror. He felt as if he had just walked, from the clear and joyful light of day, into the casings of a nightmare. Willi appeared stretched, elongated and twisted in some strange, unspeakable fashion, made into an incredible, eccentric creature who might have been plucked from some horrid comic strip—a surreal and frightening being, a gross caricature of humanity spliced with violoncello.

A voice cried from downstairs, the sour, shrieking voice of the yellow woman:

"Enough of this; I am calling the police!"

Kurt turned to his friend and called out his name. But Willi did not stop; he merely looked up with a set of wild, dewy eyes and continued to play, the fingers of his right hand, lithe as snakes, dancing frantically over those strings of his own guts while his left, metamorphosed into a bow, sawed dextrously away, intensifying the galloping serenade of torment. The sound grew horrendous; a belching massacre of stammered and contorted notes; extreme abstraction and violence mixed together, like a frenzied wolf tearing apart a painting by De Kooning with its jaws; a witch's sabbath of distortion and dissonance; like some naked and helpless creature being hounded, harried by pursuing fangs through a forest of living blades.

"Willi!" Kurt shouted. "For God's sake, Willi!"

But the tune in no way faltered; on the contrary, Willi, hearing his own name shouted, responded by becoming more high-octane than ever. There was a blur of frenetic limbs; his lips were open, vacillating, and his teeth bit down sporadically on his blood-leaking tongue.

Kurt, horrified, stepped backward across the threshold, then turned and ran, practically threw himself down the stairs. In panicked speculation he wondered what sort of help was possible for that mad and mutated friend of his, and whether he should fetch a psychiatrist, plastic surgeon or priest—or simply flee from all responsibility, pursued as he was by that mad flurry of painfully exotic notes which were like a swarm of toxic, stinging things.

THE
BLACK
TIGER

It seemed to particularly prefer the tender, milk-fed flesh of the rich. Many a fine citizen, perfumed with essence of gillyflowers and oil of lilies, had been devoured, their bodies dismembered, their bones cracked. But it would not refrain, goaded by hunger, by the need to ensanguine its jowls, from slaughtering the sons of bakers, from feasting on the throats of mat-weavers' wives.

Valerius Etruscus was the governor of Numidia. His palace at Hippo Regius was sumptuous. Elaborate mosaics vied with richly hued frescoes. An imposing statue of Hercules stood in the atrium, the face of which was carved to have a strong resemblance to Valerius himself, who claimed this hero as his ancestor.

He was intrigued by the stories he heard concerning the animal, how it delighted in eating his citizens, and determined to have it captured, thinking he would have it sent back to Rome as a present to Antoninus Pius, to be killed in the coliseum.

Legionnaires and hunters: they went out with nets and spears. Half of the men were eaten, and the rest savaged, bodies furrowed with ghastly wounds. Hands missing, eyes gouged from their sockets. Those survivors re-entered the city, looking like a pile of gristly, cast away meat from a butcher's shop.

"What a brute that creature must be!" Valerius said.

"Well, you govern over a country of wild beasts," his daughter, a delicate-looking beauty, commented.

Her name was Livia. Slim and pale, she never smiled and seemed always to be oppressed by a great sadness. She liked to go alone, to the edge of town, and wander through the olive groves. She was reminiscent of a solitary puff of cloud against a blue sky, a piece of fine glassware balanced on the edge of a sharp blade, a pool of clear water in the midst of the desert in which is reflected the emptiness of one's soul.

When the sun rose, light gushed over the land. Though awake, she did not rise from her bed until almost midday. For lunch she ate figs and drank water stained purple with wine. Afterwards she tried to amuse herself by reading the poetry of Sulpicia and fiddling with her cosmetics.

Then, in the midst of filing her nails, she stood up to leave the walls of the palace.

"Do you need assistance?" a short and ugly slave, a rascal named Tychaeus asked.

"No. I will walk. Through the olive groves. Alone."

He handed the thing to her and murmured some words pertaining to self-defence and then, as she walked away, followed her with his eyes, running a hand through the huge bush of his beard.

Now the day was hot and the blades of sun lent the dust-filled air the appearance of molten gold.

Livia glided through the streets; then to the edge of town. She crossed over a little brook and saw that the reeds which sprang from there were stained with blood and heard the water murmur sadly, a song as desperate as that of murdered kisses.

Presently, she came to the olive grove. Mute trunks reached out from the earth, pallid green leaves were clasped by crooked branches.

She was not startled when she saw it there sleeping, curled up in the shade of the trees. It was huge, with black fur. Its tail was as big around as her arm.

Delicately her feet took her to it.

Alert, it sensed her, lifted its head and then raised its body from the dust. Its eyes, roral gems, were like courage incarnate, and glistened with sharp intelligence.

The tiger approached, inhaled the scent of the silk-tressed virgin. She looked at him boldly and, dazzled by her beauty, he purred.

She knelt before him and offered him her hand. He licked it with his huge tongue, warm and rough to the touch—licked her hand with that tongue which had licked at dead human flesh, lapped up quantities of human blood. It was clear that he was enchanted by the young woman, and with his moist, whiskery nose nudged at the little pyramids of her breast.

"A woman could love you very much," she said.

It purred, stretched out its limbs and showed its claws.

"Ah! But how can I love you? Your claws are so sharp that they will tear me to shreds when you hold me close. Why, you see how I treat mine." And she showed it how she filed her nails.

The beast stretched forth its claws and she, holding them between her dainty fingers, filed the sharp points away.

Blinking his big, soft eyes, he pressed his muzzle to her throat, so she could feel his hot breath.

"But my dear—how can I kiss you," she said coaxingly, "when you have such sharp teeth. I might very well cut my lips in the process! If we are to be coupled together, you must let me do something about this."

The tiger opened its mouth wide, and she, smiling prettily, filed away its sharp teeth.

It rubbed itself against her, rolled before and showed her its belly which she scratched.

Then, removing a dagger from the folds of her peplos, she drove it into the tiger's neck. The animal opened its eyes wide with astonishment as blood gurgled out of its mouth.

Livia, her face distorted with hate, proceeded to slaughter the beast, driving her little tool again and again into it, piercing the rich folds of its skin, tearing through its flesh. Panting, the virgin let her cruelty blossom. Bright red petals spread themselves over her skin; her face became freckled with gore; garments dyed, sprinkled with festive colour.

Finally, she rose and stumbled out of the shade, raising her arms, letting her splayed fingers meet those of the sun. She cried out in a loud and piercing voice, a cry like the mad melody of a fife, summoning the people to see. This music, which drifted to the edge of town, and then through rumour, spread from ear to ear, alerted the lazy populace. Awoken from their midday dreams, they came running. Riding on a tide of murmurs, they approached; seeing the body, jumped around with delight. Then they began to tear it to pieces, scattering its fur to the wind. One woman cut out its tongue, another smashed open its skull with a rock and reached in for a handful of brains, while a third, with fingers like hooks, plucked out its eyes.

The men, elated, savage, ripped wildly at strands of bright pink flesh; galloped, danced with sandaled feet in the disgusting pool of gore.

Tychaeus was among the number, his eyes wide with excitement, blood lust. He approached Livia. He pulled her towards him and sucked her mouth into the depths of his dingy beard.

THE

PUTRIMANIAC

"I don't see him anymore. I can't."

"Can't, or won't?"

"He is repulsive; I find it physically impossible to be in his presence."

"Ex-girlfriends always say those sorts of things."

"No, really, he has changed."

"Another typical remark . . ."

When Millard left the café he walked along the Via Odescalchi, towards the Piazza Duomo. He had been away from Como, where his family had a holiday villa, for over two years and found pleasure in seeing all the familiar places and people—the Torre del Comune, the old city walls, all the beautiful and stylish women, the loud and laconic vegetable sellers at the market, the rich and aged bachelors who walked slowly down the streets, unswerving, with eyes frozen and introverted, like somnambulists.

Alfonso di Leopardi had been one of his best friends. They had had long philosophical discussions together and sat over bottles of old wine until late in the night. Alfonso spoke English fluently; he was extremely knowledgeable in matters of art and literature; and had impeccable taste in clothes, cars, houses and women, compounded with money enough to indulge his tastes. He had always been an odd character, able to eat a pound of Camembert cheese at a sitting, devoted to fringe-chemistry and the study of fungi, a man who found beauty in an extravagantly shaped mushroom or a woolly bit of mould—but Millard would have never considered him repulsive. Alfonso was too good looking, too well mannered, too brilliant for that.

"He is an eccentric, and that frightens women," Millard said to himself as he looked up at the superb Gothic façade of the Duomo and the pair of statues adjoining the main portal—on the left Pliny the Elder, on the right Pliny the Younger, those two brilliant, ancient citizens of Como wrought in marble, their features plastic, more silly than noble, but still certainly carved with a touch of fantastic genius.

49

It was early in the evening, toward the end of September, and the air was warm and pleasant. . . . He walked on, through the Piazza Cavour, until he came to the lake, a serene, gently undulating sheet of water that curved through the steeply descending hills, its banks encrusted with villas. To the right appeared the Tempio Voltiano, that neo-classical monument dedicated to Alessandro Volta, and a short way out the water was cut into by the newly constructed pier. A hydroplane was just taking off and he watched as it rose out of the water and then arced toward Bellagio. His gaze wandered over the mildly dramatic landscape, and then to his right, where he saw the Villa Leopardi, a stroke of yellow and red high up on the hill—certainly one of the best positioned dwellings in Como.

A taxi was driving by and he hailed it. Ten minutes later he was let off at Alfonso's gate. He walked up the path, flanked on either side by huge, man-sized amphoras, arrived at the door and rang the bell. And then, moments later, he was in his friend's strong embrace, had sight of that same healthy smile, those same candid grey eyes he was so familiar with and which he had always found so appealing.

The two men sat in the living room and smoked, looking out the great picture window at the lake below, a vast splash of blackish-blue dotted over with white dabs, boats.

"You have one of the best views on earth here," Millard said, hooking one leg over the next and blowing out a long stream of smoke.

Alfonso pursed his lips, and then, flicking a bit of ash into the soil of a potted plant by his side, replied, "Do you really think so? I have grown to hate this view. Generally I keep the blinds drawn."

"Well, if you are bored of it . . ."

"Bored is an understatement. The calm blue of the water, the dark-green pleasantly surging hills . . . disgust me."

Millard thought of Monica. 'Disgust'—it was the same word she had used to describe Alfonso. Yet he was handsome, virtually unchanged, though an eccentric to be sure.

"I suppose," said Millard, "that men of genius grow bored with things more rapidly than most. Personally though, I find the view quite enchanting. With your good taste, I would think you could tolerate it."

"Because it is pretty?"

"To a high degree."

"You say 'good taste,' . . . 'genius,' . . . but what are these? . . . Pablo Picasso's *Guernica* is atrocious, crude, and yet at the same time so truly noble, inspiring. . . . Vincent van Gough, in his *Night Café*, used the most appalling colours, a hallucinatory blend of pond-scum green, butcher-shop red, and puke brown, but it is a masterpiece of the highest order. Because, when ugliness is taken to the limits, it turns into beauty. This is something uncultivated minds do not realise. Vulgar people delight in the smell of roses, the sight of tawdry watercolours, the unambiguous taste of fresh strawberries or breast of chicken. A truly sophisticated person however turns away from all such things with disdain."

Millard smiled. "A new type of elitism? But you can't seriously tell me . . ."

"Maybe I should explain things. If there is anyone who would understand my present state of mind it is you. . . . Even as a boy I enjoyed the smell of rotting fish; liked the sight of ants ransacking the body of a decaying frog; the poetry of flies as they buzzed around some vile bit of excrement. . . . To me it was all very interesting, that dark, ominously intellectual side of the universe that makes men turn their heads away in ignorant revulsion and unfounded shame, that cause beautiful women to elevate their pert little noses and squeal with apprehension. . . . You remember my love for old cheeses, how fond I have always been of St. Felicien, of Munster, of pungent and spicy Epoisses de Bourgogne, of sharp and citric Bruxelles Kaas. . . ."

"Yes, I recall your fanaticism for odoriferous cheese."

"And mycology, the enthusiasm I have always had for mushrooms, fungi and moulds—odd shaped cones, colourful spheres, popsicle forms, bright yellow fuzz far more beautiful and noble than the most precious lily hybrid or exotic orchid. That xanthic and slimy blob *Physarum polycephalum* . . . or *Aleuria aurantia* which looks like some pink, freshly severed ear lying on the ground . . . *Urnula craterium* with its resemblance to charred and broken eggs . . . and the utterly bizarre *Mycoacia copelandii*, like a hanging fleece of sharp icicles or stalactites."

"But this theory of yours, that ugly old rotting things are somehow in the best possible taste . . ."

"You think it is nonsense?"

"Well . . ."

"No, it is not nonsense. Go to Milan, to the Galleria Ambrosiana, and you will find there one of the most delightful paintings, a priceless masterpiece by Caravaggio. It is a still life of fruit. Not fresh fruit mind you, but decaying, rotting fruit. And this painting is the artist's finest work, his most tasteful quadro. . . . Old fruit, oranges, apples, grapes, their acrid smell, the little insects skirmishing around those moulding rinds, that overripe luxuriance . . ."

"In art yes, I agree that some rather unpleasant things can be shown in a profound light. But in human affairs, you have to admit that fresh, pretty things are much nicer."

"Are they? . . . I used to go around town, go from café to café, from bar to bar. . . . But not to drink or keep company. No, my sole purpose was to visit the restrooms, those atrocious hidden holes which, for us Italians, being such a superficial people, are places where cleanliness matters not. . . . And I would visit these simply to savour that vile aroma, to inspect those filthy stains."

Millard moved uneasily in his chair.

"Oh," said Alfonso, responding to his friend's obvious discomfort, "I realise perfectly well that this was a perversion, a habit completely unworthy of me, and that is the reason I discarded it. When I do something I do it properly. These evil odours and sights were for me delicious, something that mere vulgarians could never appreciate. It was something to be cultivated, not indulged in clandestinely like a criminal. . . . As you know, I have always been something of an amateur chemist. To determine the responsible chemicals inside the vapours of burning hair, rotting flesh and other exceptional and pleasing items was no terribly difficult task. By combining a variety of sulphur compounds, I created a perfume of rotting garbage. I admixed n-valeric acid with trimethylamine, and found myself in possession of a perfect imitation of the odour of a decomposing cat. To recreate one of my most successful smells, that of human waste, I mixed a chemical called skatole with certain fatty acids and treated it with sulphuretted hydrogen."

The sun had already sunk behind the hills; the room was filled with a soft and mysterious light. Alfonso removed a small pink phial from his pocket, undid the top and took a sniff, his eyelids half-closed, a blissful expression spreading over his face.

"Simple butyric acid," he murmured, "the same chemical butter releases when it goes rancid. . . . So acrid . . . with its sweetish aftertaste. . . . Better than the best wine . . ."

He handed the phial to Millard, who, after gazing for a moment at its oily, limpid contents, cautiously undid the top and feebly sniffed. His whole head was suddenly suffused with the extreme smell of foul, disgorged food; he felt sickened, dizzy, as if he was about to lose consciousness. For a moment his mind was plundered of its reason and he was filled with an overwhelming sense of panic.

"Easy fellow," Alfonso murmured. "When you are not used to the stuff . . ."

"Revolting . . . almost hallucinogenic . . ." Millard gasped.

Alfonso lit another cigarette, and from within the murky clouds of smoke he had created around his person, continued talking, his voice soft and meditative.

"And my diet gradually became more refined. . . . Fresh foods, in whatever form, no longer found their way to my table. I, like the Europeans of old, realised that my meat needed to be well aged before it was fit to touch my palate. . . . Fly-blown beef, fermented fish, fowl made tender by time, its enzymes turning the flesh and muscular fibres soft as pudding—all these piquant things I came to relish, every day refining my luxury. In my upstairs chambers, where visitors never go, I have my works. Currently under a glass case I possess a Berkshire swine decomposing, maggots tumbling through it most madly. . . . I have a rare example of a chihuahua, that race bred by the Aztecs of Mexico, so small that it fits in a tea-cup, and I will watch as it putrefies, first turning to a rotting stinking little ball, then a colourfully moulding frivolity, and finally mere dust and blanched bones, like those of a sparrow. . . . Each creature, when in a perfect state of corrosion, is like a masterpiece—not only visually, but also aromatically. . . . Kangaroos, Komodo dragons, zebras . . . eventually I would like to experience them all."

The two men now sat in almost complete darkness. Millard, horrified, listened to his friend's voice and he imagined that sitting opposite him was not so much a human being as some sort of corrupt demon; a man who, in his search for the ultimate refinements of taste and beauty had turned into something far less than the most miserable beast. It seemed that his friend, after all, was nothing more than a scavenger poised on a pedestal of lofty ideas, the gaps of his teeth filled with rotting flesh and his own skin purposely soiled in heinous decadence.

"Are you listening?" Alfonso asked, in a soft and delicate tone.

"Yes," Millard replied.

"Well, I imagine these aesthetical adventures of mine are of some interest to you, as you yourself have always been somewhat of a connoisseur of sophisticated sensations. . . . So . . . odours, flavours, sights—and then there was the matter of women. —You remember Monica I am sure, the adorable little thing I was with just before you returned to England. . . . She was deeply in love with me, but could not understand my predilection for rot and decay. She did not have an artistic sensibility. So she left, she said I disgusted her. And this was all very well, because she bored me. Her features were a million times too smooth and fresh to make my blood tingle, and her breath was always adorned with the plebeian scent of mint. . . . I needed not the ripe, but the overripe. In order to satisfy my natural desires I sought out creatures thrice my age, tempted by their maternal wrinkles and veteran matrixes, but even they seemed far too fresh. The easy readiness of older women was rather tedious, because they always insisted on competing with their younger counterparts, perfuming themselves, stuffing their breasts into stiff bras and hips into reinforced corsets, blanketing their deteriorating features with make-up, doing everything they could to make their forms and physiognomies more appealing—which for me was less appealing. . . . So I longed for something more, some exotic mound of flesh dug freshly from the earth, cosmetised with the holes of worms and bejewelled with the slime of snails. There was only one way to indulge this passion and——"

"Stop!" Millard cried, springing from his seat. "Don't tell me. I don't want to know. Enough horrible revelations for an evening, really!"

There was a moment of silence, and then Alfonso turned on a reading lamp. He still sat in the same chair, a pleasant, somewhat mystified expression on his face.

"But really, Millard," he said, "your nerves are on edge. I should have never let you have a smell of that butyric acid."

Millard shrugged his shoulders. Monica was right, his friend was repulsive—though certainly in a highly refined way.

"It is late. I should go."

"Late! It is only eight-thirty. . . . You aren't going to stay for supper?"

"I don't think I will. I am not feeling very well."

"Poor fellow. . . . I have disturbed you!"

Alfonso walked his friend to the door.

"Did you drive?"

"No. . . . But, please, don't worry. . . . I will walk. . . . The fresh air will do me good."

Millard grasped his friend's hand, shuddered as he shook it, and then turned and walked down the path, the huge amphoras rising up darkly on either side like so many strange hunched beasts. . . . When he got to the road he did not look back. He walked along the smooth black asphalt, his hands in his pockets, his mind a chaos of grotesque thoughts and images.

Three days later he left Como and did not return until the following spring. His first day in town he saw Monica gazing in a store window on the Via G. Rovelli. They greeted each other and began talking as they walked toward the Via Vittorio Emanuele.

"You heard about Alfonso?" she asked.

Millard made a face. "Heard? . . . I saw him after we talked last time. He was a real mess like you said. Thoroughly disgusting. Is there something more to know?"

"He committed suicide three months ago."

"My God!"

The pair walked for about fifty metres in silence, then Millard asked: "How—how did it happen?"

"He sealed himself in a large glass case, and apparently drank a great deal of poison. It was the postman who first alerted the police. . . . The smell was awful. The authorities could only enter the house with gas masks. A room on the third floor was filled with rotting animals. . . . And a woman . . ."

"How horrible!"

"It was very wicked."

"Alfonso . . ."

"He wrote a note, poetically describing his suicide, and directing the authorities to that glass case. . . . Inside there was nothing but . . . mouldering jelly."

Millard felt revolted. A brief vision of his friend shot through his mind,—his friend transformed into a kind of putrefied blob, a blue-green stinking mass mysteriously endowed with candid grey eyes and a healthy smile.

"They broke the glass and Alfonso oozed out onto the floor," Monica continued. "I suppose the sight was intolerable because a few of those present panicked. They screamed in revulsion and, pushing each other aside, tried to get out of the door all at the same time. There was a shelf lined with beakers, beakers of chemicals, and this got knocked over."

"His perfumes," Millard murmured.

"Yes, they were his perfumes. They splashed everywhere and seeped through the floorboards. The stench was so awful that it would not go away no matter what cleaning agents were used. . . . It became necessary for them to tear the house down."

"And Alfonso?"

"I don't know. The authorities would not say what they did with his remains. . . . The Leopardi family was very upset. . . . They wanted to put up a small monument in the cemetery, but the Comune di Como would not let them. They said it would be sacrilegious to honour Alfonso in any way."

Millard looked at Monica's face to see if there was any sign of emotion, but she appeared cold and distant. . . . They hugged and then parted ways. . . .

The news of his friend's death deeply disturbed Millard. He wandered through the narrow old streets, which wound amongst the buildings like a coil of intestines. And then he found himself at the lake, looking out over that expanse of heavy-blue, almost black water. He turned his gaze toward the hill where his friend's villa had sat and he could see nothing, save the yellow arm of a crane, undoubtedly digging away the very earth, so tainted, to be hauled off to some distant and uninhabited location.

A DISH
OF SPOUSE

After Mrs. Shapiro had eaten Maurice, her husband, she felt a sense of regret. It was not that he had tasted poorly; no, it was not that. She had taken all the care in the world over his preparation. She had fed him on nothing but milk and cereal for ten days before killing him, despite his childish protestations, and then bled and cleaned him ever so well. It was a good deal of trouble stringing him up by his legs from the fig tree in the back yard, but she had been determined to do things properly. Removing the intestines and innards was unpleasant. All the same, she had to admit to smiling when cutting off his genitals.

She scraped, parboiled and dressed him, and, with an apron strapped over her healthy chest and a show tune on her lips, stuffed him with a mixture of sausage, bread crumbs, chopped onions and celery, seasoned with a little savory paprika. It was only upon seeing his big green eyes staring up at her that she realized that she had neglected to remove them. So, berating herself mildly for her silliness, her lack of attention, she plucked them out and cut away the lids.

She sewed him up, skewered his arms and legs into a crouching stance, and stuck a wooden block in his mouth to hold it open. Then she rubbed him with oil and a cut clove of garlic and dredged him in flour. Covering his ears and rump with aluminum foil, she put him in her biggest pan and roasted him, at 325 degrees, until he was tender, basting him every fifteen minutes with drippings. When he was finally done, she removed the foil and block of wood, stuck an apple in the mouth and cranberries in the eye sockets and garnished him with watercress.

The guests all knew Ellen to be an exceptional cook, but they had no idea the trouble she had gone to on this particular occasion.

They arrived, removed their coats, and sat talking over cocktails in the living room. Many compliments were made on the aroma floating in from the kitchen, and guesses as to the nature of the dish. Mrs. Shapiro smiled good humoredly, stirred her Tom Collins with her little finger, and, like a good hostess, diverted the talk to other matters.

When it came time to eat, the party filed nonchalantly into the dining room. It was only as they seated themselves that Dick Rethause, a long time friend, commented on the absence of the host.

"Ellen, where in God's name is Maurice?" he asked, with an appearance of genuine concern.

"Right here; coming through, coming through," she replied, wheeling her husband in on a dining cart.

His skin was a lovely golden glossy brown and, with the apple in his mouth and the cranberries for eyes, he looked quite festive.

"He's beautiful," said the women, clapping.

Of course it was Dick, the self appointed authority on meat, who did the carving, slicing off generous portions for each guest, and an especially generous portion of the left buttock for himself. The question arose as to what wine would be best drunk with the meal. Red was essential in regards to beef and game, but white often preferable with pork, lamb or poultry. Ellen settled the matter decisively by setting several bottles of a lovely California Burgundy on the table.

"We bought these on our last trip to Napa," she said. "It's a bit heavy, but I think fitting to the occasion."

Toasts were made to the host and hostess and knife and fork played their tune. By the guests' silence, and the rapidity with which the plates were cleared of flesh, Ellen Shapiro knew her dinner to be a success. When the guests could eat no more, at least not without appearing out and out gluttons, dessert and coffee were served and conversation resumed, voices uttering out of grease-shined lips.

"A really wonderful choice," said Dick's wife, Charlotte. "You'll have to give me the recipe."

"Well, for myself," chuckled Dick, "this is the kind of meal I would much rather eat at another's house than have eaten at mine."

As the guests filtered out, bellies distended and eyes half-closed in torpid satisfaction, they each gave Ellen a hug and final compliment. She stood with her back against the closed door and listened as motors started and wheels turned out the driveway. It was then she felt that vague sense of regret, the after effect of almost any well planned event or party, when all has been done and passed through and little more than enjoyable memories remain.

She went into the dining room and began to clean up, stacking plates and collecting soiled silverware. The table was scattered with odd orts of meat and stained with splotches of grease and gravy. A bit of bread with teeth marks lay there, as did several half-drunk glasses of wine. The remains of Maurice sat devastated on the dining cart.

"Well," she sighed, looking at the carcass, still rich with shreds of him, "at least this will make a wonderful bone soup."

THE GIRL
OF WAX

Prince Tolfi lounged, his unexercised body well wrapped in furs, one hand, highlighted with a gem-crusted lion head ring, straying to a dish of confection, sugar coated coriander seeds soaked in marjoram vinegar, which sat at his side. Occasionally his head would cock back to admire the panelling which had recently been installed on the ceiling of his bedroom: lxxvj beautiful paintings from the workshop of Paolo Uccello: sumptuously dressed youths, figures mythical, posing against a swimming blue background, landscapes executed with jewel-like perfection.

He lifted a small bowl of black wine to his lips, let the fluid enter the florid grandeur of his mouth and trickle down his throat, which was long and thin like a water-bird's. His eyes were frozen ice on stagnant pools, their visual strategy that of the sensualist: impassive. At the knock on the door they defrosted slightly, and grew to faux-liquid as he said, with the most elegant of Tuscan accents: "Admit her."

The door opened and she walked in, the very girl he had seen near the market that day, only now properly dressed, as befitted her unquestionable beauty. He, being impetuously royal, maniacally whimsical and equipped with a heart nourished on shallow sentiments masked as great feelings, immediately synthesised within himself emotion. Her swelling outgrowths inspired lust; her creamy complexion simulated the beauty of art so closely, that he had requested himself to love, and had requested his valet Wolframio to see that she was delivered, right virginal, to his chamber that night.

"Come in," he said in his most gentle voice, rising from his seat and letting the furs drop away, in order to better expose his hipshot, boyish frame attired in close-fitting garments of brightly dyed silk. "There is no need to feel awkward here my little mouse, as I am your most sure protector, having become enraptured by your beauty from when I first espied you, like some violet springing from the filth of the market streets."

Her round cheeks became suffused with a blush and she advanced closer to the royal personage before her, her glance straying over the luxurious furnishings and extraordinarily lavish odds and ends that were placed tastefully about the room. It was apparent from the stunned glitter of her eyes and the unsure movements of her feet as they trod the Persian carpets that she had never in her days been exposed to such wealth, even in the capacity of a cleaning woman, let alone one invited to exist in it on the footing of an enjoyer. That she showed modesty was true: for she did not speak, and she was obviously shy of Tolfi's presence. But whether this modesty was a natural part of her character, or a mere reaction to the situation, could not be determined. And, indeed, the prince did not try to determine it. He took the girl for what she was before him, a charming, innocent beauty, and did not so much as consider that she existed apart from his gaze or had a life apart from the idealistic one he had built for her in his mind.

He came to her and took her in his arms. She sighed.

"Flower," he murmured and, fearing he would bruise her with his kisses, gently led her to the bed. "You will be my bride."

The fact that there was no priest in view to consecrate the union did not seem in the least to inhibit the young woman, possibly even the contrary, for she gave the prince a smile, the language of which he could not mistake. He embraced her.

"Tell me dear," he whispered in her ear. "What is your name?"

What belched forth from that mouth, more red and soft of texture than rose petals, would be difficult to describe. Its smarmy accents, to Tolfi's well-polished ears, sounded rude in the extreme. He had never been one for slumming and, lending his attention to art and the picturesque, had not yet had his smooth exterior directly contact the abrasive textures of the lower levels of peasantry.

"Please. . . . Please be quiet," he said, aghast, his skin visibly yellowing.

But once started, the beautiful, gruff-voiced girl did not seem to have it in her power to refrain. In gross slang she let loose the indelicacies of her tongue, not even aware that they were the cause of the deepest agitation to the prince who sat groaning at her side—that handsome young man who, moments before, had been ready to devour her with love. Fancying that her words were adding spice to his desire, she lay them on in profusion, letting whatever thoughts came rising to the surface of her simple mind spill forth from her mouth.

"Quiet," the prince hissed.

Thinking he was joking, she laughed. Her laughter struck him as the most immodest, indelicate thing he had yet heard. That it issued forth from those beautiful lips, that it was the by-product of that gorgeous, goddess-like face, only made it all the more disturbing.

Nervously he twisted the ring on his finger and then, biting his bottom lip, stretched the hand towards her. She clasped it in her own, bent her head down, and kissed it. He tightened his grip.

"Ouch!" she whined. "Your ring pricked me."

He withdrew his hand, his eyes straying down to the mammoth, gem-crusted lion-head ring, now inverted, its jaws, just tipped with blood, turned towards the palm. Rising from the bed, he tore it from his finger, flung it on the floor, and strode to the window, where he buried his face in its embroidered sash and wept. He heard her calling to him and madly smothered his head in the rich cloth, blocking his ears. A quarter of an hour later, when he turned his pale gaze back towards her, her body was going through the final spasms of death, her eyes wide with pain and terror. He watched her dazzling skin ripple and her precious eyes grow glassy as she expired.

Gasping, as if he had just risen from the bottom of a lake, he rang for his valet.

"Wolframio, you fool," he cried out when the other had entered. "Why did you not tell me she had such a wretched voice?"

"Why, Your Excellency," the page replied with a quivering voice. "I thought you knew she was the daughter of a cheesemonger."

"The daughter of a cheesemonger," the prince sighed wistfully. "By the incomprehensible laws of attraction, it could only be the daughter of a cheesemonger that would attract the son of a lord."

He looked at the pale corpse lying on the bed, a lock of blonde hair flowing over one shoulder.

"She is so beautiful," he said. "At least now I can look at her without fearing that she will open her mouth. That vile accent!" he concluded with a look of disgust twisting his features.

"I will see that she is properly disposed of, Your Excellency," Wolframio said with a bow.

"Yes, do; please do." Prince Tolfi's eyes strayed over the fine figure of the girl. He could feel the longing she had inspired still within himself, like a bubble unable to burst. And now she would be cast in a hole, food for the worms, without him ever having . . .

The page moved to the body and began to wrap it in the sheets of the bed, moving the limbs gently, out of respect for his master who still looked on.

"Wait Wolframio," the prince said, raising one finger. "Leave her for now. I will tell you when you may take her away."

"As you wish, Your Excellency," the valet replied, and departed with a bow.

In the mid morning of the next day, Mester Donato di Niccolò di Betto Bardi, called Donatello, was shown into the chamber by the prince himself. He looked ruefully at the object pointed out to him.

"I can make a likeness, certainly," he said. "But . . ."

"But?"

"But to comply in complete regards to you request seems to me— frankly, not in my calling."

"Are you not an artist?" the prince asked haughtily.

"I am an artist," Donatello replied with gravity, "but I am not able to step into the shoes of the divine. I am not able to restore flesh back to life."

"That is not what I ordered."

"But it is——"

"But it is not you who makes the decisions," Tolfi curtly interrupted. "You will receive coin of the realm enough for your labour. My only requirement is that you do the work, make it your masterpiece, better than anything you have yet done, more sweet of body than your David, more noble than your Saint George—and utterly and ideally feminine. Make it superb and you will be rewarded; but do not fail." And, grandly sweeping his ermine cape over one should, Tolfi left the room, and the brilliant artist to contemplate the grim task to which he had been assigned.

Truly it must be said that, upon completion, this figure in wax was more beautiful than anything Donatello had yet created. As it sat in his studio, naked, with contours more graceful than those of a swan and an angelically seductive look on its painted face, the master sculptor cried, "Come now! Why don't you speak to me?" hardly able to believe himself that what was before him was but the product of bees, and not an idol of flesh and blood.

Prince Tolfi, upon seeing his girl of wax, was enraptured. For him she was far more beautiful than her predecessor, particularly as she carried about her the perfume of honey rather than that of Parmesan. The joints of her limbs were made so that they could move. He could situate her in any position he wished. He kissed her lips. They were succulent. He whispered in her ear and the smile remained, immovable on her face, without giving vent to vulgar reply.

The figure settled down magnificently into the household routine. The servants, not daring to question their master's predilection, treated her as the lady of the house. A chambermaid thrice a day brushed her yellow hair (which had in fact been transplanted from the head of her predecessor). At night, while enjoying a glass of Vin Santo, the prince chatted volubly to his mistress, filling the air with witticisms to his own infinite delight—for his favourite sound in the world was that of his own voice. Chucking her beneath the chin, he would tell her all sorts of romantic endearments. Taking her upon his lap, he played the part of a naughty yet dignified child. Dipping a pen in lavender ink, he wrote poems, nearly as good as those later written by Francesco Berni, telling of how, finally, he knew what it was to adore, to love.

Taking the magnificent gold-handled dagger from its sheath, he cut up the roasted venison, liking very much to eat it in that fashion, which he considered to be jaunty. The blood meat coursed down his bird-like throat, and he washed it down with heavy drafts of Montepulciano, a light, purple wine that always sat well with him at meal time. After letting a dozen or so sparrows al pomodoro and ij black birds slide into his mouth, he attacked the fish, a great braised turbot set on a bed of sweet, green olives.

"It is a shame you do not like fish," he said across the table, which was covered with blazing candelabra. "This turbot is really something special."

Like the perfect woman she was, she did not reply but only smiled.

He toasted her good health, drained his glass of wine and, after refilling it, set about devouring the jellied pig, which was his favourite, and of which he had ij portions. For green meat, a great bowl was brought before him containing baby lettuce, radishes and finocchio; for dessert pomegranate seeds in peach juice and a pineapple from Sicily.

71

"It is such a pleasure to dine with you darling," he said, leaning back, massaging his now distended belly and propping his legs, one atop the other, on the table, which the serving boy was just beginning to clear.

"Be gone with you," the prince shouted. "Cannot you see that you are interrupting my admiration of her beauty!"

The boy made off, bowing with profuse and obsequious apologies. Tolfi gazed at the woman through the flickering candlelight, his ideal of love, and closed his eyes, which were heavy from wine and feasting. Her smile was there, frozen, an exquisite forgery of romance; and laughter prismatically turning to the cackling of a witch; the bickering of a cheesemonger's daughter.

When he awoke, the table was aflame. His foot had disturbed the candelabra. Wolframio ran in, pulled his master away from the table and then, together with the serving boy, proceeded to fetch pitchers of water which they cast upon the fire. Through the dance of the expiring flames the prince saw his beloved, hair fried, its very odour reaching his nose, eyes shedding waxen tears, cheeks gouged out, melted, lips abolished, now a mere pinkish stroke. And down below the fine garments, crackling, acting as a wick to the heavenly torso and now drooping, dripping breasts; the whole image having the likeness of a flaming, rotting corpse or member of the undead—demonic, ablaze in a glimpse of hell.

He gasped, shuddered and reached forward. The dagger, which he had but an hour earlier used to cut his venison, was in his hand. And, with madness reflected in his ij eyes, the sharp tool he drove into his breast. The black panther carpet, upon which his body fell, was stained with the true red of blood, not in the least bit artificial.

THE

TONGUE

I.

"As a man, I am far too passionate for this contemporary life," I murmured to myself as I strolled along the Viale Carlo Cattaneo. "As an artist, I am of the highest order, up-to-the-minute, the 100,000 follicles of hair on the human head obeying my commands as so many helots might those of a Spartan king. . . . Raised on the over pungent sauces of antique philosophies, I could have been anything: soldier, spy, diplomat or adventurer; but the seeds I plant in the little garden of my profession are those of updos and chignons, elegant hairstyles for sophisticated women and . . . men."

I turned and walked past the library, into the park. It was autumn and, in the light of the late afternoon, the leaves of some trees had the appearance of cascades of gold and copper coins. The scene was as charming as one of those seasonal paintings by Boucher—or really, more truly, a certain piece by Claude Monet—a shimmering display of colour, almost outrageously, radioactively bright. And I was in optimum spirits, making my way forward with buoyant steps, widening my nostrils—though it was not so much the lake air that I sniffed as the bouquet of my own thoughts which, sensorial as they were, emitted perfumes of cinnabar and sericato, odours such as Ty, that famous ancient hairdresser, probably anointed his patrons necks with.

Exiting the park, I crossed the Riva Giocondo Albertolli, onto the Via Stauffacher and into the city centre. Rapid motion of pedestrians. Faces. Fur collars. Hair: grey, red, black. Improperly tended. Needy. And like a good little scout I moved on, guided by my desire to be amongst men, human beings.

As I was passing the Café Down Town, I sighted Marsyas in the window, sitting with a young woman of Praxitelean appearance, the equivocal symbolism of their profiles rich with nuance. I tapped on the glass. He gestured frantically and then came rushing out to greet me. He gripped my hand in a brotherly fashion, and I had to move my head to one side, or his nose, which was excessively long, would have poked me in the eye.

He said, in his flute-like voice, that he was glad to see me, and I would have liked to have replied, but could not. "She is vain," he continued, nodding towards the young lady in the window, "but twice a day she allows me to reap the corn of her passions, and of this the chine of my scythe, which is well polished, never grows weary. For truly Elba (that is her name) is as venereal as a rabbit, an animal as delicious in its own way as any shellfish. . . . Oh, I had seen her before, in the snowy bosom-shaped peaks—the Bietschhorn, the Aletschhorn, but to have such a creature nestled up against one, to have the opportunity to melt her glaciers with my mercury, is a sensation that makes a dreamland out of days."

I listened to his words as the Japanese poet Jōsō might have the song of a thrush. And then I attempted to give a suitable response, to comment knowledgably, with a hint of disdain on his indiscreet exultation; but no sound was forthcoming. At first I imagined it was just some temporary case of ankyloglossia. I endeavoured to run my tongue over the roof of my mouth and then experienced a lack of sensation. Alarm. Wonder. I felt for it with my teeth, but it was not there.

Marsyas asked me if something was wrong. A sensation: of blood rushing to my face. I motioned him away. Through the corner of one eye I saw Elba observing me: a circle of imitation marble framed in chestnut hair. I turned and made my way down the street, around the corner in the direction I had come, checking pockets, front and back, as I went.

A mild aura of panic descended on the city; and I was upset. To lose one's tongue is an especially unpleasant experience (as: a painter losing his eyes; a duellist, his sword; a farmer his land). . . . It was the tool with which I expressed my desires, my wants, my hates and antipathies; and surely it was my body's loveliest muscle.

I rapidly retraced my steps, my eyes panning over the sidewalk, the events now taking on the appearance of some antique Cecil B. DeMille silent. Hand-tinted. Low-key lit. Crowds directed. I looked around at the people on the street, wondering if one of them had picked it up. There was a fellow with the demeanour of a dog and a mane of long black hair; a woman with an overt bosom; a Chinese man wearing a bright pink tie. . . . . . Or could some animal or bird have taken it? Cat. Child. Thief.

Anyone who found my tongue would love it, very possibly be adverse to parting from it.

My mind flew over the incidents preceding the mishap. . . . I had last used it on the Viale Carlo Cattaneo, while murmuring to myself before entering the park. Had I left it somewhere along the way; had it dropped out?

Biting my bottom lip. Speculating curiously. Anger and fear.

I saw something red on the ground and picked it up. It was the skin of a persimmon.

I carried my legs along and the cars swirled past me, them greeting the new night with their headlights, like so many grotesque devotees of the goddess of misfortune. Through the dark streets I wandered, those I passed transformed into monstrous toads, giant heads attached to swift-stepping feet; me, without the ability to shriek as I dove from shadow to shadow.

That evening my home was an unhappy one. I ate a green salad, a lambchop, drank a bottle of Bordeaux, but without tasting any of it, without enjoying any of it;—and then afterwards I sat in front of the fireplace, swallowing enumerable cups of chamomile tea and smoking cigarettes. It rained and the liquid occasionally came whisking against my windows. I went to bed and tried to read myself to sleep, switching from Restif de la Bretonne to a book of poems by Robert de Montesquiou-Fézensac to a play in Paduan dialect by Ruzzante. Finally I settled into a sort of dream-like torpor in which I spent many aggravating hours prancing over twisting tongues of flame and then collecting screams from the garden and wrapping them in a batiste handkerchief.

"Screams of beasts," Elba said.

"Lovers and beasts."

"Dogs."

"Shame."

"Squealing."

"But shame never?"

"No."

The next morning I placed an anonymous add in the paper. I mentioned that an organ of allocution was missing, was terribly missed, and described it as strawberry red, U-shaped, exquisitely supple and offered a suitable reward for its return.

Afterwards I went to my studio and taped a hand-written sign on the door, claiming an indisposition and begging my clients' patience. The day was overcast and I was possessed by a feeling of inadequacy. I threaded my way through the streets, gazing at the tips of my shoes, depressed by the sensation of not having anything with which to lick my lips. I dreaded encountering someone I knew, a client, a friend, the jeers of an enemy. . . . I avoided the crowded Via Nassa and the Piazza Riforma; took small byways, unfrequented alleys; then along the Via Gerolamo Vegezzi; the Via Canova; into the park with my collar upturned and a whiskered five-o'clock-shadow look to my person—appearing, I imagine, vaguely like Napoleon on the day after Waterloo; and hoping, somewhat desperately, that I would see the red jewel lying about in the grass or hanging from the branch of a tree.

There are days when the world is reduced to cinders and we stalk across it inhaling the smell of our own burning flesh. At such times our sense of identity is mutated, awful, and we are guided by odd magnetic principles—pushed forward like lonely clouds.

I saw: water, sky, earth; heard the distant sound of motors; looked over at: a man with a square-shaped chin on a bench. He wore a sort of loutish sloppy-Joe jumper. He seemed to have fallen asleep; probably some labourer resting on his lunch break after swallowing meat sandwiches and cheap Merlot. His mouth was open, and I could clearly make out his tongue lolling from it, a glistening somewhat brownish item, like the liver of a cow. Though I am normally a veritable phoenix of politeness, on this occasion I acted the part of a son of nature, following my first impulse. I grabbed the thing, turned and made off with it, my legs moving in express mode over the grass. . . . Exit stage left. . . . At the Corso Elvezia, crossing, avoiding speedily moving cars. . . . The sound of the wind in my ears, my steps on paving stones. . . . I put the tongue in my pocket, darted into the Casino. Lazy croupiers, black-jack tables and the dim lighting of decay. I needed some place to hide and, after dodging the inquisitive glances of a few gamblers, ushered myself through a door. A room whose walls were painted with hills and trees. A group of youths and girls were sitting around a fruit and wine loaded table which was set in the middle of the floor. To one side of the room stood two young men, one dressed in a waistcoat and tailcoat, limp and too large, and a great shiny hat, the other in a work-a-day costume of centuries gone by. On the other side stood a man with a baton between two pretty ladies who sat on the floor. One played the guitar while the other was frozen in the act of singing a cadenza, her eyes raised towards heaven.

"And who are you?" cried the man with the baton, looking at me. "Can't you see that you are interrupting a charming tableau based on the description in Eichendorff's *Aus dem Leben eines Taugenichts* describing the tableau based on Hoffman's *Die Fermate*—the story about Hummel's great painting at the Berlin exhibition in the autumn of 1814!"

A few drops of sweat flew from my temples and my lips twitched uneasily as I receded back over the threshold. . . . And through the Casino I went; the smell of air-freshener and cigars; searched and found the back door.

More turns; more frantic movement; more distance gained. Furtive glances from side to side. No danger. . . . I leaned against a wall and exhaled air through my lips. . . . And then I took out my prize and held it up to the light. It was certainly not pretty, certainly not an Annika Irmler tongue, but I had turned renegade and would settle for relieving sows of their ears when there was no princess to divest of her silks. . . . So, without wasting time, I shoved it in my mouth, and considered myself once more to be an articulately speaking man.

With long strides I now made my way forward. I would drink, eat and live. Not like a foul, silent brute, but as an individual at the highest level of development, able to reason and speak.

An aged woman, in a helmet-like wig, stopped me and asked for the time.

I looked at the elegant silver circle on my wrist.

"It—half—past—three," I said, my words rolling clumsily out, heavy as stones.

Clearly I was not capable of singing an aria from *Figaro*; the organ did not function so well as I would have wished.

II.

It could not appreciate good living: It salivated every time I passed a hunk of ham or was in the presence of fried potatoes. I imagine he had been a dirty feeder. . . .

○

I felt as if I were some kind of human bell or drum.

○

To educate that beast, make my pupil repeat the sounds I wished; with what difficulty instil in it the proper pronunciation of vowels

○

"If—I had been—born in the time of Tuthmoses III, I would have been Supervisor of the Dancers of the King." My voice clunked along. Stunted words fell from my mouth. "My neck—heavy with necklaces. Razor of flint and oyster shell in my—grip."

○

Realisation: there is nothing rarer in this world than a supportable tongue.

○

My custom began to fall away. As far as manual and artistic skill went, I could match the best of them, Allen Edwards, Fekkai, Sergio Valente, Alba, but with a tongue like that I would never be able to rival them in fame, never be able to utter those lisping phrases à la mode which differentiate the master craftsman from the common barber.

III.

After work, I made my way sadly home.

There was a letter for me in the mail box. I opened it as soon as I entered my flat and read the following:

Dear Lorenzo,

This is a difficult letter to write. Sincerity is always difficult; and I embroider my words with the utmost care, the needle of my pen not wishing to agitate your already scarred vanity. You see: you did not lose me, I was not stolen from your grip, but rather left of my own free will—something you should know about, having once made me read Diderot out loud, in the sighing tones of a heartbroken theorist.

Oh, you treated me well enough, bathing my flesh in wine and cream, letting me now and again roam across the lips of some beloved, but still: for long I had felt I was meant to serve a greater master. You never did satisfy a particular part of my being which I will leave unmentioned, and specific cravings drove me from your side.

I know my dear Lorenzo that you will suffer. If you can, do not think me merely fickle; because truth be told I have always put a great deal of thought into my every motion.

A Tongue

I cast the letter aside with disgust, feeling that, veiled behind those soft zibeline words, was a spirit full of bitterness—one who, like a cannibal feeding on human limbs, was nurtured on pretended wrongs. A groan came from my mouth, not the groan I would have liked, something artfully lyric, but rather the pathetic howl of a road worker whose thumb was being crushed by a steam roller.

I went to the rest room, doused my face with water and dried it with a great fuzzy towel.

There was a knock at the door. It was Marsyas, dressed in puritanical black and white; his hair in poetical disorder. Gone was his sparkling enthusiasm.

He glided around the apartment talking of white things in his flute-like voice, his shadow rolling over the wall, looking like that of a flamingo, something fantastic, monstrous.

"We were very high up," he said.

"You fell."

"She—her flesh like bread made from the purest flour—is unattainable, as some mirage that recedes as you approach, always maintaining the same distance from the observer. Clouds. Foam. Sheep. And her ghostlike vapour swirls around me as the dust of platinum scattered to the wind. . . . But I dare not flush the precious remnants of that metal from my eyes, for blindness matters nothing to me; only her kisses, with their flavour of fire and honey."

"So, she left you," I said roughly, pouring him a glass of Cliquot. "Come. Sit. Drink. Etiquette—did you have etiquette? Did you lift up her hair when she put on her jacket? When you danced, did you put your hand over it—or under?" I barked out my words. "And your bed linen—I would guess that—it is not of satin, that material so fit for long-haired women, brides, virgins and whores!"

His Adam's apple quivered in his throat.

"Lorenzo."

"Marsyas."

". . . don't understand."

"Perfectly. . . ."

"No."

"Pungent amours. There's common ground here. Both losing. . . ."

"How can you lose what you love?"

"Christ was also pinned up like a butterfly. It is all a matter of interior decorating."

IV.

I have carefully cultivated my neuroses as others might flowers and have dwelt in my autistic fantasies like a snail in its shell. When the door closed behind Marsyas I felt sumptuously sad. I washed my hands three times, slept, woke, and it was day. The bells of churches rang out endlessly and I took to the streets, bought a paper, sat in a café. Articles. Words. Black liquid stained with white. Then rising, moving slowly down the sidewalk.

I felt a hand on my shoulder. I turned. There was that square-shaped chin, that sloppy-Joe jumper. And then that awful moment of mutual recognition: me, pale with apprehension, him, white with rage. And so a giant fist came hurrying towards me. For an artist, all experiences are exquisite: The pain—his fingers groping between my teeth—the absurdity of my role a minor revelation as two oily tears slid from my eyes.

V.

Obviously stealing another tongue was out of the question. I considered the possibility of purchasing one on the black market, maybe some lithe little South American piece able to utter liquid consonants and the occasional rolling wave of 'r's. Undoubtedly there were many fine and inexpensive specimens available from Asia,—Chinese tongues used to complex four-toned pronunciation,—or the Thai tongue practised in the eleven ways to say 'only'.

But of course all that would take time. The only tongues that were available immediately were those of farm animals—dull and oversized.

There was nothing to do but claim that I had an inflammation of the larynx which prevented me from speaking; and I decided that the part would be best played with a colourful new scarf wrapped around my throat. . . . So I went to the ancient and not far distant city of Como, centre of the Italian silk industry. . . . The weather was very cool, most certainly the type for knitwear. I sheltered myself in the English primness-twinset-vibe, found myself behind the old city walls; walked by the house where Pope Innocent XI was born on the 16th of May in the year 1611.

But where was Pliny born?

I turned, made my way along the Via Independenza, to the Via Vittorio Emanuele II, passed by several shops, gazed at the silks in the windows, with their million patterns: those of birds, and insects, and phantastic shapes, wads of paisley, tiger-striped flowers, cosmic wonders, imploding stars of ultra-marine and pink.

I entered a reputable establishment. A saleswoman moved smoothly towards me.

"A scarf?" she asked. ". . . For a woman?"

I brushed the issue aside, shrugged my shoulders, pointed to my throat, gestured. . . . She dragged out box after box, each one loaded to overflowing with richly designed silks and I felt like diving in, making my bed, my home amidst those soft and colourful quadrangles. . . .

After a reasonable amount of deliberation, I opted for one that seemed particularly suited to my state of mind: a crown of thorns pattern with a faded pewter boarder.

Leaving the shop, I wrapped it around my white throat and turned down the Via Rusconi, carrying with me a sense of resignation. I wandered through a crowd of fur coats, through tall women and fat men. Via Pietro . . . Via Fratelli Cairoli. I looked over the lake. It was beautiful and I wished I could have cut off a piece and sent it to my mother. I walked eastward, with the water to my left, then turned, crossed back over the street.

In the window of a café, people were knotted together like in a Veronese painting. A group of students came by me. I heard Lombardic expressions; pigeons cooing; it seemed that everyone had a voice but me.

My legs led me into the Piazza Duomo, past the pink striped Broletto, to the church, its façade artistically acceptable, and I decided to venture in, knowing full well that there were a few decent paintings inside. I sighed as I entered the cool Gothic interior of the temple. I walked by the numerous grand tapestries, stopped before the *Holy Conversation* of Luini, gazed at the great organ, inspected Gaudenzio Ferrari's *Flight to Egypt*. I sat down in the midst of that Latin cross and abandoned myself to my dreams. Beautiful Absalom with his two hundred shekel head of hair . . . Solomon . . . hair like a flock of goats . . . Lilith . . .

I heard the combative click of a woman's heels and looked over. An elegant figure was making its way towards the confessional. She made obeisance, crossed herself and approached. Long chestnut hair, which had the soft shine which comes from a sage rinse, fell over her shoulders; her profile was pale and cold.

She knelt; the black sleeves of a priest slithered out from the edge of the box.

The two proceeded to murmur together like conspirators, she undoubtedly revealing to the black bandit her most sacred mysteries, which he surely drank in with glee, soaked as they now were in the savoury blood of Jesus. . . .

Ah, to be able to tell another one's secrets, the hidden shade of one's dreams! Indeed, at that moment it would have given me great satisfaction to have poured forth a chronology of my sins—from the harmless little items which chirp like scissors, to those grave manias which are launched like ships.

I thought thus as vague and familiar accents reached my ears— tones which moved through the air like tulips cast in slow motion by children in far away places. . . . Then, the criminal communication ended, she rose to her feet. . . . A shadowy figure slipped from behind the curtain of the confessional . . . began to walk . . . not towards me, not towards the presbytery, but rather in the direction of the front exit. . . .

Then I too was in motion. I went towards the woman. I nodded my head and she bestowed on me a cold smile. . . . There was a frozen moment. Revulsion. Rapture. Flame. I then moved on, inhaling her quietly as I passed.

The priest glanced over his shoulder and began to walk with more rapid steps—through the door and out onto the piazza. But I had seen his profile and did not wish him to escape. A moment later and I was in the open air. A group of German tourists stood admiring the church and blocking my way. I pushed through them and saw the beast scurrying away, its cassock flying as if it were being carried off by a strong wind. Exerting myself, I advanced after it at great speed. Several times my grip closed on empty air, several times it merely grazed the cloth. . . . But then I seized, collared it and it squealed like an animal. It flung itself about. It slipped from its garments, slipped from one of my hands and I grabbed it with the next, me joyful, thrilled to feel the warmth of that red meat. . . . It tried to wiggle away, acting like some loathful red toad in a putrid swamp, but my fingers, fit for tending the beards of kings, were strong and agile and not adverse to being covered in tepid slobber.

VI.

Now I sit sunk in a plush chair, writing these words in a notebook with a large gold fountain pen. The creature is currently chained up in the corner. It sits and whines like a little victim, without recalling the suffering it has these past weeks granted me. Pleading and soft words will not alter my resolution. Experience is wisdom. As soon as I lay down my pen I will chastise it . . . bid it welcome to this cage of teeth.

THE

SKIN

COLLECTOR

"Yes; come in," Professor Black said. "I had forgotten that today was the day."

Lum followed his host down into the sunken living room, which was decorated sumptuously and with refined taste. It was apparent that the man who dwelt in this house was, if not out-and-out rich, certainly well-to-do. The art that hung from the walls was a blend of the romantic and contemporary; the furniture comfortably European; the rugs stylishly Asiatic. The plants, lined up against the large windows, were lush and tropical. The whole place had an air of uninviting comfort, as a stage set might.

"So, you are interested in tattoos?" the Professor asked, after the two men had sat down.

"Yes," Lum replied, self consciously, as he looked into the small, hard eyes directed at him. "I explained it all over the phone. . . . I want to interview you; for the book I am writing. I have wanted to meet you ever since I first heard about your collection. I brought a camera so I could take photos."

Professor Black let his eyes descend to the body of the apparatus that hung from Lum's neck, but his features showed no inclination towards approval. They were a grim blank that did little to sooth or welcome.

"I understand about the book," the professor continued. "But the photos we will have to see about. I am willing to show you my collection, but you will have to keep the camera tame. —Art does not always benefit the masses."

Lum thought that Professor Black did not look like the kind of man who cared very much for the masses, but let the comment slide. If the collection were really what it was made out to be, then it would certainly have been a shame to leave without a few pictures. But of course it was the professor's call, and he did not appear to be a man to cross.

The room into which Lum was led was very large, windowless, but well ventilated, with a humidifier set in one corner. A smell, like that of old leather, permeated the atmosphere, and the track lights, which lined the ceiling, gave the room the feeling of a studio or gallery.

"These are some pretty good examples," Black said, gesturing vaguely toward the glass frames which lined the walls, like so many paintings.

Lum stepped up to the first and examined it, initially finding it hard to believe that this strip of parchment was human skin. It looked more like a page torn from some ancient illuminated manuscript. —The colours were so brilliant! The details so fine! The depiction was sublime, of two naked and winged little boys dragging a soul from a man's morbid carcass. The background was a pure azure, with minarets and bold domes rising up out of the clouds. On the ground kneeled the clergy, with heads turned upward and palms pressed together.

"It is four hundred years old. Taken off the chest of an Italian priest," Black sneered. "I suppose the fellow had a streak of pagan in him, as the rules strictly forbade any such practice amongst Christians. —The picture is what it is,—though not entirely to my taste. What interests me about it, what makes the tattoo so unique, is the shade of blue. It is very rare, and was apparently derived from a blend of indigo, comfrey flowers, and a small amount of human urine."

The next frame over contained what was obviously the scalp of a human head. The picture thereon was morbid: a scene from the pits of hell. Countless demoniac monstrosities gathered around a small fire, kindled from heaped up bones. The flames, which were of a vivid yellowish-orange, shed light on the creatures. Some were like giant flopping toads; others had the heads of rams mounted on lascivious male bodies. Women huddled off to one side, their breasts split each in two and resembling the tongues of serpents. Ghouls, plump and with wagging tails, licked their chops. The creatures were countless and varied, disappearing back into the darker shading, made up of caves and cliffs, and then more reappearing in the background, at other fires that burned off in the distance of that joyless waste.

"And this?" Lum asked.

"This is also from a priest," Professor Black replied, with the coldest of smiles. "A German. The design is taken from a painting by Bruegel the Younger. The man who executed the work certainly knew his craft. The chiaroscuro is really quite remarkable, not to mention the detail. —But of course you can see for yourself."

Ranged around the room was a complete and varied assortment of skins: Those from all periods of human evolution, as well as geographical location. The most ancient was very small—little bigger than a postage stamp—and taken from the corpse of a hunter-gatherer found in an ice pack on the Swiss Alps. It was of a little bird. . . . There were also tattered shreds taken from Chinese and Incan mummies; others, strange Christian logos, disinterred from the catacombs of Italy.

There were those that were simple, showing the straight-forward, pagan roots of the art; and others, elaborately complex, tapestries of colour, supreme skill and imagination, embossed on the epidermis of man and woman. Truly, this was the architecture of the flesh, where dragons and gorgons guard the gate of the human frame, and emblems of mortification and salvation tile its hallways. The skin, after all, does not hide, but reveals.

"Your collection is even more incredible than I imagined," Lum commented, in a low and bewildered voice. "I knew that it was supposed to be more complete than any museum's, but this . . ."

"This is just a showing;—a few prime examples. "The complete collection is back here;—over ten thousand two hundred specimens."

A door was opened and another room revealed; print drawers lined in aisles, each one labelled alphabetically and categorically.

The professor took a few out and set them down. Inside lay delicate stacks of skin, like dried leaves, each a unique and precious item: the representation of a life, a mode, a belief, or sometimes simply a fashion. Some were from long ago and others modern. Some depicted language— the hieroglyphics of Egypt or the Sanskrit of India,—others birds, fish, horses, or other varieties of animal. There were insects by the hundreds— the beetle, the wasp, the child-of-the-earth,—and an equal portion of flowers, blooming in flames of crimson and spikes of forest green.

Religious and occult symbols were plentiful. The cross, the pentagram, dice, the thunderbolt, and other signs of secret societies,—as well as Madonnas; Christs, thorn-decked, with blood secreting palms;— then deities of the far east: a certain wrathful goddess, thrilling red, holding her skull cup and sacrificial dagger; Ganesha with the head of an elephant, one tusk broken, a serpent curled up, rising at his side. Or the many others, obscure and strange to western eyes: Some having the heads of jackals, eagles or bulls—or multiple heads, of even multiple creatures,—four arms, up to one thousand, often detailed to the very fingers thereon. Or another, coal-black, winged, the head of a goat and body the blade of a knife.

Lum feasted his eyes, became excited, and broke out in a sweat.

"Yes," Professor Black said, noticing the other's discomposure, "I believe I have at least one prime example of every subject ever taken up for the tattoo. I consider the collection to be complete."

"Maybe not," Lum replied with an uneasy smile. "I can hardly believe it myself, but I have never seen the tattoo I have on anybody else, and I don't see it here in your collection. Correct me if I'm wrong, but I think I have a tattoo that you haven't."

With foolish conceit the younger man set down his camera, unbuttoned his shirt and removed it. The chest and arms revealed a modest proportion of décor,—an arrow pierced heart, a toad with tongue extended, the head of Jimmy Cagney,—but the major item of attraction was on the back, which was offered to view without the slightest pretence at modesty.

"What do we have here," the professor said, his normally impassive voice modulating toward interest. "A plant of some kind?"

"Yes," Lum replied proudly. "But it is a special plant,—a Venus fly trap."

In truth the object decorating the skin of his back was especially strange. A sheaf of lime-green stalks ascended and spread out from the base of his spine, each one terminating in a claw-like cup. Several of the cups, or traps, were closed;—the legs of a daddy longlegs stretched out of one. . . . Others were open, the centres of those spring-like traps a vivid, almost bloody, pinkish red. A fly sat nonchalantly on one of Lum's shoulders, poised just above its gaping, outstretched doom.

"Most unusual; the fly looks real enough to swat," Professor Black commented, with a strange twist of his mouth. And then, after an awkward stall: "I suppose we might as well get on with the interview portion now."

"Yes . . . but . . . what do you think about the photos?" Lum asked nervously, replacing his shirt and picking up his camera. "It would really be nice if I could just fill up a roll or two."

"Of course, after the interview."

Without leaving opportunity for further debate, the professor led the way back to the sunken living room. Lum had many questions on his mind as to the collection, and the modes his host might have used in making acquisition. At the right opportunity he would ask; just then he sat himself down on the couch, with a rabbit-fur pillow tucked behind his back, and listened, while Professor Black prepared drinks and told his tale.

"As a child," he said, uncorking a bottle of old brandy, "I always had a fascination for animal stuffs: feathers, bones, leather, shark teeth, fur. —It is not uncommon in boys to pick up a little something while out on a walk; a bird's nest, with a few robin's eggs and some strands of down.

"I had a collection of such things," he continued, handing Lum a glass of the amber liquid. "I kept them in a small tin chest. It was rusty and painted with an old-fashioned map of the world. Yes, inside there was the inevitable skin of a snake, a few skulls of small rodents, and a dried-up claw—I suppose it was a badger's."

Lum sipped his brandy and listened, jotting down notes on his pad.

"To be honest," Black said, "I believe my initial interest was more in touch than sight. Things are curious that way. I remember clearly: During a certain period of my childhood, when I was quite young, my mother shared her bed with me. I believe that I was afraid to sleep alone. One night I awoke from a nightmare—I was being devoured by wild beasts,—and the first thing I came into contact with was a sort of soft, hairy mass. Of course it was only my dear mother's arm, but it frightened me;—as well as intrigued."

The voice echoed in the high-ceilinged room, and seemed to linger in space before entering Lum's ears, and subsequently becoming part of his thought process.

"At the circus I saw the Zebra Man, and later the Tattooed Woman. She was beautiful, or at least I thought so, and I might as well admit that she piqued more than just my young curiosity. . . . Amazing, isn't it, that decades later, she could still stand foremost in my mind?"

Lum tried to make sense of this question, but could not quite bring it all together. The pen stuck out from between his fingers, immobile, and the glass sat empty near him. It must have been shortly thereafter that Professor Black's dialogue terminated. He looked at his guest's sagging form with eyes devoid of sympathy. The rays of the setting sun slashed in through the window, and glinted off the scalpel held in his hand.

THE NASTY
TRUTH ABOUT
DENTISTS

People have told me that I write well and I think, to a certain degree, this is true. Though I am no Mark Twain, I do know how to bring life to words and dimension to flat pages of copy. So I am going to write down what happened, not for anyone's sake but my own. Because I am not a philanthropist. Frankly human beings disgust me. We are a self-destructive species, clever but not wise and, while we progress in terms of technological advances, we unquestionably retrogress both intellectually and morally.

I am in my mid-forties, not especially handsome, but not absolutely ugly either. I am gentle. Particularly with animals and women. I wear glasses and have a rather large nose. Norma used to say that she loved my hands, which are small and white and very soft. She also said that she wanted to have my baby. . . . Needless to say she never did have my baby. Instead she became a dental assistant.

Norma was younger than I and had straight, long blonde hair, a pretty though somewhat naïve face and a mind-boggling figure. She was a very upbeat person and had an absolutely delicious smile—the sparkling variety so often exploited by toothpaste manufacturers, dairy leagues, and other underground pornographers. . . . I still think of that smile, absolutely against my will, and imagine the teeth splintered and gums bleeding, the whole turned into a jagged red maw. . . . But this is just fantasy, my subconscious fears assaulting my conscious thoughts, and really has nothing to do with the story.

I suppose she liked me for my mind, my intellect. By profession I am a reverse speech technologist. In college I studied palindromes a great deal and contributed articles to the now defunct journal *E. Borgnine Drags Dad's Gardening Robe*. I wrote my master's thesis on that perfect sentence *Sator Arepo tenet opera rotas*, and then, after graduating, began to study backmasking. It is true that I had a lot of time on my hands, but I also found the subject both fascinating and full of profound implications. When I first discovered the now famous *It's my sweet satan* on Led Zeppelin's *Stairway to Heaven* it felt as if a door to another world had opened up to me revealing a vast and unexplored expanse of infinite possibilities. I spent months listening to, reversing every rock album I could find, leaving my apartment only for food and small quantities of healthful exercise. To unearth those clandestine communications, those cleverly secreted assertions buried amidst abrasive guitar solos and shrieking lyrics was like finding gold in a butcher shop, or tropical flowers growing amidst beds of broken glass. When I published my book *Concealed Boulders* it caused a small sensation; my face appeared on the cover of *Family Weekly*; and, a month later, I found myself working for the Society for the Protection of Christian Youth, who were deeply troubled over the surge in popularity of demoralising music and the effect it had on their children. I personally did not care much about the society or their children, but the pay was somewhat phenomenal, so I could not refuse, and found for them ungodly messages on Aerosmith's *Toys in the Attic*, Cheap Trick's *Dream Police*, AC/DC's *Dirty Deeds* and a large number of other recordings. Then there was the lawsuit against Judas Priest for embedding subliminal messages into their songs and thus causing Sean Cowie to disfigure himself with a shotgun and later die in the psychiatric unit of the Washoe Medical Centre from drugs and complications from his numerous surgeries. The *do it, do it* on the *Stained Class* album was obvious, but hardly solid evidence of purposeful malfeasance. . . . After weeks of laborious analysis I found a handful of menacing backmasks, including the now famous *Sing my evil spirit*, (expletive) *the Lord* and *God is evil*. . . . The 6.2 million dollar lawsuit was rejected. . . . The backmasking boom came to an end. . . . But my own career path was set. I began doing corporate work, finding reverses in the speech of potential clients and employees that revealed their subconscious minds. And I believe my somewhat glamorous line of employment helped make me attractive to Norma.

From the beginning I was extremely supportive and tried my best to understand her needs. She wanted to find direction for her life; she wanted to do something that was meaningful and I backed her one hundred percent. It is true that I threw forward a few alternative suggestions, but I certainly did not insist—I simply wanted her to know that there were many options. When she told me that the dental profession was what really appealed to her, I simply kissed her and said, "Whatever you think is best for yourself." That was very naïve of me. I have never been attracted by dentists and really, to be absolutely frank, have always loathed them. So why did I not object to her choice of profession? Because, being very much in love, I wanted to take part in fulfilling her dreams; and had no way to prophecy that for me the entire situation would turn into a nightmare.

She began to attend dental school and I actually paid for the courses. It was a full-time six month program in clinical dental assisting to be followed by a six week internship in a dental office. She was very enthusiastic and in the nights we made marvelous love. It was all very beautiful. We set a wedding date for the following spring and began to write out a list of guests to invite. We decided that we would go to Italy for our honeymoon, and I started to take Italian lessons twice a week.

But things changed. She changed.

"You seem very preoccupied," I told her.

"But happy?"

"Yes."

Maybe inside herself she was pleading for help. If she was, I did not know how to read the signs. She did seem happy, but distant. She was studying very hard for her exams and told me she had a yeast infection. So the love making came to a halt and I had to take recourse in my old bachelor's habit of drinking late night glasses of water mixed with apple-cider vinegar.

Then it came. It was a Saturday afternoon; I was eating a ham sandwich when she told me.

"Maybe we should wait," she said.

"Wait?"

"To be married, Ron. It might be too soon."

"But I have been taking Italian lessons."

"We could still go to Italy . . ."

My lunch was ruined. I put down the sandwich and pushed the plate away.

"Does this have anything to do with dental school?"

She laughed uneasily.

"Of course not."

Things started to become clear to me. That little ailment which would not go away, that so called 'yeast infection', was just an excuse. I looked in the medicine cabinet and her purse, but without finding any special medication. Still, I continued with the Italian lessons, bought a guidebook to Italy and pretended that everything was okay.

Norma started coming home late from school. She said that she was spending a little time off campus with other students, going over tooth numbering.

"I can help you with your tooth numbering," I said, and smiled.

"Ron, being with other people is good for me."

That night she spoke in her sleep. At least six times she uttered the name *Hesi-Re*. I turned on the bedside lamp and looked at her face. It was radiantly gorgeous and I felt desperately attracted to her. Noiselessly I got out of bed, went to the kitchen and drank a glass of water and vinegar.

Two days later, while looking through a notebook of hers, I found an extremely disturbing entry. The notebook was, I suppose, private. It had a half-finished letter to her grandmother, a not very good poem, and a few recollections of her childhood. Most of the pages however were blank. On one page, towards the back of the book, I discovered the words *Oh, Hesi-Re!* sitting naked, disjointed and alone.

Was she seeing another man, some Middle Eastern fellow from her school expert in oral soft tissue anatomy? I looked in the phone book, but found no such name. I searched on the internet and found the following on a site called *Brush & Floss & Fun*:

> *The first known dentist was Hesi-Re, an Egyptian who lived during the reign of Zoser, the pharaoh who ordered the building of the great Step Pyramid at Saqarra (2600 B.C.). Hesi-Re was known to be an expert at removing problem teeth, and he also drilled holes in the jawbones as a means of releasing pressure caused by abscesses. Gum swelling he treated with a concoction of cumin, incense, and onion.*

On finding this information, I was very troubled, but did not say a word to Norma. She would have been justifiably angry that I had looked through her private notebook and our relationship was already several degrees cooler than I wished.

It was obvious that she was keeping something from me. Since confronting her directly was impossible, I determined to probe her subconscious using backward speech technology. For three evenings in a row I clandestinely recorded our dinner conversations and then, later, while she was out of the house, listened to them in reverse. Though there were probably a dozen or so excellent examples of reverse speech in these dialogues, two stuck out in particular.

> *Ron* . . . (indistinguishable gibberish) . . . *love* (these were fragments of the forward words *normal* and *evolve*)
>
> *Pupils* . . . (indistinguishable gibberish) . . . *risk* (these were fragments of the forward words *slip-up* and *thick sirloin*)

This made it quite clear that she still loved me and that the problems she was having originated at the dental school. I had two choices. I could either confront her directly and demand to know everything, or else I could take covert action. The latter option naturally seemed the best and so, one day just as she was getting ready to go to school, I slipped my TCS-60DV into her purse, the record button already pressed down. I wanted to find out what was going on in the school and this seemed as good a way as any. That night, when she came home from school (late as usual), I secretly extracted the recorder from her purse. Late the next afternoon I set to work deciphering the text. Unfortunately the tape had only been 60 minutes, which meant that the one side that was recorded on was a mere 30 minutes. She had obviously taken her time to get to school, because there was only a good 10 solid minutes of school taping, and half of this was her talking to the receptionist at the school entrance about cold sterilisation procedures. Finally, however, I did get a minuscule chunk of what seemed like prime material. Apparently, in the hallway, she had come across one of the teachers, a certain Dr. Keith, who, after greeting her and mumbling a few indistinguishable words, clearly said:

"Are we not drawn onward, we few? Drawn onward to new era?"

"But if people don't agree?" Norma asked, "is it okay?"

"No," the doctor replied, "it is opposition."

The tape ended there, with those words, but I felt that I had found something disturbingly solid. The forward words were menacing in themselves. I salivated at the thought of what they would bring by backward play. With trembling fingers I pressed the reverse button. Dr. Keith's voice clearly said: "No, it is opposition." I looked down, and the tape was playing in reverse. There was the gibberish of reverse Norma, and then Dr. Keith saying, "Are we not drawn onward, we few? Drawn onward to new era?"

A queasy feeling came over me and I would have surely broken out in a cold sweat if I had not been interrupted.

"What are you doing?"

I turned around. It was Norma standing at the door of my laboratory.

"I came home early," she said. "I thought we hadn't been spending enough time together lately. . . . What was that voice I heard? It sounded familiar."

"Nothing," I murmured.

"Why are you acting so funny?"

I licked my lips. "Norma . . ."

"Play the tape, Ron. I want to hear what you were listening to."

There is no need to describe the scene that followed. I tried to explain things, but she would not listen. She cried, but would not let me comfort her and I spent the evening talking to myself in triangular tenses, stalking the house in my slippers, drinking Paternina Rioja adulterated with vinegar through a straw.

When she told me that she wanted to move out it felt as if the world was coming to an end. I went for a very long walk in the rain. The streets seemed like miserable fissures; cars drove by and splashed me with mud. I got to the park, visited the rose garden where we used to sit and hold hands, now completely without leaf or bloom, a great maze of thorns.

When I came home she was very nice to me. She prepared tea and we sat in silence with the cups steaming in front of us. Later she started to pack her things into boxes and that was the last night we slept in the same house. The next day she said goodbye and we hugged.

"Is it because you are in love with another man?" I asked. "Is he a dentist, some sort of professor of occlusion?"

"Ron."

"I won't quit with my lessons. —*Ti piace?* —So we can still go to Italy together. —Do you love me? —When will I see you again? —Do you think there is a possibility of us getting back together at some point in the future? —Can we meet after your endodontic procedure exams?"

"Don't ask me any more questions, Ron. Just let me go. It's over."

"Why? I am not going to let you go without an explanation."

"Your spying on me should be explanation enough."

"But you love me!"

"Ron, I like you very much, you are a sweetheart. But you are just too weird and I am just not attracted to you anymore."

I let her go. I knew she was lying to me, but I let her go.

That night, it was very difficult for me to sleep and so I took a dose of quazepam. I awoke late the next morning, with an absolutely clear recollection from my adolescence, one that had disappeared from my memory for many years.

When I was about seventeen or eighteen years old, I went to the dentist to have my wisdom teeth pulled. They gave me a general anaesthetic and I lost consciousness. When I awoke, I had violent scratches on my face, arms and chest, great red furrows where skin and flesh had been gouged away as if with a chisel. The nurse told me that I had struggled a great deal and they had been forced to contain me. Groggily I went home and for several weeks after that lived in a half-conscious, dream-like state, eating mashed potatoes and codeine and rinsing my mouth every day with warm salt water.

This episode came back to me. I saw all the particulars with absolute lucidity and under them a blurry, indistinct second level as if I were staring through a glass-bottomed boat at a forbidden, turbulent ocean beneath. I was in the dentist's office, chained naked to the wall. Two figures wearing exotic masks, performing some sort of odd aboriginal rights, harassed me, poked me with metallic instruments and stuck unpleasant substances, bizarre objects into my mouth, sticky liquids, cloud-like balls of cotton, brightly coloured spheres. As I said, this part of my recollection was somewhat vague, but I felt sure it was none the less real. My dislike for the dental profession was apparently based on an experience that lay buried in my subconscious mind.

Relatively certain that Norma was mixed up in a nasty business, I set to work to get to the bottom of it. I loved her and, to use a cliché, would not abandon her without a fight.

I drove by the dental school every day for a week hoping to catch sight of her, but I never did. She had left no forwarding address or telephone number. I bought myself a false moustache and a green overcoat. It was a silly disguise, but it really did make me look completely different.

The vestibule of the dental school was set up very much like the waiting room of a dentist's office. For a visitor to enter the school they would first need to get past the secretary. She was a woman of about fifty years of age with a hare-lip and a quantity of flaccid flesh that hung loose beneath her chin. When I told her that I wanted to look around the school she became visibly uncomfortable.

"Are you an aspiring student?" she asked.

"My son is considering the dental profession," I lied, "and I want to know a few things about this establishment before I enrol him."

She pulled out a prospectus and offered it to me.

"Still," I said, caressing the bright, glossy pages with my finger tips, "it would be nice to look around the place if you don't mind."

"We have a special introductory tour once a month for aspiring students. If you would like to leave your name and telephone number I would be happy to——"

"How about I just walk through the place for ten minutes," I interrupted. "I am sure I won't get in anyone's way."

"Sir, we have classes in session and it is absolutely prohibited to have non-students or non-personnel tour the premises without a guide."

I walked out the door without saying another word, the secretary calling after me, persisting, practically demanding that I leave my name. My car was conveniently parked two blocks away and I made certain that no one followed me. When I got in I looked at myself in the mirror. The moustache had been a brilliant inspiration. It made me look ten years older, somewhat grave and stupid, like a bankrupt building contractor.

It was obvious that the dental school had something to hide. I recalled how enthusiastic Norma had been when she had come back from one of their 'guided tours'. She had been given a prospectus as well, a masterpiece of typography bristling with the language of picks and drills, which I had briefly looked through. That sterile, matter-of-fact language was truly as seducingly hypnotic as the well-regulated metre of some ancient religious poem.

I waited a week without going anywhere near the school. In the meantime I did my homework, reading John Hunter's *Natural History of the Human Teeth* and both volumes of Fauchard's *Odontology*. On the following Thursday night, after my Italian lesson, I drove by the school. It was completely black and nobody was in sight. I parked in my usual spot and, with the aid of a flashlight, applied the false moustache to my upper lip. I took out my wallet, put it in the glovebox of the car, got out and walked to the school. The night was moonless and somewhat chilly and a thick mist hung in the air, giving halos to the street lamps and making the school itself appear especially sinister. While circling the premises I discovered a small window, higher than my head, that was cracked open. There was a garbage receptacle near the front entrance of the building. I took this and placed it upside down under the window, so it now acted as a kind of footstool with which I could raise myself high enough to access the target. I pushed the window open, lifted my body up and worked it through the opening.

I found myself in a restroom, standing on top of a sink. After lowering myself to the ground and washing my hands, I removed the flashlight from my pocket and stalked forward. I walked through a long, cheaply carpeted hallway, opened a door, a broom closet—bucket, mop, a bottle of Duracryl-25, etc.—, closed it, opened another and found myself in a classroom, standing in the midst of neatly aligned rows of desks. I ran the giant ray of my flashlight over the walls. To my right was a chalkboard on which was written: *K. John Greenwood, 1789 —dentures for George Washington.* Towards the front of the room a sort of altar was set up before a green chlorite image, chipped and obviously of great antiquity. Screwed to its base was a plaque on which the name Hesi-Re was engraved. On either side of his figure were portraits, one of Archigenus, the inventor of the dental drill, and the other of Paul Revere, the most renowned dentist in American history, and placed slightly to the left and somewhat before the display was a species of throne, painted gold and set on a richly carpeted platform. To the right was an upholstered red leather dentist's chair with a steel and rubber headrest and a two-step foot rest, framed in steel and covered with rubber.

Seeing all this, I felt extremely uneasy, as if I was violating the precincts of some awesome and cruel god. *The music is reversible . . . but time is not. Turn Back! Turn Back! Turn Back! Turn Back!* Those were the reversed words from Electric Light Orchestra's *Fire on High.* My mind recalled them; my feet, almost of their own accord, led me out of the room. Back in the hallway, I moved forward. There were other doors that I did not try and then a door, at the very end of the hall, that I was magnetically attracted to and opened.

It was an office. Against one wall was an aquarium with several very pretty dwarf gouramis in it and what looked to be a black tetra, though I am not absolutely certain. On the opposite wall hung a giant portrait of H. Charles Goodyear who, through his discovery of vulcanite rubber, made false teeth available to millions. The picture itself was in the poorest possible taste and had a strong resemblance, stylistically, to a cheap print of some false Indian guru or god—a smiling, almost ecstatic face wreathed in gaudy colours and speckled with dental symbolism—a painting that, for all its ostentation, was both emotionally mute and artistically dead. There was a closet which I explored, finding hung within several hooded lilac robes, the dental ensign emblazoned on the breasts. Aside from this, the room was sparsely and plainly furnished. On the desk was a pamphlet, *Sedation of Phobic Dental Patients With an Emphasis on the Use of Oral Triazolam* by Gary Sussex, D.D.S. F.A.G.D., F.A.S.D.A., F.I.C.D.

I opened to the first page and read:

120 million people worldwide are dental phobics. Another estimated 120 to 240 million suffer from dental anxiety. Coping with the difficult-to-manage patient has long plagued the profession. Phobic dental patients come in all sizes, shapes and colours and are phobic for many different reasons, both psychological and physical. Often these phobias stem from traumatic childhood dental treatments. In some cases, troubles start much later due to an especially difficult treatment, particularly if pain control was incomplete.

I turned to page 13 and read:

The high incidence of retrograde amnesia on conscious patients further endears it to the dental practitioner. Patients do not have to be asleep for their dental treatments if they can be relaxed enough for us to do the required procedures and not have any memory of the procedure.

I closed the book and, sitting down, rifled through one of the drawers. There were a few pencils, a girlie magazine, a professional atomic digital wire weather station, numerous papers and a bag of potato chips. I opened the latter, ate a few and propped my feet up on the desk. I closed my eyes and thought of Norma, her long blonde hair flowing over me like rays of golden sunshine. I wanted so much to be with her, to be able to cook for her and hold her close to me, bathe in the depths of her white skin, approximating a lake of milk of magnesia. I was dunked beneath the surface, spanked with a red-hot tongue suppresser as I watch her being seduced by Guy de Charliac. I tried to explain things to her, but every word I uttered came out contrary. Then I found myself lost amidst a crowd of men in white, knee-length jackets who were all running backwards. One looked at me in the face, his eyes great blue emotionless disks, and he said quite clearly, 'Slow down; last one to the finish line wins,' and together we coursed across the rhythm of my dreams, dreams in dripping mauve and shattered sea green. . . . Oblivion. . . . Dentists know about comfortable chairs. . . . I was jarred awake by the sound of laughter. The light of day filtered in through the window. I could hear students arriving, talking outside.

I cracked open the door and looked. Figures clad in hooded lilac robes marked on the breast with the dental ensign glided mysteriously along the hall; a number disappeared into the classroom I had visited the night before. Without hesitating for an instant I went to the closet, pulled down one of the robes I had seen there, and slipped into it, adjusting the hood over my head. I then left the office and walked forward with my head down so that my face would not be seen, nodding to other robed figures as I passed them. Though this would have been a good time to find my way out of the school, I did not, emboldened as I was by my flawless disguise. Instead, I moved into the classroom.

Both the image of Hesi-Re and the portraits of Archigenus and Paul Revere were now richly adorned with fresh garlands of mint, and the smoke of incense curled up in front of the triad. The throne was now draped in white silk and built up with luxurious cushions.

The students all sat at their desks and, seeing that several were still unoccupied, I did likewise. Luckily for me no one exchanged words with their neighbour. It seemed that respectful silence was requisite. I looked at the figures around me, wondering which one of them, if any, was Norma. At least ten of them had marked protuberances of the chest, and I had little doubt that under those robes could be found various grades of female figures.

A person, an obvious dignitary of some sort, in a hooded crimson robe adorned with golden braid, walked in, followed immediately by two subordinates wearing black robes. All the students sprang reverently to their feet and stepped to the left-hand side of their desks. The crimson-robed being approached the image of Hesi-Re and threw himself on his knees before it, letting out a loud, almost orgasmic cry as he did so.

Both of the black-robed figures and all the students fell to their knees and prostrated themselves before the image, and I followed suit as best I could, imitating their movements, touching my forehead to the floor, quickly rising to my feet and falling once more, three times in succession. After this, all the students sat at their desks while the crimson-robed being seated himself on the throne, attended on either side by his subordinates.

For the space of about sixty seconds no one made a noise and then, when that leader, teacher or priest—I could not say exactly what he was—spoke, the crisp, clear and thoroughly grave enunciation of his voice broke the silence like a bell clanging in some lifeless wasteland.

"Praise be to Hesi-Re; praise be to Paul Revere; praise be to Archigensus, who more than one thousand nine hundred years ago invented the dental drill. Praise be to these, our fathers, from whom we have descended and in whose names we prepare ourselves for the coming singularity. May my words fall upon attentive ears and may they be cherished in wide-awake hearts."

"May it be so!" everyone in the room cried in unison.

He then began to lecture at some length, his speech a mixture of dental history and crackpot techno-transcendentalism. He marched through great, superficially profound generalities and then moved on to vacuous specifics, fragile balloons of logic that, while being very pretty to observe, would surely burst at the slightest pinprick of discrimination. In the same sentence he would mention the 25,000 RPM air-router drill of Dr. Robert Borden and the proceedings of the first European conference on artificial life. "When Abucasis first invented the dental file . . . and Vesalius . . . now, exponentially increasing the ability of our machines to make calculations . . . an equally profound magnification of our knowledge and power . . . to alginate impressions and diagnostic casts. . . . And, through science, select humans will be enabled to live forever. . . ." I regretted not having my TCS-60DV, as surely there were some wonderful backward gems buried amongst all that forward drivel. . . . Backward I would have taken an interest; forward it bored me. My mind wandered. I began to think of other things, such as my childhood, my aborted romance with Norma, the reversed lyrics from the Backstreet Boys' *Everyone* (*the sadness and madness*), the fact that I had not eaten breakfast that day. It seemed like the best thing to do would be to just slink out the door, go home and fix myself a bowl of cereal. . . . Everyone stood up in a body around me and I in turn rose, trying once more to concentrate on the crimson-robed being's words.

"Now it is time for the second initiation, the initiation of the first level dental assistant in which you receive your Dentocomm Dental Chip together with your password. . . . In the not-too-distant future, upon the occurrence of the singularity, you will be able to communicate with other league members without even opening your mouth. You will be able to communicate with league members across the globe in any language you choose, and have vast ability and knowledge. . . . This dental chip will be the bridge for future brain-computer interface and will be sealed in your 2nd bicuspid, not only with an amalgam of silver, tin and mercury, but also with your unbreakable vows."

One of the creatures in black wheeled a small cart covered with dental paraphernalia towards the upholstered red leather dentist's chair and the other spoke: "Will the first initiate, her who is known as Indonesia-39, step up to the chair."

One of the lilac-robed figures stepped forward.

"Woman who is known as Indonesia-39, are you prepared to be initiated into the second mystery, the mystery of the dental assistant, and thereby receive the Dentocomm Dental Chip, that sublime item developed by our own most illustrious Dr. Keith?"

The figure nodded, lifted up her arms and the two black figures removed her robe. Long blonde hair streamed over bare shoulders, skin blindingly white. She wore nothing but sneakers and socks. It was her, Norma; and a moment later she was seated in the chair. . . . Whirrr! . . . The drill started; and she smiled; and something inside myself simply broke. I was stunned and for a moment lights danced in front of my eyes and my knees became weak. I thought I saw a great jet of blood spurt into the air. Two or three loud, guttural sounds escaped from my lips and bounced across the room; I lunged forward, but after a brief instant of movement, found myself on the floor, my hood thrown back.

"Ron, is that you? Where did you get the moustache?"

"Do you know this man?"

"He's my ex-boyfriend—the one I told you about."

"The reverse speech technologist?"

"Yes, Dr. Keith, it's him."

"Norma," I murmured.

"You will not talk to the young woman known as Indonesia-39."

"To hell with you!" I screamed and my head surged with waves of heat. It felt as if the earth was opening up beneath me, my body hovering suspended in fathomless space. I struggled, but there were too many of them and I found myself unable to speak or properly move my limbs. I was carried through the sea of desks and into the cheaply carpeted hall; the broom closet was opened, the bucket, mop, bottle of Duracryl-25, etc. hastily removed, a secret hatch revealed; and my body and mind were both dragged down a flight of stairs, through a narrow corridor and flung into an unlighted room.

I collapsed on the floor and gasped for breath. I heard the sound of some sort of nearby engine or motor. The words from Marilyn Manson's *Dope Hat* mercilessly went through my head. Forward: *Ouwa, Ouwa, Ouwa, Ouwa.* Backward: *Prepare to meet your doom.* In the darkness I thought of all the possible tortures dentists could inflict: attaching electrical wires to the tri-geminal nerve, prodding the LX nerve with the cold and barbed steel of a cooley pick, sending cracking pain through the pink of my gums, making my jaw rigid with anguish as wolf-like howls break away from my blood-coated throat.

The door swung open; my eyes were suddenly dazzled by light. The room was completely empty except for a table, a chair, and an old Krüger dehumidifier that sat working away in one corner. Dr. Keith loomed over me; he flung back his hood and for the first time I saw his face clearly. He had the cold, unflinching eyes of a butcher buried in a handsome and intelligent, clean-shaven face. His head was crowned with a helmet of perfectly tended brown hair, that was certainly either dyed or bogus.

"I am Dr. Keith."

"I know."

"Why have you intruded on my school?"

"Norma . . ."

"You love Indonesia-39?"

"I love Norma."

"If you really loved her you would have let her lead her life without interference. By spying on her, you have shown yourself to be a selfish, narrow-minded man."

"Maybe she is the one who is selfish."

"Norma is as selfless as I am, Ron."

I bit my bottom lip; wished for my TCS-60DV.

"Turning that around in your mind?" he asked. "For all your expertise in reverse speech psychology, I don't think you have ever considered that the only reason you love her might be because her name backward encompasses your own." He smiled and his teeth, two rows of perfect white cubes, sparkled. And then: "You realise that, at the moment, it is virtually impossible for me to set you free?"

"So then I am a prisoner?" I murmured. "Or a dead man?"

Dr. Keith laughed. "No, not at all," he said. "Dentists are not monsters. We want to benefit humanity, to fill cavities, perform root canals, and prepare ourselves for the coming age when the weight of the whole human race will rest upon our shoulders. . . . Kill you? Not at all. Actually, for all your meddling, you are going to receive a great reward, something many people pay large sums of money for."

Directing me to follow him, he opened the door, outside of which were now stationed his two henchmen dressed in black. To the immediate right was a second door, which he led me through and into a large, brightly lit room full of numerous metallic cylinders that looked like giant thermoses.

"These are our cryostats," he said. "If you went to one of the many companies that offer this service commercially, you would be charged between thirty and a hundred and fifty thousand dollars for initial suspension and then an additional four or five thousand dollars a year for maintenance. Under the present circumstances however—due to your own foolishness and this organisation's philanthropy—you can enjoy the benefits of cryonics for absolutely free. —But you don't look very keen on the idea."

"You want to freeze me?" I asked.

"Exactly. And then, in thirty or forty years, after the singularity has occurred and our organisation has taken its rightful position in world government, we will defrost you. —At that time you will no longer be a threat and you will be reintroduced into society."

He patted me on the shoulder and showed me back to the other chamber. He pulled a pre-prepared syringe from his pocket.

"This is benzodiazepine, a harmless anaesthetic. I would like to inject you with it."

"What if I don't want to be injected and frozen?"

"I am hoping we will not need to go down that path. . . . You are an intelligent man, and I am assuming that reason will make you see———"

He had turned and set the syringe down on the table. In one incredibly swift instant I picked up the dehumidifier and let it come crashing down on his head. He fell almost noiselessly to the ground. I picked up the needle, stuck it in his arm and injected him. Five minutes later he lay asleep on the chair, him wearing my lilac robe, I wearing his of crimson. As a final touch I tore off my false moustache and applied it to his upper lip.

I opened the door.

"Is he ready?" one of the black-robed figures asked.

"Yes," I murmured. "Give him five minutes until the sedative has completely taken effect and then put him in the cryostat."

Resolutely, I marched down the corridor. It seemed incredible that they were not running after me, and every second I expected to be seized by the shoulder. When I reached the stairs I could barely keep from bounding up them three at a time. I walked through the cheaply carpeted hallway, the lilac-robed students bowing reverently to me as I passed. The ante-room was easy enough to find—a few doors tried, and I was there.

The hare-lipped receptionist looked up, startled.

"Dr. Keith . . . your robe!"

I exited the building and walked rapidly down the street; my walk turned into a jog, and then I started to run. Once in my car, I headed straight for the highway, too terrified to even stop at my house—which was of course the first place they would look for me.

The sky was a dreary grey. I drove past fields out of which grew the white necks of cranes. Huge semi-trucks roared alongside me; the road stretched out in front, a great black line that shot off into infinity. For me there was no turning back. I could never return to my home. So I moved to Italy where I now live under an assumed name. For the moment I lie buried away in the vast and almost impregnable maze called Roma, as it is very close to love spelled backward and is also rich in art and culture. The food, though somewhat lacklustre at times, is quite good and one can buy a decent bottle of wine for a very low sum. My Italian has greatly improved and I believe that within the next year or two I will speak it fluently. I have a pain in one of my incisors which is, ironically, probably due to a cavity. But the last thing in the world I would ever consider is a visit to the dentist.

THE NANNY GOAT

I.

She had always been ugly. Now, at ninety-eight years of age, she was hideous. A lizard in a dress; a piece of twisted tin come to life.

A shrunken yellow head sat atop a neck that looked like a bundle of cords. Her chest was punctuated by two long, flaccid breasts. An odour of rotten fruit and propolis hung about her, as if she were an old nun.

And, indeed, she had led a life of the most acute abstinence.

Martyring herself in her own virginity, she had always relished the idea of sinners going to hell—the eternal torture of lubricious women and homosexuals. A smile would come to her lips when she thought of them there below, roasting over hot flames, their skin blistering and their tongues sticking rigid from their mouths.

She, Carla Necroforo, had never known the touch of man and was convinced that she would some day ascend straight into the sky.

II.

Mendrisio is a small town situated on the southern most tip of Switzerland, in Ticino, the Italian speaking part of that country. The town's origins clearly date back to Roman times, as can be deduced from the marble slab dedicated to one Publio Valerio Dromone, on the old bell tower on the Piazza del Ponte.

The population lazily stroll down its main lane, which is paved with bricks, lined with numerous bars and cafés. They sit, murmur to each other in low voices over glasses of dark Merlot or, sometimes, let out guttural cries and in times of festivity sing songs of farmyard romance.

Though the town is blemished by a fair number of modern edifices, which protrude like warts from its visage, the buildings are for the most part old, with thick walls and long, narrow windows.

Her house was a gloomy stone object left over from the 18th century. Dark red shutters eternally closed. Chilly as a tomb, it seemed to suit her to perfection, for she was a sort of hobgoblin, afraid of the light, murmuring prayers like a recluse in a cave, shunning human kind, living creatures, sucking on her own gums as she read about how Jael smote off Sisera's head when she had pierced and stricken through his temples.

III.

One morning, after breakfasting on black espresso and dry toast smeared with peach jam, she heard a whining outside. She opened the shutters, and looked, espied a havoc of fur. A pair of dogs were coupling in her yard.

"Beasts," she murmured.

But she did not raise her voice, did not try and chase them off and, somehow, was unable to remove her gaze from the spectacle, the power of the dog, a quivering blotch of brown against bright verdure.

IV.

The days that followed were difficult for her to bear. She could not get the image out of her mind. It haunted her. At night she lay awake in a state of profound agitation. All of a sudden, desire had awoke in her, as if she had been a girl of sixteen summers instead of a woman of almost a hundred winters. She tried to fight away the thoughts, but ended up succumbing to them, losing herself in the wildest fantasies. She bit her pillow, felt as if fire were burning her loins—for indeed she was like a piece of ancient timber that only needed a spark to ignite it.

"I must have a man," she murmured to herself, her voice as brittle as the wing of a long dead moth.

Restlessly she began to prowl outside her house, haunt the piazzas, espy young men and smack her meagre lips in a frightening, lurid fashion.

Several times she tried to accost them, but was only met with looks of amazement, disgust.

"Excuse me . . ."

"Eh?"

"If you could . . ."

"*Mamma mia, che schifo!*"

V.

Her eyes were ringed with scarlet, though she could shed no tears.

She sat in her living room, nursing her unclean thoughts, wondering if she, who had always prided herself on her cold virginity, would end by dying in that state now that she craved to rupture it—see it burnt to dust in the blast of some able youth's lust.

Her eyes wandered over her scrawny thighs, then along the floor . . . up the wall. There were a few very bad religiously themed paintings as well as a dark portrait of a broad shouldered man with a huge moustache.

She gazed at the portrait.

It was of her great uncle, who had inhabited the house some seventy or eighty years before, had been a great scholar.

Vague memories from her girlhood came to her—a mélange of words, phrases, images. She recalled imprecisely that her great uncle had carried with him a reputation, as one to be feared, as one who had certain occult powers.

She stretched out her tongue, wafer thin and reddish-brown, and dampened the thin threads of her lips.

"I wonder . . ." she murmured.

She arose from her seat, wandered into the library.

The bottom shelves were stocked with her books, religious tracts, lives of saints, etc. while on the top were those which had belonged to the family, some to her parents, mostly to her great uncle—row upon row of great, leather-bound tomes.

She climbed on a chair, tried to reach, but the books were still too high for her. She took a broom and knocked them down—a mass tumbled to the floor, almost crushing her, letting off a faint odour of mould. She kneeled down, touched the dusty leather covers, passed her fingers over the yellow paper, her eyes darting over the titles, over the words.

"Ah, ah!" she croaked, a strange sparkle appearing in her sharp eyes.

She lifted up a volume titled *The Magic Cauldron*.

VI.

The bathroom was lit with seven candles.

A lamb was tethered to the door handle.

Into the tub already half full of water she poured treacle, tossed daffodil, rhubarb and hellebore, a dead mole, the embryo of a mule, the hair of an eight year old child and scrapings of silver.

She cut the lambs throat, and held it tightly as its blood flowed.

The bathtub now filled with the vile liquid, she let her dress drop from her shoulders, undid her stiff, wire-rimmed undergarments, stepped gingerly in, soon submerged her body—felt as if a thousand hot little worms were burrowing into her skin, felt her withered flesh begin to swell.

VII.

The vines became heavy with clusters of dark purple spheres, which hung down like the overly ripe breasts of some tribe of aboriginal women and the days, somewhat shortened, gave more time for the stars to laugh at night.

It was towards the end of September. Evening. La Sagra dell' Uva—the festival of the vine, the grape. The central streets of the little town were crowded with people. Men grimaced behind huge moustaches. Hollers and thick accents; the racy idiom of Medrisiotto. Younger adults, the more sophisticated crowd, sampled the finer wines from booths while the men from the hills drank whatever came their way, without worry of the wherewithall. From within the scrambled sounds of an accordion and a guitar we see mouths agape, blurting out the fatalistic lyrics of peasants.

Jacques Montebello was a handsome young man with soft eyes and somewhat feminine lips which contrasted in a pleasant way with a prominent chin which often wore a day or two's worth of whiskers.

He wandered through the crowd. He was to meet some friends—to eat polenta and beef in one of the bustling courtyards.

He stopped at a booth and ordered a glass of the better Merlot; turned, sipped at the beverage while letting his eyes dance over the passers-by. For the most part, the women were the sort that a man would need to drink a few glasses before he could appreciate their attractions. And so, on his first glass, Jacques stood. But his eyes, no longer dancing, were arrested—shackled to flesh which might have been hewn from moonlight and movements like sunshine reflected in a northern sea.

It seemed as if a more beautiful woman had never before walked the earth. Her body, which gave off a fragrance of flowers, of sweet things and summertime, seemed a fecund temple—a place which cried out for worshippers, those devotees of love, to come, enter its doors. She had long flowing hair and eyes in which one saw the flutter of a butterfly's wings, the glint of jewels, rolling sand dunes kissed by the sea.

In an instant, he forgot—not only about his friends, his supper, his plans for the evening—but even about his past, any hope he had for the future.

She winked at him, smiled an invitation and he approached, murmured a few indistinct words. Taking his hand, she led him away; offered him some bizarre enchanted fruit, the intoxicating flavour of which he had never before known, knew existed.

VIII.

"My name is Carla."

"My Carlita!"

"Yes, with me you can both eat and drink."

"And this big house . . ."

"Do you like it?"

"I thought it belonged to a wretched old woman."

"My grand-aunt. She is gone and I am here."

"Thank God!"

She pressed her mouth to his, almost swallowed him whole.

IX.

Her house became like a bee-hive, with men constantly coming and going in a frenzy of excitement. An old woman's lusts hidden in the body of a young. She shed estrus, threw herself into the activity with an abandon that truly astonished her partners—demanding of them the most complete compliance to her dirty wishes.

Her aroma attracted men from all quarters, like wolves who can sniff out a lone fawn in the forest, little suspecting that the palace of her body contained the most filthy of chambers, halls coated with cobwebs, latrines overflowing with the sanctimonious refuse of a century.

Young lads barely just licensed to drive, swarthy construction workers whose muscular legs stretched out the fabric of their pants, then blond men of effeminate manners and exquisite taste. She offered herself gladly to every comer, provided they were youthful, handsome and hungry for cheesecake. She was like some sponge which had sat many years in the desert, insatiable for liquid.

A young Japanese man by the name of Ryō, a student at the Accademia di Architettura, was one of her most ardent admirers, abandoning his studies, tapping at her door at all hours, losing himself in the folds of her skirts as he murmured strange, poetic protestations of love in broken Italian.

With a sinister smile playing on her lips, she would make him race through all the stages of humiliation until, after he had licked her clean with his tongue, he would collapse in tears of quivering joy.

Then there was Paolo, a lumbering young man, the son of a farmer, who came to her door still smelling of cow dung and hay.

From him she demanded Herculean tasks, the sort of muscular love prized by female orangutans and others with a reversed sexual dimorphism.

In her new body, which was as flexible as a snake, she became exceptionally extrovert, finding herself at clubs, quickly picking up the latest dance moves. The woman who had never drunk anything stronger than tea with lemon suddenly found an appetite for burning liquors, for brandy, vodka and tequila drunk to the cheers of her masculine companions.

On those rare moments when she was alone, she would snigger, cackle to herself as she dug her nails into her own plump breasts, exulting in that plastic youth. She marvelled at how she could have lived so long without tasting the pleasures of the world, simply waiting for those uncertain of heaven.

She wanted to make up for all that she had missed in her life and more, throwing all cares to the winds, as she lunged forward, laughing, tongue lapping at the frenzied lips of her partners.

X.

She moved a goddess and she looked a paradise. Her gynecic attractions made men lose all self respect and, indeed, she took keen delight in humiliating them, thinking them toads at her disposal.

"Crawl at my feet, Apollo."

As she stuck her toe in his eye the man whimpered with joy.

"Imbecile!"

And like a cat in heat she clawed, the cries which issued from her pretty mouth darkly fantastic like those of a creature from hell.

XI.

Her worshippers sat around her with lascivious grins on their faces, each one hopeful for the most wild indulgence, an evening recalling the ancient days of Messalina, when the last comer was even more welcome than the first. They clicked their tongues, scratched themselves, behaved like so many primates—their intelligence struck down by the heavy hammer of their desires sauced with wine, them filling glasses to the brim, swallowing down the purple liquid, dribbles running from the corners of their mouths. They stuck out their tongues and showed their teeth, scratched themselves and made strange, lewd jokes, which would have only made sense to the initiated.

"Some music!"

The radio was turned on, an old Blaupunkt.

Corrupted with static, the sound of bass and drums waddled around the room, the voice of some Italian crooner drifted from ear to ear.

"Who wants to dance?" Carla cried.

Jacques came eagerly forward and took her in his arms. They skipped about as the others howled, moved their hips synchronically forward, each eager to bump with her; hounds sniffing at bitch-amourette.

She freed herself from the grip of Jacques, shook her breasts and hips madly, shimmy rippled, her body possessed with maxixe-like movements, tempest-tossed mammillae and the plea of zooidal jelly.

The young men grovelled in front of her, like maggots eager to infest some enticing piece of ripe red meat, eyes bulging from swollen faces.

And then something very strange happened.

Reality sometimes disgorges itself in the most awful way.

As she danced, her hair began to fall from her head.

The smiles of those fellows evaporated. They stood back, warily.

Great patches of skin peeled away from Carla's face and bare arms. Her plump lips peeled back to reveal a mouth full of unpleasant, disarranged teeth.

Jacques gazed at her flaccid breasts with profound dismay. Ryō shivered. Paolo was nauseous.

A very old and repellent woman danced before them, grinning with gross carnality.

The most horrible thing about the spectacle was the fact that she, half-drunk, aflame with desire, clearly did not realise the transformation that had taken place, for she continued to act the coquette, speak perversion; an obscene spectre. As she moved, her dress fell away from her dried-up form.

The young men were sickened.

"Come now boys, touch me," she cried, her mouth twisted in the most ghastly expression.

Jacques gritted his teeth. His soft eyes became hard.

"You ugly old bitch!"

"Eh!"

She looked at her hands, her boney fingers, down at her spindly legs. Turning, she caught sight of herself in a mirror which hung on the wall, then shrieked and covered her face.

Those young sportsmen forgot all the weird pleasure they had received, now filled with extreme, unthinking agitation, violent antipathy.

Ryō lunged at her, bit her ear.

She pulled herself away and, with blood running down her neck, turned and sped from the room, spilled out the back door of the house.

The sky drizzled rain and dawn was just breaking.

Our heroine ran, lifting her thin, repugnant legs as high off the ground as she could, her unclean zeal turned to fear. She scrambled over and fence and dashed through a neighbouring vineyard, now a maze of dried twigs and dead leaves.

The lads, yelling and screaming in a babel of languages, pursued. And the woman was not very difficult for those robust bodies to catch.

Paolo stormed at her, like an enraged bull, head down, clenching his fists. She gave a lamentable yell before being flung face foremost to the ground.

They kicked her and beat her with sticks, then spat upon her corpse, mutilating it with savage blows. And afterwards—some in silence, some with mad laughter or with faces bathed in savage tears—they disbanded, stumbling their separate ways as the rain stopped, clouds cleared and the light of the sun came over the hills.

MESH

OF

VEINS

What would you like to be,—pig, buzzard, clown or millionaire?
—Honoré de Balzac

The first tattoo was fairly benign. Still, Dee procrastinated and trembled considerably over the decision. In a sense it was the sacrificing of one's flesh, the marking, branding of the only thing that could truly be called his own. It was not unlike the loss of virginity; certain things can never really be undone.

The falcon on his shoulder was no work of art. Yet Dee felt proud of the object that coloured his skin. He oiled it, lending the hues bold definition. A tank-top shirt was worn out of doors, exposing the bird to open air.

It is said that human beings are the only creatures to become involved in self-scarification. This sort of knowledge is espoused by some as further proof that we are the only bodies to house a soul. Strange to say, the Jews and Christians of old outlawed tattooing and all forms of self-scarification, except circumcision. . . . The Romans used tattoos to mark slaves. Undoubtedly this stereotyped and embittered the process for many centuries.

Humans are a habit-loving species who cling to their addictions, making trends of them. Dee did not have his first tattoo for long before he desired a second. The epidermal raptor drew a little attention to him, which was not unwelcome. He was partial to birds of prey, and had a kestrel imprinted on his left breast, directly over the heart, emblazoned around the nipple.

To pass from having one's body daubed with permanent ink to the piercing of an ear is hardly a significant step. Instead of being a mature progression it is almost a retrogression. Dee went from piercing the lobe of the aural orifice to the cartilage of the septum. Later, though not much, a stainless steel ring was inserted in the tip of his phallus. . . . To some it might seem akin to infibulation, the buttoning of the penis in the male, or, in females, the padlocking of the pudenda. . . . Dee however did not see it in this light. If anything he believed that it made him all the better developed. The rumour current in his circle ran that it was a tool sure to enhance the voluptuous pleasure of both participants. Some clues are left to the fringe to verify.

One morning, while absorbing a cup of coffee, he saw a man with the teeth of a cat. This thrilled Dee. He lost no time in striking up a conversation, asking for details on the phenomena. The Cat Mouth, Karl Ledux, was very friendly and offered his services if they should be needed. The following week our protagonist's teeth were filed into sharp, even rows, in imitation of the archaeopteryx. The smile was genuinely intimidating, glimmering with a carnivorous lustre.

The bird theme in general caught Dee's fancy. He had, on several occasions, seen a man, to immediate appearance ordinary, riding the 7 train. As soon as the fellow disembarked however, he would begin cawing. Up the escalator he would go, on to 42nd Street, his feet stepping lively. The sound issuing from the man's throat was so genuinely crow-like that, if you happened not to see him, mouth moded in articulation, you would be sure to think a dark scavenger was pecking and flapping around the vicinity.

Forking from the corner of each eye, Dee had five lines per side seared into the skin. A large coil of stainless steel, bent to a crescent, was implanted in his forehead, just above the eyes, the brows of which he shaved and waxed. These markings were inspired by the head of the male Andean condor.

From his teenage years he had smoked cannabis and drunk alcohol. Later, experimentation was made with other drugs. The books of Carlos Castaneda were read around the same time that he became involved in body alteration. This inspired him to partake of a small quantity of the *Psilocybe cubensis* mushroom. He saw what he believed to be the fibre of the universe, sympathetic filaments connecting mankind to plantlife, the spirit world and the kingdom of animals. Thereafter he ate the mushroom on an almost weekly basis, believing that to regularly and dramatically alter one's consciousness promoted emotional well-being.

His back and chest were tattooed with intricate vanes, of which every barb was discernable. Not wishing to be gaudy, he chose the delicate colouration of the wren: dun patched with cinnamon, dark barring, occasional tints of white and grey. The shafts he had cicatrized on his skin with a razor. Around his neck he opted for the turquoise of the cassowary blending into fleshy pink. The sum total was a bizarre and haunting plumage, jointly delicate and brazen.

He went through a good deal of trouble and expense over his eyes. Finding a specialty optomologist able to create contact lenses that adequately replicated the eyes of the *Rupicola peruviana*, or Peruvian cock-of-the-rock, was not easy. Yet, once they were in place—that mysterious and eerie light-blue, a tiny ink-black pupil ringed by a sliver of milk—the outcome was dramatic.

A number of his acquaintances had split their tongues, lizard fashion. Naturally this would not fit into his projects, his theme. . . . He had it trimmed, from the back forward, in a diagonal motion. Due to the highly sensitive constitution of the muscle, it became necessary to rub cocaine in his mouth before each stage of the operation. . . . The final result was a V-shaped organ, tapering off into a thin and delicate point. . . . Of course there were unforeseen results. Strangely enough, the reduction in the number of papillae, instead of reducing the sense of taste, made it all the more keen. Bitter and sour things suddenly seemed too strong, to the point of causing repugnance. Contrariwise, things normally considered bland and uninteresting, such as peanut butter, plain bread etc., assumed the flavour of delicacies, rich and delicious. . . . Probably the most disturbing aspect of the tongue carving was the manner in which it altered his speech. He lost almost the entire ability to pronounce dentals. His palatals, the semivocals in particular, sounded strangely guttural, like those in the speech of one deaf from birth. The sibilants and labials on the other hand became the defining mark of his speech, carrying with them all sorts of strange inflections never much heard in the English language. The sound of his voice was a kind of hissing, chopped up by the popping of lips, highly unusual and certain to make eyebrows rise. His mouth would open, a slim and xiphoid muscle, strawberry red, tapering to a pinpoint, curling and bending like a pinworm between two rows of violently serrated teeth.

Dee cicatrized bands around his calves, thus simulating the scaly rings of many tarsi. His legs he shaved and waxed as swimmers do. This further enhanced the scars, making them shine with a certain measure of brilliance. He let his toenails grow to morbid length, filed them into prehensile curves, and then stained them black. . . . Yet this was not intense enough. . . . After meditating darkly, he cut the first phalange of the first and third toe off and stitched the first toe to the second, then the third to the fourth. This left him with three toes, or talons, on each foot. To further enhance the effect, he separated the flesh between the second and third metatarsals about half an inch up from the base phalanges of the corresponding toes. Between the fourth and fifth metatarsals he separated the flesh half an inch into the plantar arch, completely through the ball of the foot. Of course he did not do this all at once, but in stages, letting fissures and wounds heal, re-opening and elongating them. . . . Over time he stretched apart the three toes of each foot, inserting chunks of wood of ever increasing breadth, until each digit was permanently separated by a good two or three inches. They splayed out, resembling the foot of a crake. . . . To finish this dark handiwork, Dee pierced the outer edge of his heels, inserting into each hole a piece of stainless steel jewellery resembling the talon of an eagle. These he also painted black. . . . As a matter of course, shoes were out of the question, the range of workable possibilities. He wore sandals instead.

Karl Ledux returned from a year long stint in the Northwest, carrying a large quantity of the dried *Psilocybe cyanescens* mushroom. This variety, growing almost exclusively on the woodchips of the afore-mentioned region, is reported to be around seven times more psychotropically potent than its sister, the *Psilocybe cubensis*, which flourishes in cow dung and is much more common. . . . When Dee traded off his weekly dose for an equal portion in weight, he multiplied many fold his intake of the primary acting component, psilocybin. . . . Select North American Indian tribes have long regarded this fungus as a sacrament. . . . Modern men often tamper with the nocturnal flipside of the human organism, which former generations have tapped with infinite caution. Revelation, invisible, casts a perceivable shadow; damnation.

Certain African tribals insert disks of wood into their lips to expand them to fantastic proportion. Dee carved himself a bill, curing it heavily with linseed oil and waxing it. The maxilla was as curved as a hawks. The mandible was gentler of aspect, but of course had to facilitate the maxilla. Before installing the beak, he graduated his lips to the necessary flexibility with plain pieces of waxed wood, ever increasing in size. When the flesh seemed ripe, he riveted, with piercings, the bill in place. The process was gentler than he had expected, though the maxilla ended up blocking off the major portion of oxygen from his nostrils. He found it necessary to trim away a reasonable amount of the cartilage in order to breathe freely.

The gold-hungry wisps of upright tissue paraded themselves across the strips of sidewalk, down below. The light, almost cowardly, seeped from the sky, through the rectangle of window. . . . From the street his figure might be seen, a blotch against the pane.

Yes, the glass was his frame and he was a portrait, no, a painting. —He was most like a horrific etching by Dürer.

He stepped back, wetting his lips with a strand of tongue. A wave, as if from the ocean, coursed through the room. A liquidity wriggled through his spine and he shivered. The mirror was nearby. —That was where he found himself, the black balls of his pupils.

He stared at himself, and in a frozen second, which compressed reason to bursting, knew the meaning of true fear.

THE FLATTERER

*Your belly is your god and thus misleads your
better sense to acts of shamelessness.*
—Archilochus

The second chin of Pithyllus, governor of Halicarnassus, seemed to have a life all its own. It would dance and ripple, move with motions truly apart from those of its proprietor, but which certainly corresponded to his gross sensuality. He had a round head, draped with orange curls, quite false and kept in place by an elegant bandeau spangled with gold. He had a covering especially for his tongue, a kind of glove, made of snake skin, with which he wrapped that muscle for the sake of luxury.

"Take it off," he told Cleisophus, his most devoted parasite.

"Yes, yes!" that simpering and obsequious man replied. He quickly obeyed the command and, after removing the precious glove, set it on a small table aside.

Pithyllus rolled his tongue over the bud of his lips. All the dozen or so fawners about him clapped in delight and squirmed on their comfy, ivory-footed couches.

"Oh," said one Telemon, a beardless young man. "Oh, but does not Pithyllus have the nicest tongue of all!"

"It is more red than Lesbian wine!" cried Cleisophus, dramatically clasping his hands in front of his own heart. "And his words, those artistic combinations of sound, give nearly orgastic pleasure."

Pithyllus the governor laughed. "Speaking of pleasure, speaking of wine—let us drink."

All present cooed at the idea, and forthwith two nimble slaves trotted into the luxurious hall: One carried cups of gold, a second a great oiochoe, or pitcher, full of the scented drink—a mixture of one part sea water to thirty parts mariotic wine from Alexandria.

"Oh, drink," lisped Cleisophus, "drink, you exalted male ruler!"

The governor lifted the cup to his haughty mouth.

143

"Egh!" he exclaimed, making an unpleasant face. "This beverage is far too free from heat, and does disgust me."

"Egh!" cried Cleisophus, in imitation, and threw himself down at the governor's feet. "Spit it out upon this creature before you, and thereby cleanse your palate of what is unworthy."

This the governor did, spitting strongly on his favourite parasite's cheek; and the act filled them both with extreme pleasure.

"You are so absolutely despicable, Cleisophus. You are such a low reptile that I do love you. —Now, quick, a decent wine and food for us all, for we must swallow more than just words!"

Soon another oiochoe of drink was being carried around the room, though this time it was from Mendaea, of which Hermippus says:

Mendaean wine such as the gods distil;

and all were thoroughly pleased with the powerful and aromatic liquid that sloshed down their throats and made them even more foolish than was their normal state. Some seasoned their wine with onions or pistic nard, some drank it as it came, but none diluted it with water, as was the custom amongst temperate men. The talk became general, spiced with cleverly coarse jokes, and shrill laughter rang throughout the hall. Platters of foods of every variety were presently brought forward: roasted hares, calves' feet, fried meatballs upraised, tender thrushes and delicious rooks, anchovies and nettles steeped in oil, cuttlefish, well-seasoned sea urchins, smooth-mouthed pina and univalve limpets, swines' brains, black-pudding, asparagus in sauce of pennyroyal and rue, artichoke hearts steeped in Carian oil. And there were also Chelidonian figs in close-packed baskets, sweetmeats, cakes steeped in milk, pomegranates, acorns of Jupiter, arbutus berries, pears, Naxian almonds and grapes.

Pithyllus, who was very fond of sea food, ate a dish of roasted harp-fish, a few sea frogs and twelve fig leaves stuffed with young shrimp and raisins. He recited some lines from the comic poet Ephippus, guzzled down a full cup of wine, and then dipped his fingers into the paunch of a gelded pig, which was well boiled and white and basted with pungent cheese.

"Some of that bean soup!" he cried, pointing to a tureen that was just then making the rounds.

"It is delicious, with lovely bits of beef swimming around in the broth," said Telemon, who was just then eating a mouthful. "It makes me wish that I had a throat three metres long, so I could enjoy its flavourful warmth all the more."

The guests all laughed at this, and one cried out: "And I wish my throat were equally long so that I could swallow more wine in just proportion!"

"Bring in the magodi and musicians," murmured Pithyllus, and licked the gravy from the tip of his pinkie.

Before many minutes had passed, the entertainers and musicians filtered in. First came the magodi, three young men with cymbals and little drums. They were dressed in women's clothing and thoroughly effeminate in manner, one with the swagger of a whore, the next the mincing gate of the toy boy, the third the stride of a slattern slut. These three paraded about the room and sang a comic song, all the while giving show to lewd and ridiculous postures which very much amused both the governor and his guests. Next the poet Myrtilus stepped forward, wearing a crown of ivy, and recited a very moving iambic. This man was followed by Amoebus, the harp player, who wore a veil of thyme and a garland of violets, and his body was covered with a Tarentine robe that reached down to his ankles. He played beautifully, a luscious Ionian harmony, and was presently joined by a short, chubby singer named Sinepas, which means mustard, for that man had a reputation for singing lyrics of the spicy variety.

He began with the lines:

To you Bacchus, are praises due,
And the melody here, the song I sing,
Is for virgins thoroughly unfit.

All present applauded, for to everyone the piece was both familiar and loved. Two of the guests set down their wine, stood up and proceeded to dance the igdis, while Cleisophus, in high spirits, did the 'Dance of the Master of the Ship'. A few men became sentimental: Youthful Charmus rubbed the feet of Orcus, a grey old lecher.

"If there were some other boys here willing," said Telemon, "we could do the gymnopaedica, which is surely the best dance of all."

145

But no one was at all eager to lend themselves to the sport, which not only required that those involved strip themselves naked, but also that they exert a great deal of energy and take on the indecorous attitudes of wrestlers—a task that was incompatible with stuffed bellies. There was however another source of amusement, for the governor had a certain coppersmith brought before the company in chains. The culprit had had the audacity to engage himself in noisy work within earshot of the palace—a serious crime under the rule of Pithyllus, who liked no uncouth sounds to interrupt his luxurious peace. The smith was made to kneel in the middle of the hall, where he was flogged to the sound of a flute.

"Come," said Pithyllus, "we must now eat more. —Why, look at this lovely hashed eel which my slaves are toting out!"

And so saying he began to attack the dish with vigour. His jaws worked, his cheeks shook like plates of disturbed jelly.

Cleisophus, in dramatic style cried out: "Heracles, slay that plate of eel, which we have secured from the briny deep!"

This inspired all with laughter, and the governor, spirited, laid waste to the fatty food before him. He then applied himself to a course of pickled fish, as well as a pâté of weasel. He pursed his lips, blinked his eyes and moved on his couch with unease.

"Oh, dear me. I seem to be somewhat full. That will not do. No, that will not do in the least on a day when my cook is at his best, and there are so many nice things to taste."

So saying, he stuck two fingers down his throat and proceeded to vomit into a silver trough that was by his side, especially for this purpose. His guests watched with great interest.

"Oh, it is like honey," murmured Cleisophus as he licked at the mess, down on his hands and knees in the fashion of a dog.

"Cleisophus is most certainly the prince of flatterers," said Orcus, with mingled admiration and disgust.

The governor chuckled. "No man of means should be without such a base scrounger at their elbow. He knows how to make me feel my own worth, which adds pleasure to this life, and pleasure we must take now while we breathe, for in the afterlife we will get none of the luxuries we get here on earth."

"Excellently said."

"Excellently said, and now excellently put into action. My belly has been somewhat relieved. Bring forth fresh dishes," he cried to a slave. "Some shark, and sea-cuckoo. A bit of squid. A pike steeped in oil and clothed in marjoram."

A musician struck up a tune on the magdis, an instrument of many strings, and a second round of food was ushered forth, this time accompanied by a twenty-five year old Chian wine which tasted like nectar.

"Delicious, delicious," said Orcus as he nibbled on a split saurus, or lizard, anointed with asafoetida. "A simple and straightforward food, perfect for the priming of my lazy manhood."

"Has anyone tried this dish yet!" cried a balding gentleman, who until then had been for the most part silent. "I do not know what it is, but its taste is the most delightful that has ever crossed my palate!"

"That," said Pithyllus, "is the secret weapon of my cook. He calls it a Dish of Roses. It is made from the boiled brains of pigs and jays mixed with a quantity of pounded rose petals, as well as eggs, wine, pickle juice and pepper, the whole then doused in good oil."

So saying, the governor had a bowl-full of the soft and piquant mixture set before him, and devoured it with relish.

A giant tray was being carried about the room burdened with slices of sow's womb.

"None for me," said young Telemon. "I could not eat another bite."

"Oh," cried Pithyllus, "young men these days are as temperate as Pythagoras; they would be content with honey and turnips! —For me, a slice of that sow's womb, and some ovaries of swallows, on the double."

Though the governor was as voracious as ever, and Cleisophus continued to nibble obsequiously, most of the guests had eaten far more than their fill. Lamps with balsam oil were lit, and great globs of myrrh ignited in incense urns. Slaves brought out basins full of hot, soapy water mixed with lily oil, followed by stacks of perfumed towels for each to dry their hands.

"No water or towel for me yet," said Pithyllus, "for I have only begun to enjoy these products of my kitchen."

And so saying he proceeded to lay waste to a dish full of testicles, swallowing them by the pair and chasing them down with great drafts of blood-red wine. With drooping eyelids and hanging jowl, he then polished off a casserole made from the entrails of roasted tuna, followed by a heaping dish of small octopuses in vinegar.

"And now for the candaulus," said he.

"But what is candaulus?" Telemon enquired.

"Candaulus my boy is this most delicious food which you see being placed before me. It is a Lydian dish, a ragout, made from boiled meat, aniseed, honey, grated bread, and Phrygian cheese."

"And it is an amatory food," Cleisophus added, winking in all directions.

"Catamites beware," murmured Orcus pithily.

Palm wine was being served and of this Pithyllus drank two cups, while munching down three pyramid-shaped rolls. Lentils with onyx he also ate, as well as milt of lampreys.

"I believe Pithyllus, that no man has ever been blessed with a more healthy appetite than yourself," said Orcus.

"You are wrong," the governor replied somewhat gravely, "for Milo of Crotona is said to be able to eat twenty minae of meat, twenty minae of bread and drink three choes of wine. After the last games held at Olympia, he ate an entire bull by himself, to the astonishment of all present."

Cleisophus giggled. "He ate a coarse bull, but I am sure that when it comes to fine dainties, you my lord, could eat more than even the gods."

"Be quiet fool, and help me, for my jaws have grown tired from this extraordinary exercise, but my belly is far from content. Take that plate of marrow there, that lovely white mass well sprinkled with cheese, and pour it down my throat, so I need not exert myself with masticating."

Cleisophus was naturally thrilled to be of service, and with great alacrity poured the plate of steaming marrow down the governor's throat, the latter simply swallowing and gurgling, eyes blissfully closed. A thin film of sweat appeared on his brow and on the bridge of his nose and his hands sat lax on his great belly.

"Now," he murmured, smiling uneasily. "Now . . . rub my throat with essence of wild ivy, to loosen the muscles. . . . And then drop in a lump of fried cheesecake. . . . And pour me a goblet of yellow wine."

The eyes of all present were on the governor as Cleisophus fulfilled his bidding. The cheesecake was scooped into that cavern of sensuality, that mouth, quickly followed by half a thericlean goblet of the cool yellow wine.

Telemon clapped his hands.

"Marvelous," sighed Charmus.

"Pithyllus my friend," said Orcus wisely, "you have eaten enough."

"Yes," said another man, "cheesecake is very filling."

"Cheesecake," gurgled governor Pithyllus. "Cheesecake. . . . Another. . . . This time one with black sesame seeds crusted over the outside. . . . And a plate of honeycombs. . . . And a plate of camels' heels . . . with truffles. . . . A stewed owl. . . . Bring me a stewed owl."

A slow and romantic tune was struck up on the lyre, and another cheesecake was brought out, a beautiful black confection, which somehow found its way into the governor's stomach, as did the other foods, even the owl, whose flesh a slave diced finely so it would be easier for the great hedonist to swallow.

"Scrumptious," governor Pithyllus sighed, with a shallow burp.

Cleisophus, always the imitator, gave a little burp as well, though hardly genuine.

"But Pithyllus," Orcus said thoughtfully, "your countenance has grown rather peculiar. I do not think those camels' heels have agreed with you—they are very indigestible."

"Yes," lisped another guest, "the governor looks far from well."

And this was true: Pithyllus's eyelids drooped heavily. His second chin, that garland of fat, hung limp. He stretched out his legs and, attempting to rise from the purple couch, fell to the carpet-covered floor. He ran his hand over his face, then pushed it back over his head, disturbing the bandeau. The false hair fell away, revealing a nearly bald scalp fringed with grey stubble. With glassy eyes filled with lazy fear he looked around him, and his lips quivered. The man let out a gasping croak. He trembled, his obese body undulated, its bulk seemed to swell. The balls of his eyes rolled back in his head, showing whites veined with red and tinged with yellow. There was a kind of a hiccup, and then hot blood gushed from his nose and one corner of his mouth.

"It is pure ichor," said Cleisophus as he proceeded to lap up the red fluid with his tongue. "It is a veritable sauce of the gods!"

THE LAST MERMAID

Carlos II, King of Spain, Naples and Sicily, was the product of an incestuous and syphilitic marriage. He was sovereign of over thirty-million subjects. Until the age of six he had been fed on nothing more coarse than the mellow teats of Sevillian wet nurses. He never stood on his own legs, of soft bones and feeble joints, until he was ten years old. His head was enormous and misshapen. His tongue was so large that he was barely able to speak. When Juan Carreño de Miranda painted the king's portrait, it was all that that artist could do to make a likeness without depicting a monstrosity.

The king's passion was hunting. He enjoyed watching his dogs rip out the entrails of stags and boars. It would make him drool to see one of his hawks swoop down and pink the white fur of a rabbit. At the bullfights, he would clap his hands with delight when a horse or matador was gored and surveyed with interest the spasms of the dying toros. But what gave Carlos the most pleasure of all was to observe his favourite verdugo, Alonso de Alcalá, at work, breaking arms in the mancuerda, or wrenching off toes with the balestilla. The king laughed at the poppings and wails produced by the pulleys of the rack, and liked personally to apply the red-hot pincers to the nipples of the unfortunates.

But, though he found it amusing to watch other creatures suffer, he was not adverse to possessing certain living specimens. In his bedroom he had a caged kinkajou which he would feed from his own hand. His menagerie was one of the finest in Europe. There were flying squirrels and fighting polar bears. He had hyenas and porcupines. There was a cat from Majorca which laid eggs, and a pig-faced rabbit which the Emperor Leopold had given him as a birthday gift.

The king was also an avid collector of diminutives. He had a Mayan midget from Mexico, perfectly formed, a tiny replica of an ordinary man, whom he had dressed all in lavender. There was a pigmy from the depths of Africa who could play the flute. He had a dwarf from Japan named Morerino; but one day this runt made an impertinent comment and Carlos had the fellow nailed by the tongue to the wall of his picture gallery.

His Catholic Majesty was wed to Marie Louise d'Orléans. In honour of their marriage there was an *auto público general*, in which eighty-six victims were roasted alive.

The grandees aligned with the court were well pleased, and prayed daily to heaven to grant the royal couple offspring.

The young woman had the broad, flat forehead of an idiot. Her beauty fascinated the king. He would adorn her with jewels, with bracelets of manganised gold from the mines of Peru, the finest diamonds from the marts of Amsterdam, and old family heirlooms, cameos and tiaras, great sea-green emeralds, necklaces of sapphires and rubies so heavy that they would drag down her head, like a sunflower saturated with rain. At night, after heating his brain with a glass of spiced raspecia, he would make her dance in front of him quite nearly naked. The queen found her husband repulsive but, out of a sense of duty, and possibly because she hoped that even such a beast could gratify her, she did all she could to inspire him with lust.

The royal doctors would examine the couple's bed sheets and undergarments, sniffing at them and holding them up to the light, in the hope of finding evidence as to the issue of the affair. Marie's confessor asked her about the most intimate details of her unhappy life. She was reluctant to talk of such things, but at last ventured to say: "Strictly speaking, I believe that I am no longer a virgin. But things have proceeded in such a way as to make it, if my understanding of the matter is correct, technically impossible for me to produce a child for the king."

The queen's face became like a dripping candle. Unhappy in love, she turned to gluttony, stuffing herself full of rich foods, goslings steeped in Saint Merry's sauce, great lumps of pâté de foie gras, and lampreys fried in butter. She would wallow in the depths of down cushions all day, eating oreillettes, and it was said she became so lazy that she would never lower her hands beneath her own navel. She was like some strange little doll. She was obese and, in the manner of a prize-winning piglet, pretty. And finally she died, but whether from indolence or unhappiness it is difficult to say.

The king became prone to fits. Sometimes he would go into spasms and writhe on the richly-carpeted floor of his audience chamber. After one especially violent paroxysm he became deaf in one ear. Some nights he would not sleep, but walk about his castle naked, whipping his own misshapen body with a gold-handled cat-o'-nine-tails. In the morning he would say Credos until he was dizzy and then fall asleep on the cold stones of his private chapel.

He missed Marie. Sometimes he would make his way down to the gloomy vault where her embalmed corpse lay, in order to gaze on that fat form arrayed in silks and jewels. He would press his lips against her dead flesh and howl at her feet, the echoes of his voice mixing with the smells of incense and must.

A new queen was found for him, this time a German princess, the daughter of the Elector Palatine. But this second was as fruitless as the first. The queen despised Carlos, ridiculed him for his deformities; and it was rumoured that she used the court dwarves for unmentionable purposes.

His Catholic Majesty fasted three days a week; on the other four he had a boy to chew his food for him. His physical and mental health, never strong, steadily declined. The vilest thoughts would fly through his disordered head. Himself impotent, he wished to see women couple with wild beasts. He claimed that demons visited him in the night and that the devil himself had asked how many andarmes his soul weighed. He was exorcised according to the forms of the Church and, after that, never went to bed without having three friars placed in his room to guard against the forces of evil.

The royal doctors administered to him countless cordials, extracts of pellitory, powdered skink and concoctions of amber. His complexion was turning from yellow to green. It was clear that his health was doing the very opposite of improving.

A spiritualist named Juan González Díaz was brought to the court. He wore an outlandishly tailored weasel-skin cap on his head and a long black beard on his face and asserted that he was able to converse with ghosts and other incorporeal beings. After questioning Berith, Forneus and Paymon, he informed the king that he was under a spell, which had been cast on him during his childhood by an English warlock, with the objective of discontinuing the royal line of the Spanish Hapsburgs.

"A potion made of the brains and kidneys of a human corpse was given to you in your chocolate. The fountain of life has dried up within you. There is only one thing which can cure you, which can restore that vitality which is rightfully yours. . . . You must eat the flesh of a mermaid."

The king asked what a mermaid was. He was informed that it was a very rare aquatic animal; so rare in fact that one had not been sighted since the year 1608, more than ninety years previous.

A proclamation was issued in which a reward of two thousand reals was offered for a single fresh mermaid. The fishermen of the ports could talk of nothing else. You could not make two thousand reals in two lifetimes catching mullet and conger. Before six months were out, every sea-man and fisherman from Europe to the Americas had news of the prize.

All sorts of odd marine creatures were delivered up to the court; vast, bright yellow things gasping for air; giant sea turtles stripped of their shells; a fish with extremely long pelvic fins that hung down like arms; a sleek and silvery arowana with strange barbell-like extensions protruding from its mouth. One man, in an attempt to deceive, brought in the head of a porpoise stitched on to the body of a woman. He was fined three hundred reals and exiled for twenty years from Madrid, Murcia and Cuenca.

The king began to despair. But one day he was told that a genuine mermaid had been procured. It had been caught, by a Portuguese privateer, off the coast of Brazil, near Ilha de Tinharé, and kept preserved alive in a barrel of salt water in the ship's hold.

His Catholic Majesty asked to see the creature and it was brought before him. It was speckled like a mackerel and seemed to be possessed of milk secreting organs. Its head was covered with numerous fine, black cylindrical filaments. Carlos poked at its belly. It gasped and shuddered.

The king stared with languid eyes. "It looks like a small lady," he murmured.

"It is very pretty," said the queen, and then suggested that they teach the creature to kneel before the crucifix.

"But . . . if I am to eat her . . ."

"No," a friar commented, "it would not do to eat a Christian."

The mermaid blinked.

"Is . . . it nice to eat?" asked Carlos.

"It is a mermaid; a very good fish," said Juan Díaz with confidence. "If you eat it, it will do wonders for your health; it will inject your frame with vigour."

"Then have it taken to the kitchen."

When Fernando de Uceda, the king's master chef, saw the fish he merely shrugged his shoulders. He was instructed to prepare it *deshecho*; but like all great chefs, he ignored instructions and did what he pleased. He could not bear to overcook such a pretty vertebrate. He gutted and scaled the creature, placed it in the oven, and then set about puréeing oil, chopping garlic, and pounding together walnuts, almonds and bread soaked in meat broth in a mortar.

The mermaid was brought out steaming on a great silver platter. It was fringed with parsley and baked wardens. Its aroma filled the room. A rivulet of drool descended from the left-hand corner of the king's mouth as he looked at the beautiful glazed cheeks of the mermaid, her back dripping with ajada sauce. He drove his pre-masticator away, insisting that he would eat his special supper without help from another. He didn't bother to use his golden trencher, but ate directly from the serving dish, washing down the unchewed food with liberal drafts of an antique Málaga.

The flesh itself was not like that of other fish. It had the texture of pork. The king found it deliciously succulent, and swallowed greedily. With the point of his knife he worked out the creature's eyes and slipped them between his lips. With his long, tapering fingers he tore away the breasts and stuffed them down his throat. His chin and some locks of the hair of his wig became stained with sauce. He sucked the meat off bones and, at every mouthful, snapped his mouth shut like a famished dog. He licked at the fins and took in the crispy tail.

That night he slept well; far too well for his wife.

When he awoke the next morning he had a terrible headache, and throughout the day was indisposed. In the evening he became feverish. It has already been said that the king's skin had become somewhat green. Now from green it progressed to a sickly shade of turquoise with spots of blue appearing on his forehead and feet, like the hide of some hideous lizard.

His Catholic Majesty complained that the fish he had eaten was indigestible.

The doctors applied compresses of freshly slaughtered pigeons to his head and the steaming entrails of he-goats and horses to his stomach. He was bled. Twenty leaches were applied to his buttocks. The king said that he was on fire. The last sacrament was issued, but he vomited the host. He strained his feeble voice and said, "I am bewitched and suffering."

So died the last mermaid, and the last of the Spanish Hapsburgs.

THE

CRUELTIES

OF

HIM

When fishes flew and forests walked
And figs grew upon thorn,
Some moments when the moon was blood
Then surely I was born.

—G.K. Chesterton

I.

"So this is your third adoption from the agency?" smiled the woman, from behind her administrative desk.

"Yes," replied Ruth, the doctor's wife, "we love having children around the house. I thought that when I mentioned the idea of a third to Donald he would say I was crazy. But not at all, he thought it was a wonderful idea. . . . He's so understanding you know—about my ovaries," she blushed.

Dr. Blanche patted her hand sympathetically. Yes, he could very well understand what it must have felt like to be an infertile woman. He himself was a sober individual. Yet his face showed that he was capable of shedding a few tears, should the appropriate occasion arise.

○

That afternoon they took home the third child, a baby boy, hands grasping innocently and mouth puckered with bubbling spittle. . . . The nurses flapped their own paws, in his face, as an expression of parting, let their lips curl up in semblance of joy, and stood at the door of the agency, uniforms chalk blue, to watch the infant be submerged in the Blanche family car.

II.

Dr. Blanche was a well respected physician. He had awards to his name and works of repute on the shelves of bookstores. Colleagues sought his advice. He and his wife were greeted with effusion bordering on sycophancy when arriving at a dinner party.

His receding hairline exposed a broad and intelligent forehead. The eyes in his head were a dull shade of green. They bespoke a calm and methodical mind, a potential compassion that lurked beneath the pink of his skin. . . . Ruth was infinitely matronly. Old fashioned, neighbourly to near blessedness. . . . It was seldom that her face did not beam, irradiate the warmth of a country hearth, the charm of Middle America.

It was said that she was a bit simple for the likes of her husband. But who can rightly discern the ways of the heart? Better to let nature's elemental laws of attraction work their will; and be happy when two beings find shelter from the cold of night in each other's embrace.

○

The doctor let his knife wriggle through the roast, the weight of the slice of beef, infinitely thin, depositing itself onto the serving fork. His right hand lifted it onto the plate held by his left. This was his second helping, and the meat lay wrinkled in folds in the light violet of its gravy.

"So what do you think of the little fellow?" asked Ruth, a forkful of oven-baked stuffing held in readiness before her mouth.

"He's a beautiful boy," the doctor replied as he cut through a portion of the brown, grey and red rainbow of flesh. "Really, he is in much better health than the others were when we received them. You remember how sickly Pedro was. The way he ran through those diapers was awful. . . . And Cynthia was not exactly a prize as I recall. Getting rid of that rash became a genuine trial."

"It was hard alright," agreed Ruth. "But you did want to begin with healthy children."

"Of course," he said, his jaws stirring a mouthful of beef, "with all the stress they were to go through, it would hardly have been right not to root out those little ailments. . . . It's funny they should give a doctor unhealthy babies though. If I were a differently motivated man I would have returned them."

"Well, at least this one is fit."

"Exactly."

○

After dinner, the doctor climbed down the steps that led to the basement. He flipped the light switch and a battery of phosphorescents buzzed into play. The chamber was fully subterranean. Two tables, covered in coarse white fabric, sat end to end against one wall. Medical apparatus, often antique, hung from hooks and nails. Industrial sized mayonnaise jars lined the tables and other shelves, grim metallic objects bristling out.

There were syringes, obscene in their length and throbbing glint. Odd-shaped scalpels lay about, the ends curved like the Malaysian tjaluk. Others glistened with the obscure complexity of the African mongwanga, or the ends of certain European halberds, such as the guisarme, chauves souris, or the Lucerne hammer. Many of the implements could be described as nothing less than medieval, primitive. . . . It was an inspired collection that would have been the envy of any museum's chirurgical reliquary.

The walls of the room were of red brick, thus making them outskirts of shadow. In the centre sat a doctor's chair, lamps stationed around, leather straps with buckles hanging loose from its body and arms. Off to one side, against the wall opposite the tables, were a series of cages. The smallest, in the forefront, showed mice, a gerbil or two, and various other rodents. A forlorn monkey strutted across a residence much too small for it, chicken wire, fortified with re-bar. A few yellow warblers, perched in a jail on a string, quite still, apparently asleep. The larger two cages, of seeming professional make, were adumbrated by the play of light through their very bars.

A faint motion was detectable from that direction. There was evidence of life manifest behind those fingers of steel. A gurgling whine reached his ears. Soon this unpleasant noise became blanketed by a bizarre twittering, a frantic mutilation of musical song.

The cage birds awoke, joined in with their more elegant calls, beat their wings against the surrounding net of copper wire.

III.

Pedro had been the first to come under their roof. Despite what Ruth might have said to the adoption agent, the doctor was the primary advocate in all those acts of offspring collection. Whatever state his wife's ovaries were in was without significance; he needed children. Unformed minds, unformed flesh—these called to him; they were of vital importance.

The boy was sickly to be sure. Dr. Blanche, like many modern physicians, believed that environment could overpower atavism. He did not want the creature to hear nasty language—or any language. The ear is delicate. Our doctor knew anatomy like few men. Others might have the ambition to restore, but he would take away. The stapes are the smallest bones in the human body, more minute than grains of rice. He removed these, thus severing the connection between the malleus and incus, or the hammer and anvil, and the inner ear. Sound could not reach those delicate labyrinths, the utricle, saccule and cochlea.

The monkey, a male mangabey, was named Chako. The first years of Pedro's residency were spent in near intimacy with him. They shared the same cage. Dr. Blanche made sure to limit his own contact with the boy to a bare minimum, making it clear to Ruth that she follow suit.

With Chako for a guide, Pedro learned to show his teeth, bob his head, and slap the ground with his hands. The monkey would groom the youngster and he, in turn, enjoyed picking lice from his mentor's fur, decimating them between his bared teeth. At feeding time Chako took charge, setting the larger portion of raw eggs, frogs and roughage down his own gullet, while leaving the little *Homo sapiens* enough nutriment to remain relatively vibrant.

Pedro's hair and nails were left to nature. Without sun, his skin grew to cotton whiteness—apparent subsequent to his monthly washing down, via Ruth. . . . Her husband was sensitive to ill odours. . . . He was growing his own wild boy, but chose to be sanitary about it.

IV.

The smudge advanced into the slashes of light, its mane hanging thick around the shoulders. He strutted back and forth on all fours for a few moments, his buttocks prone in the air, then lurched up, grabbed the bars and oscillated his trunk like one intoxicated, a hideous grin riving his face.

The doctor however was not interested in Pedro's antics. Though they gave him some measure of satisfaction, they offered but small amusement. He had come to attend to the other, Cynthia.

She had entered the glow of the family hearth a few years after Pedro. Her adoptive father had been plummeting deep into the alchemy of the flesh. From the principles laid out by Thomas Vaughn, he delved into the old Chinese texts of Black Taoism. He possessed an unknown manuscript in the hand of Robert of Chester, which offered vital hints, as well as the Arabic works of Jabin Ibn el-Hayyan and the Persian of Ghazali. Of course the branch of the art that truly interested him he found laid out in uncompromising detail in a series of unique pamphlets. These documents, of anonymous authorship, were written in cyanic script on pages of vellum. The language was a sort of hybrid Latin, a post-pagan vernacular, combining bare Imperialisms with quaint strands of Middle English. Certain lines read eloquent, poetic. So much so that they could have been composed by a man such as William Dunbar. Others were blunt and trim, grammatically perfect, pure Latin, in the style of Tacitus or Quintilian.

◎

She was more timid and let herself be heard before seen. The chaotic whistling and clucking came from the shadows. The songbirds responded from above. Slowly the girl waddled out, her hair straight and golden, body sheathed in a banana-coloured jumpsuit, a strange and xanthic being, with pale blue eyes and a simply innocent forehead.

He had stitched up the sides of her mouth when she was a baby, cutting the width of the aperture in half, transmuting the orifice into a puckered bud. The doctor and his wife had never spoken a word to her for the first years of her life. The cage of warblers hanging above her quarters served as masters of elocution. She heard them and replied, listened and imitated.

He elongated her neck, using the ring method of certain African tribes, stretching the item a portion further with every quarter year.

The tibula was extracted and re-inserted at the pit of the leg. Of course he had to alter the base of the femur to make the operation mechanically sound. But her bones were supple, young, and responded well to the chisel. . . . The fibula and tibia he turned one hundred and eighty degrees, snapping them into alignment with the patella. When these bones turned, the gastrocnemius, peroneus longus, all the minor muscles and the entire foot also turned. The result was a leg that swivelled in reverse. . . . Her heels faced what she approached. . . . In order to keep proper balance, she became forced to tuck in her pelvis and stick out her chest. . . . As this operation had been performed on her when she was an infant, these postures became, if not natural, at least habitual.

When Dr. Blanche opened the door of her cage, she shied away from him slightly, tucking her head to her shoulder in a fit of modesty. The doctor patted his knee and whistled. At this she sprang forward, attaching herself to his leg. He hoisted the frail creature into his arms and brought her over to the surgical chair.

From the linen-covered tables he took a sponge, which he infused with chloroform. This he placed over Cynthia's nose and the button of her lips. . . . The lamps clicked on, closed in, brightening that centre of activity, that little sentient being. . . . And the scalpel flickered in his hand.

166

V.

The black disk spun, a band of light playing on its grooved surface. The mellow sounds found passage through a fleck of diamond, created a silvery atmosphere within the room, a guitar plucking away, Gabor Szabo's *More Sorcery* album emitting its exotic, somewhat sensual melodies.

The doctor sat in a leather armchair, a Gauloises cigarette burning between two fingers, a glass of rye whisky, half-consumed, set on a coaster on the table next to him. One of the kidskin pamphlets sat open on his lap. He turned the pages with great care, reading over material he already knew by heart. These were the root texts of jester anatomy, the design manuals for the construction of court clowns, circus freaks and necromancer's toadies.

The rap at the door and the sound of his wife's voice were simultaneous.

"Dinner is ready," she said.

The doctor glanced at his wristwatch and, after extinguishing his cigarette in a nearby ashtray, rose with a sigh, depositing his precious copy on the bookshelf.

A large platter of fried chicken was just being deposited on the table when the he made his appearance in the dining room. The miniature body parts had the rich hue of unadulterated gold. A crockery bowl of mashed potatoes steamed on a second trivet. The cobs of corn were cut in half, a few strands of silk still clinging to the kernels.

He sat down, settled a napkin on his lap and scanned the food spread out before him.

"Have you thought of a name yet?" Ruth asked, gnawing at a leg of fowl.

"Tarquin," the doctor replied coolly from across the table.

"Tarquin?"

"Yes. I believe that it is a suitable name for the little fellow." He methodically buttered a cylinder of corn, running a thick pat over the rough surface with his knife. "Lucius Tarquinius Priscus," he continued. ". . . And then there is Tarquinius the Proud, Tarquinius Superbus, who came along a bit later. . . . Roman kings you know. . . . Tarquin." The corn rotated between his teeth, manifold seed coats bursting, embryo and endosperm stripped from the cob, puréed together.

"And you'll begin soon?" she asked, her voice flavoured with wifely concern, fingers setting a chicken bone down on the side of her plate.

"Yes."

VI.

Tarquin was his human clay. A ball of flesh, malleable; a satchel of blood, bone and brain to be transmuted.

Dr. Blanche tampered with the facial muscles, crippling the right side of the boy's mouth in an eternal grin, the left an unalterable frown. The lips formed a sideways 'S', the twisted neck of a swan. . . . Those eyes, gentle brown, became sockets of horror. He removed a generous portion of the skin at the height of each cheekbone, thus straining the bottom lids of the visual apparatus, pulling them so that the sheltered pink became prominent, the serous edge of the ball exposed. . . . By taking away the tip of the nasal cartilage, at a descending angle, he caused the nose to acquire a radical snub. . . . The result was morbid, forlorn, the countenance of a lost soul.

His scalp was cicatrised with a web-like pattern. Hair would not grow from the scarified skin, but clumped out pell-mell from those blocks left untouched.

His feet and hands were regularly injected with a mixture of cayenne pepper, procaine and excrement. They became inflamed, numb and infected, bloated and cankerous. The doctor was careful not to let the infections become too malignant, and made sure that they stayed local, though in the end the damage was permanent. . . . The hands and feet became of a cartoon character, those of a grim Mickey Mouse.

The boy became an amalgam of comedy and horror. To see him you might laugh, if your stomach was not flopping with disgust.

VII.

The doctor would have liked to have had his intestines put under the protection of the children of Horus. —How fitting, with one bearing the face of an ape, the next that of a hawk, then the jackal, and of course man himself. . . . After his innards found themselves in protective jars, giving him the chance for a second life, his brain would be extracted, through the nostrils, then laid aside to dry.

Those seventy days swimming in liquid natron, skin taking on the greenish-grey hue, the gloomy colour of swamp water. —Yes, that epidermal tissue would toughen, to an armour for defleshed bone! Sweet spice and natron, stuffed into him, through the convenient slits made in his fingers, toes, arms and thighs. . . . The skull, filled with a pâté, a preservative seasoning of plaster and herbs. . . . Gums and spices, natron and bitumen, pounded together, packed in the cavity of his chest and stomach, through a slit in the side.

The obsidian eyes, the fingernails stained with henna, the ornaments of gaudy gold. . . . And bandages! . . . He could not help but think he had been born three or four thousand years too late. There were no high priests to officiate his desire.

"In the modern age one should be dull and expeditious," he told himself. "Prepare oneself for the pasteboard sarcophagus of the new era."

VIII.

Edward Kelly's *The Theatre of Terrestrial Astronomy*, the works of Elias Ashmole, and the *Pseudomarchia Daemonium* of Johannes Wierus sat on the most frequented corner of his bookshelves. His favorite recreational reading however was *The Life of Heliogabalus*. After opening a bottle of Château Latour, set aside for special occasion, he extracted this latter volume, to read once more.

The text itself lay amidst the stories of the other Roman emperors. Yet, in the study of Dr. Blanche, those others went largely unread. Catallus was of course interesting, the way he had boys swim in between his legs, calling them his "little fish," and the newborn babies he nursed rather lewdly. . . . But the old pervert was no match for Heliogabalus in matters of decadence.

The young ruler had momentum.

Camels' heels appeared on the menu as well as peacocks' tongues. He would lay back on cushions stuffed with rabbit fur and partridge down, eating sparrows' brains, flamingos' brains and thrushes' brains. Him and his base entourage feasted on the heads of parakeets, pheasants and peacocks. Meanwhile the dogs were fed foie gras.

A smile played on the doctor's lips as he read of this dish: Wild sows' udders and wombs stuffed with pearls.

Heliogabalus never had sex with the same woman twice. We know however that he was more consistent with his boyfriends.

On an evening he would bath in a swimming pool perfumed with wormwood, feast with his friends on a meal of six hundred ostrich heads, eating out the brains, and tie a number of beautiful naked women to his dogcart, cracking a whip in their ears as they pulled him around the living room.

That lickerish youth met an unpleasant end, as grim as his life had been indecent. . . . The jewel-crusted court that he had had constructed beneath the tower, to meet his flying body when the time came, proved unnecessary. . . . In the filth of the gutter his corpse was dragged.

○

The pages pressed themselves together and the book sat closed on the doctor's lap. The blood coursed languidly through his veins. Blinking his weary lids, he arose, putting the volume aside.

With bare feet, he strode to the bedroom. She was there, the thick, down stuffed duvet covering her to the chin. He smiled sourly. He knew it was a personal weakness to let his curiosity take hold of his better judgement, but those very failings were in fact the perfume of his life and genius.

Within an hour he had her somewhat plump figure strapped to his medical chair in the basement. She was well anaesthetised and would certainly not awake.

It had long been his fantasy to see her other than how she was. He would lie next to her, or in the embrace he jokingly referred to as love, and time and again the vision would flash upon him. It wormed its way into his brain, and he gradually found it delicious.

The instruments were arrayed around him, vicious and clawlike. He adjusted the light, took up a pair of callipers and made measurements of her cranium and neck, jotting down the figures in a nearby note book. His palm glided over to a sawlike tool, of incredibly ferocious aspect, and he set to.

The operation was an incredible challenge. There was the entire vertebral body, which had to be readjusted, bit by bit, inside the living flesh, with all the intervertebral disks as well as the esophagus and trachea which needs not be over tweaked or deranged for fear of terminating the flow of oxygen. —And then the axis of the brainstem (though he never thought she made much use of it) was vitally important to stretch to some degree, without however severing; and turning the spinal column while preventing it from corkscrewing, in order to mitigate the odds of utter disability—which would in no way serve his designs.

IX.

During the week that followed, he slept alone and was satisfied with freedom of movement, being without one hundred and eighty pounds of woman flesh pressing upon him in the night with an over abundance of warmth.

○

He fixed himself a bowl of muesli and yogurt for breakfast, washing it down with unsweetened cranberry juice and black coffee.

"She stirs," he told himself as he heard the cries resonate from below, muffled and miserable.

He swallowed the last of his coffee, set his bowl in the sink, and proceeded down the steps to the basement.

"Donald!" she screeched, panic stricken.

"Coming dear," he called and, with a show tune whistling from his pursed lips, flipped on the lights.

The songbirds, awoken, began to twitter with maniacal pitch and soon Cynthia was in motion, parading about her cage, lending the recital her own musical mutilation. The monkey, Chako, joined in with a furious cackle. Pedro rose to his feet and craned forward, jaw protruding, simian, salient, the boy's eyes marbled with unnatural ignorance. Though unable to hear the sounds, he could none the less detect the air of excitement, and began to strum the bars of the cage with his head, like a guitar. Tarquin kneaded his bulbous hands. The hair shocked out of his head like a sea anemone. A gurgling falsetto rose from his twisted lips. —Though whether it was a cry of pain or pleasure was indeterminate.

"I care for you so much!" Ruth cried from the shadows. "Donald, I care for you so much!"

Dr. Blanche laughed callously and stepped to Tarquin's cage. Toward the back, kneeling on a heap of straw, neck bandaged, body half-covered by a white sheet, she groped, disorientated, unable to fathom the new twist to her anatomy.

"I know you do dear," the doctor said crisply, peering into the half light of the cage.

"But why?" she sobbed, tears melting down her cheeks. "Why this? . . . I'm not the same!"

He observed her torso and back and how her breasts pressed against the wall. He was satisfied to see her face thus, chin saddled between shoulder blades, eyes staring in wonder down at the soles of her feet and fleshy flipside. An exhalation of breath, whining, almost like the bleating of a goat escaped from her lips and she looked up with an entreating gaze.

"Oh, don't worry," he grinned savagely, delighted with his success. "This will in no way impede our love making."

WIGGLES

I came off the hill, that sky coal-red behind me and the crickets chirping and down into the forest I went, going pretty fast though not running. The trees took away the last light and there were the fireflies glowing along the path, sparkling like dew drops and the trunks standing black and thin. I came out and crossed through the meadow, now walking faster because I knew it was about supper time; those nighthawks flitting and feeding above, swimming in the cooling night air and me opening and closing my army knife in my pocket, thinking about the beef and gravy.

The house. Hearing the gravel and up the steps.

Through the screen door and dark living room, following the voices but not thinking about who, just smelling that beef and stepping quick. Margaret turned to me when I stepped in and I looked over her and saw his teeth, shining white and a loaded up fork moving right in.

"Joseph's come to stay with us," she said, without even worrying me about being late.

I sat down and drank at the glass of water that was there.

"He's sleeping where you were and you'll be taking that spare room. We moved your blankets already."

I put out my plate for the food and saw it steaming hot with the whipped potatoes and lots of beef brown with gravy. My fork was in my mouth and the food came in and went down into me, me going quick, not caring about him and his teeth or the way she was all spruced in blue at all. There was a slice of bread and I took it and soaked it in the gravy then asked for juice and she got me my apple juice. He was drinking a can of beer and I knew he brought it because we never had beer.

"He eats," he said.

"He does do that. Wait till you see him tomorrow morning."

"He likes breakfast, does he?"

"When it's liver he sure does."

Then there was pie and milk and they drank coffee on the porch, talking real quiet and me getting seconds and thirds on my own with no one to say different. Afterwards I went upstairs and saw his bag in the room that had been mine and flowers up on the dresser for the first time ever. So I went down the hall to the other place, touching on my army knife as I went, switching on the light and looking in to see my blankets on some old bed with my poster pinned up to the wall and shoes off to one side. There was that smell and I did not like it, almost like that mouse we once found behind the refrigerator, but different the way this new one came up on my cheek and then through just one nostril.

I sat down on my blankets on the bed and heard it and lay down and looked at the shining in the little window. Then there was them talking down below, voices drifting up from the porch, unclear, and I reached up to the light and flicked it. Then it died away and that shoot of moonbeam coming in and that smell. The way it told me I could not understand, so I just closed my eyes, seeing the blue glitter down below and all of them jumping like fleas. Someone looked in and then no one was there, just those boards against my hands and on my knees going down the stairs, the rubbery toughness, the cold rubbery toughness, and then the hay and him poking in my ear again until Margaret was at the barn door yelling and him there without his shirt on.

"I didn't know it was this bad," he said.

"Neither did I," she said and she was crying.

"He likes liver so much?"

"He never made away with it raw like this before."

"Well, just clean it up and cook some eggs and we'll be fine."

Then she came and rolled me over and took all those big brown-red pieces of liver off the ground and out of the hay and the plastic case they came in which was running wet with blood. My hand opened and there was a liver in there. The hand pressed tight, reached up and threw it at the door.

"That son of a bitch!"

"Ely!" she cried.

"That son of a bitch, throwing liver at me!"

His teeth were white, shining and filling out his mouth and I saw it thick and red inside and how it moved and then they came out of my own, deeper than the throat, not words exactly, not ones I could appreciate, but just feel: like when I found the Wheaton's dog, over in the woods, its nose all full of porcupine quills.

"If that spit gets on me I'm going to hit him."

"Don't."

"Is this one of those fits?"

"I don't know. I'll get him inside."

"Better. He's eating the hay."

My fingers took a bunch and stuffed it between lips and I felt it on my gums. He looked at me like he was mad or sick and turned and Margaret kept crying and it was sweet and I felt her hand. Through the screen door, across the floor up the stairs.

"Go in. Get back in there."

She left. I looked at the poster on the wall and grabbed at the sheets.

The smell was there and it came inside of me and then I felt them. They were in my stomach, all jumbled up and boiling and it said for them to come out so they started coming on up my chest and then got stuck in my throat. The air came in through my nose and then, all oily, the first came out. I stuck out my tongue and it climbed off it and hopped on to the floor, just like those little ones in the front lawn. Then there were more and more, coming up from my stomach, climbing up my throat and hopping off my tongue, moving on the floor with their little sounds.

Him. Him standing there; his eyes.

"There are frogs in here! That spaz of yours got frogs in here!"

"I cooked the eggs like you said. If you want them, they're on the table."

"He's got frogs; you better call a doctor."

Gone. It. Pillow in my mouth and looking up at the red in the window. Them up in my legs, one climbing on my stomach.

It told me in my ear and I looked. They were there, at the ends of my feet, wiggling around, smiling and out the window I saw a patch sky, the colour of a raspberry. So I took the army knife from my pocket and opened it. I took the smallest one and cut it, right through the core, and watched it go all over my hand, the sky, and how the other four moved quick. I dropped the first one which was just soft and was starting to cut into the next one in line, all sticky now, when Margaret came running in, saying, "Oh, my God! Oh, my God!" and the smell started laughing a little, like some old fighting tomcat.

"What the hell now?" Joseph said, running in.

"He has cut himself! He has cut himself!"

"They were wiggling around," I said. "I saw them white wiggling around."

"Christ almighty," both rows of them shining and that wet, red strip calling to me.

"Who is it? Who he . . ." (her breath just wheezing.) "Who he?"

And my legs were moving up and I heard the word, "Run," and started to do it, to really do it, him moving first, barefoot, bare-backed down the stairs, then across the floor and pushing open the screen door, it swinging shut after him. The arms of me were tearing right through it, the screen, and outside a host was flying around, the sky still scurrying liquid raspberry. Like butterflies. And the weeds all over flickering blue flame.

"Ely," she screamed in back of me, all frantic like. "Ely!"

But the legs kept moving, that nice feeling at the end of one like a nail and the ground flying under me.

Joseph lit out pretty fast across the field out front, not so much as looking back over his shoulder, but just hurrying on. My body jogged behind him, knees coming up to my chest, then legs shooting out, stretching big in the pursuit. He jumped the fence and was into the Wheaton's property, right on the pasture's edge. I came up, it must not have been eight seconds later, not really even touching post or wire, but simply soaring over. I kept going; I could feel my thighs rubbing together, knees still coming up high so I could see them.

The forest waved dark green at the far border and I was closing in, hearing it inside my ears and still smelling it, core deep. My belly bounced up and down. Their house was off to one side, with the new neighbourhood and buildings behind, stretching out from town. Their house was off to one side and I saw them both, father and son out front, staring over and they started yelling and Joseph veered off towards them. I could see the muscles of his rump and how they worked; my own gained power; I took a few big strides and leapt, nimble as a cat, agile as an adder, right on him and straddled his back.

He was glossy wet and I touched it. Him yelling.

"Son of a bitch! Son of a bitch!"

Then my army knife went behind his ear and I started cutting. He screamed out and I started cutting.

"Wiggles," I said. "Wiggles."

There was the goo and I looked over and saw the Wheatons, father and son, the young one holding a pitchfork, coming close on towards me. My foot was in Joseph's mouth, teeth up on his forehead then the ground was moving fast again, right underneath. I was running and it held the goo in my hand and spoke and smelled in my nose and the core of my head and I ran. Across the pasture, skirting the edge of the woods, the clear clean calling and me twisting the other in my hand, just a little lump. My legs moved over the weeds and then up the little hill to the pond. I saw him coming, not the Wheatons, just the son and there were fish swimming and that foot, plopping in the water and it staring at me; up from on top the fish he stared, the water cold and smell going he going, just pink clouds drifting down there and the fish feeling and coming up close.

"You better not move. You move and I'm going to stick you," he said.

"They were wiggling around," I said. "I saw them white wiggling around."

THE
WOMAN
OF
PAPER

Ewen Patrick, Professor of Orientology at the University of Leeds, was a tall, thin man, with a sombre face and somewhat outgrown, unnaturally ochre-coloured hair. His profile was like that of William III, once King of England. In his youth he had spent much time in India and China; he had lived nine years in Japan. His translations had brought him a certain amount of fame, as had his scholarly studies, on Tantric rituals, on calligraphy and tea ceremonies. He was also an able mathematician and one of the foremost historians of origami.

His mind was full of the exploits of Robert Harbin and Kunihiko Kasahara. He could quote the *Kayaragusa*, word for word, passage for passage, as if it were some holy book. His own collection of those decorative and representational forms was elaborate. He had valuable pieces by Akira Yoshizawa and Kōshō Uchiyama, a *pajarita* by Miguel Unamuno, past Rector of Salamanca University, a beautiful old mecho butterfly from a Shinto marriage ceremony, a paper soldier by Freidrich Froebel, a bullfrog by Houdini.

But he was far from being simply a passive admirer. In less then a minute he could fold together a nautilus, an elephant, a rose or a boat. He liked to make octahedrons and starfish. At all times he carried, in his jacket pocket, several six-inch squares of paper, for impromptu folding.

He sat in the teachers' lounge and ate his egg sandwich, drank his tea. When he finished, and was just clearing the crumbs from the place before him, he was approached by Agatha Moray, Professor of French Literature.

"I finished your work on Yu He's *Thousand-character Essay* last night, Ewen. I found it fascinating."

The Professor of Orientology, in a distracted manner, thanked the woman for her compliment. He averted his eyes from hers, pulled a square of lime-coloured Fontana paper from his pocket, and quickly folded a little chameleon.

In his afternoon class he endured the ostentatious smiles of a student with long red hair and spaces between her teeth. Throughout the day he observed the various females of his species, but each with distaste. One was too heavy, the next too slim. Some had breath that smelled of ham; unpleasant sounds issued from the mouths of others. Truly the females of this world held no attraction for him. And yet, he had to admit to himself, that he was lonely, and would have liked to have had some pretty woman to share company with, some woman like those depicted in the prints of Torii Kiyonaga or Katsukawa Shunchô,—some tall, elongated beauty capped with an elegant coiffure.

At home he set to work on his calculations; he made his diagrams. He went for long walks and sorted things out in his mind. He perused stationers' catalogues and placed orders.

He made her body out of the most precious gampi paper from Japan; her face from Bhutanese edgeworthia white; hair from unryu-shi, cloud dragon paper, littered with hundreds of long kozo fibres that seemed to float across its surface. Her dress, a sort of outrageous kimono, was constructed of moss-green asarakusui and was secured with a sash of sweet-potato vine paper. He gave her a cape, like a precious fur, made from deckled edged patched Yucatan huun, a paper like that used by the ancient Aztecs, prepared from sanseveria and cattail fibres. And she had jewellery, bracelets of mottled gold parchment made from sulphite pulp, bangles of daikon-based Thai metallic-silver and a necklace of Brazilian banana paper.

His creation was beautiful. Her skin was perfectly white. Her eyes were like the ocellated markings on a peacock's feathers; and their cilia exquisitely fine. The terminal members of her hands were delicate, slender, more or less cylindrical, and all tapered to points, except for her left forefinger which was circinate like the frond of a young fern.

He sat in the parlour in his armchair and sipped his whisky; the red marking-pen danced in his hand, spilled its ink over the numerous papers, his students' dissertations which he had to correct.

"What a waste of energy," he murmured to himself in disgust. "These people should not be at the University. . . . They should be tied to the plough."

That night when he closed his eyes:

He stood in a pleasure garden, on a well-kept violet lawn. Strange and exotic trees and flowers, showy yellow clusters and blue bowl-shaped blooms, sprouted from the earth; strings of peach-coloured cranes floated through the sky. There was a still and bright lake, upon the shores of which rested elaborate chalets and rising up on either side were dizzy cliffs and perched on the top of these were fantastic castles profuse with gold-crowned spires. In front of him was a tower-like building with upward-curving roofs over individual stories, the way to it lined with dwarf cherry trees in full and pastel blossom interspersed with vassals in shiny red armour, motionless, frozen stiff as icicles.

He made his way forward, projected himself up the steps and through the door. The room was splashed with the pink flesh of young waiting women; the air thick with the pale green smoke of some exotic, intoxicating incense. She herself rested on a nest of cushions, her person surrounded by a glowing cloud. She motioned to Ewen with her hand, and he placed himself at her feet, the bottoms of which he saw were marked with delicate and beautiful calligraphy, in some language which he could not understand.

"I am the goddess Billion Folded Petal," she said, "and this is the world called Paper Jewel Blossom, over which I am queen."

Ewen placed his mouth to her delicate toes; paid reverent homage; wanted to tie his arms around her waste; felt as if he were entering an advanced stage of intoxication;—a succession of images, emotions; and the scent of living flesh, the sound of sighs.

The next day he felt very light, happy. His stomach was the home of butterflies. He walked, almost on the points of his toes, like a ballerino.

The faculty at the University noted his buoyed appearance.

"The old fellow is probably in love," a professor remarked.

"Maybe," thought Agatha Moray, "but not with me."

And, while she each night turned the yellowing pages of French novels, of Les *égarements du coeur et de l'esprit* and *Follie amorose*, he, after dinner, would sit before the woman of paper; gazing at her form, drinking his whisky, his imagination carried forward as if on wheels. His bed then became a door, which led to that floating, ideal world;—and there he would see her, animated; and his feeling of profound and reverent passion matured; while they drank scented teas, strolled through fascinating landscapes, while he listened to her voice, which was as soft as rustling silk.

He sank into the deep, white clouds of sleep.

He approached her through smiling flowers. She stood against a striking, thickly-painted background of off-tinted lemon-yellow.

"I am the goddess Billion Folded Petal, and this is the world called Paper Jewel Blossom, over which I am queen. You have been celibate for many years. You have been faithful to me. We will celebrate together our nuptial rights."

"Will—will you be my bride?" Ewen faltered.

"Ewen Patrick, Professor of Orientology, I will be your loving bride."

"When?"

"You must leave your native land. When you have left your native land, for good, we will be united forever."

When he opened his eyes the room was red. His body was moist. There was a smell of oregano, almost nauseating, in the air. He climbed out of bed, went to the window, and saw the bleary light of dawn. He went to the parlour, where her form, in the almost dark room, was like a white flame.

At the University, Ewen could hardly concentrate on his teaching. He was very excited. "I will not be among you tomorrow," he thought.

He had read an article about an Indian family who, mistaking the roots of cowbane for parsnips, had made a curry of them, and perished.

That night, at home:

He bolted the front and back doors and swallowed two anti-histamine tablets.

He took the roots out of the oven, placed them on a plate and spread them over with butter. He ate in the parlour, in front of the woman of paper, and his food had a sweetish and not unpleasant taste; but soon there was a burning sensation in his mouth. Feeling weak, he sat back on the divan and closed his eyes; clenched his jaws.

The trees, now giants, were hung with paper lanterns, splashes of purple, yellow and green; some in the shapes of stars, others exotic, bloated fish, or insects with huge diaphanous wings, or serpents which seemed to coil endlessly through the branches, their glowing tails hanging down over the avenue. Short fat men, with skin tinted dark-blue, beat on huge drums that looked like the hulls of boats; and young women, crowned with fantastic coiffures, blew into elongated silver trumpets, and the notes spilled out of the ends and fell to the ground in shiny heaps. The sky flashed with pyrotechnics;—and that artificial fire bloomed into numerous images, of birds, warriors, foxes and bathing maidens. In front of a pavilion the bride waited; a delicate, pink perfume radiating from her body. Her cheeks had the iridescence of pearls; and her elongated torso appeared as supple as a vine-shoot. Ewen approached. He wanted nothing better than to consummate their relations.

"I have come to you. I have left my native land and come to you."

"Ewen Patrick . . ." Her voice was an art of sound; words like chrysanthemums being swept through the air.

"My darling," Ewen murmured. He reached out.

His life, blunt and real, resonated around him.

"Do not abandon me," she said.

"Come home," shrieked his life, showing a tongue of quivering fire.

"I do not want to," Ewen replied.

Red.

Entangled.

The hue of the cherry, feverishly glimpsed, faded from sight.

When he came to, he could not move his legs or hands. His whole body was numb. It was daylight. It was raining outside. The figure stood, in the dim light of the room, inanimate and unresponsive to his moans; the tears which rolled down his bloodless cheeks.

He needed to go through months of therapy before he could walk again; but his fingers never regained their dexterity. It was impossible for him to do intricate folds.

At the University he could be seen, a shabby figure moving unsteadily across the lawn, his face like a cinder grown cold. In class he would caress the sheets of A4 white with tenderness, feeling the sadness of lost flesh in each one, and then, in a trembling voice, lecture on the subtleties of late Tang poetry. At his home the woman of paper still stood in his parlour, but his dreams were black liquid, not only unpopulated by love, but even by fantasy.

THE
LAST
OF THE
BURROWAYS

or

A Strange History

Any man who has ever had an affair with a harlot would be unable to name a more lawless creature. For what savage dragon, what fire-breathing Chimaera, or Charybdis, or three-headed Scylla, that sea-bitch, or Sphinx, Hydra, she-lion, viper, and the winged broods of Harpies, have ever succeeded in surpassing that abominable class?

—Anaxilas

I.

"I love my daughter, is that some form of crime?" Walter Burroway said, looking hard in the eyes of the curate.

"Sir," the latter replied, licking his dry lips, "to love one's child is but normal—Yet, the manner of your living is causing no little stir throughout the community, and I do believe that you will be thrown in the Gaol before long if you do not in some measure correct your ways."

"Correct my ways!" the wiry, wild-eyed man cried, his voice jutting from his throat in high pitched incalescence. "Why, could a man push away a loving child from his arms, such a beautiful child as Alice? You might as well suggest that I quit eating as doing without the love of my only daughter."

The curate shook his head mournfully. "Then I can do no more for you," he said. "As you refuse to mend your ways, refuse to even so much as disguise their lickerish aspect, I can tell you plainly that, not only will you roast in Hell hereafter but, in all likelihood, be set kindle to at this place called Earth first. Farewell, Sir."

With these words the good curate turned and walked rapidly away, spitting along the side of the road as he went, as if to relieve himself from the very taste of the conversation he had just endured. Burroway stared gloomily around him and then, turning and walking through his scraggly little garden, re-entered his own home: a run down cottage on the edge of town; a cottage which stunk of poverty and cried neglect. Within: litter everywhere and grimly soiled bedding heaped dark in one corner. Nestling in the filth, a thin, simple creature: that frog, spawned from agitated water and mud.

"Alice!"

She was silent, and gave him a simple, questioning glance.

"Alice, gather together your articles of clothing and any little things you might care to keep. For a long time I have said that we would move, and now we must, we are compelled to."

"Compelled? But why father?"

II.

"Oh, she is too young a wife for him."

"Too young? Why no, for when I was wed to Tom I was but sixteen years of age."

"Well, you and Tom are a fit couple. But these two: There is something about them that seems not at all quite right."

So the women of Wrexham spoke.

Burroway minded his own business, did day labour when he was in desperate enough need of money, did nothing when there were funds enough to scrape by. The same squalor once cultivated in his previous home, he renewed upon translocating, for he did sully the air around him wherever he went. The girl no longer called him father, but Walter, her husband: a wild-eyed, shock-haired, drinking man, with the physical strength of the high strung, the muscular wiry.

○

"I saw your young wife at the well this morning, Burroway. . . . So when is the child due?"

Burroway shrugged his shoulders and took a tug at the small beer he was drinking. He stared before him with a sullen, somewhat aggravated look. A few jests were made at his expense and the room sounded with merry laughter.

"Who is laughing!" he cried, rising from his seat.

A young man near him by the name of Jim Buchan, the honest and simple son of the village cobbler, giggled; a silly set of red lips widened and a tongue shone between. It was bad timing. He did not realise that the joke was over. Walter Burroway, before anyone could make a move to stop him, had hit the boy on the head three times with a his half-filled beer mug. The first blow made the mug break and the boy fall back. The second blow lacerated his jaw and made him turn his head. The third blow hit his temple. The sharded handle pierced it, straight to the brain. It was the work of a few frantic instants, and the boy was dead; his hot blood crawled on the floor.

Judge Charles Parker presided over the court. He had already, in his career, sentenced one hundred and sixty-eight men and four women to be hanged, to pronounce the rope for another man, a hundred and sixty-ninth, was an easy matter for him, and one he performed without the slightest hesitation. The executioner was a small, evil looking fellow named George Maledon, who, when performing his base function, carried a cocked pistol in his belt, ready to shoot any man who might attempt escape. On the 4th day of March, 1671, Walter Burroway was taken to the gallows at the edge of town and hanged by the neck.

III.

The child was born of Alice some five weeks later: a pale, feeble little thing, curled up like a fatty shrimp, his screams like drops of vitriol. The mother was in a bad way: drawn, nearly lifeless, exhausted and incapacitated. A few good women of the parish, after rinsing the baby of its sticky brown filth, took it on themselves to provide the mother with warm broths, heartfelt encouragement, and hope for the future.

"You're a young woman yet, and handsome, though in need of colour. . . . You certainly must get some back into that flesh of yours. . . . The man suffered it out of you. . . . He's gone now, so you need not worry. . . . His sins are not yours. . . . A beautiful world is here ready to treat you with kindness."

195

But Alice, a very wilted blossom of foxglove, was not looking for kindness; she had sprung from dung.

The broth offered to her she sucked down, soon graduated to brawn and mustard, and then on to good fatty mutton to heal her sick body. She got well, her arms, hips and breasts filled out. The helpers were thanked with quasi sincerity; a few coins were wheedled together and the child, the worm-like baby, was left with a wet nurse, while young Alice secured herself a seat on the coach to London.

The woman haunted the darker regions of the city, fascinating sailors and men from foreign lands: dissolute merchants from Spain, wicked old French men, filthy-minded Germans. A certain expert in lust, one Giuseppe Struffolino Krüger, a chapless, sharp-bearded dwarf who had been blended on the continent and lived primarily off daily dinners of bulls' testicle pie, inaugurated her into the secrets of devilish intimacy. He, hiccoughing a stench of profanity, showed her a hundred and one ways in which her defiled cake might be used, not only for her own pleasure, but also to enrich her purse greatly. In a few sordid and painfully delicious months, the whole mysterious range of notes which could be played upon the male trumpet were revealed to her, and she determined to beat the said instrument into gold. The experience she gained from this great maestro of sin she was quick indeed to turn to a profit. A languid Scottish Earl she made her prey: The Right Honourable Earl of Berwick, a thin, sandy-haired gentlemen, whose eyes she made hollow and dark, whose bankbook she pillaged, or it should be said he gladly laid at the temple of her shame.

"You know Alice," he said. "You know you are dragging me into a life of sin."

"And are you repentant m'Lord?" she laughed, showing her overripe and playful tongue.

"Better to go to hell with you," he gasped, lurching forward.

He reached out his hand and touched what was there; felt his head grow cloudy and hot. No, he was not repentant. His wife and frowning sons be damned. A fly that serves forth its blood to the doxy spider was he; so corrupted, he became a shadow of his former self: sunken cheeks, eyes greedily bulging for some last acidic dip in pleasure.

Meanwhile she portioned his hours so as not to dry him up all at once, adding weekly sums to her banking account, subsidising her income with new youths on the scene, solvent at turning one and twenty, burning their way through London in competitions of degeneracy.

Her son, when he reached the age of ten, she moved to the town of Swindon. There she journeyed monthly, always bringing with her sweets and toys to lavish on the boy. A tutor was hired to instruct the young Christopher, who was in this way given the tools to show himself to the world in an almost gentlemanly manner. When he reached the age of seventeen, his supporter Alice retired from her shameful occupation. Many a noble and valiant man had she wasted. A good deal of money had been saved. A house with a small portion of land was purchased near Colchester, and there she established herself, with her son as the lord of the mansion.

IV.

He was a handsome clear young man and Alice's heart was full for him. His quiet, dignified speech was as sweet as a girl's. She felt she had done right in adopting the course she had for his upbringing and education, for the youth's appearance and manners left nothing to be desired.

"He is certainly very different from his father in every way," Alice told herself, shuddering at the recollection of the man.

In all truth, the more time she spent with her son, the fonder she became of him. She had always had a deep attachment to him, and for this very reason she had plied her wares all the more diligently in the city, so he might grow into a life of comfort and thereby circumvent the gallows which had hung their mutual father. Even though Christopher was now taller than herself, she still petted and fondled him, pleased with the touch of his skin and the even sound of his voice.

There was one thing she noticed, however, that upset her: The neighbour, a widow by the name of Mrs. Kress (a simple-minded woman, with a round, pale face—a woman living on a meagre income) —The neighbour, Mrs. Kress, had a daughter, very young and attractive. Her beauty was not extreme, but she did have all the commodities which a young man is apt to believe to be great beauty, or if not believe, certainly prefer to great beauty, *id est* a fresh and rapidly blooming body, and a beckoning, rather erotic mouth.

Christopher, saw this girl come and go from her house daily, saw her wander through the fields, her plump figure moving with a seductive twist, and formed a great longing for her. It was obvious, by the way he stood at the window with loose, parted lips and watched as she passed, and then how he hurried out, like a dog on a scent, what he was after.

V.

There was, not far from that village, a certain midwife called Dame Moore; a very old, a very ugly woman, who was often questioned regarding matters of a female nature, and seemed to be able to provide from her stock of remedies a treatment for nearly all situations. The duty of the toad has always been to huddle beneath the damp stone; the duty of a midwife, in those periods of the past, was to be well versed, not only in the workings of her patients' privates, but also to hold some knowledge of the three fold world of the Celestial, the Elementary and the Intellectual. She must know the strength of herbs, stones, creeping things and fruits, as well as what could stir the heart of man, what could freeze and what could restrain it.

☉

Alice left Dame Moore's house, repeating to herself the instructions she had received.

"Take a needle," she murmured under her breath, "and smear it with dung, and then wrap it up, together with the earth in which the carcass of a man has been buried, in the cloth which was used at the funeral. Let a woman wear this about her, and no man shall be able to lie with her as long as she does keep it so."

VI.

"It seems that my son is very much in love with your daughter."

"So it appears," Mrs. Kress said, looking down.

"He is very much in love, enamoured of your daughter, but he has no intention of marrying her. He wants her for the pleasure of it, and for nothing more, and then his intention is to cast her aside, pure and simple."

The woman looked up with frightened eyes. "My Jane is a good girl," she murmured. "If the lad has bad intentions . . ."

"Then we must divert them," Alice smiled sympathetically.

"That we must! For the honour of my house, her chastity must be preserved!"

"A girl's chastity is her only treasure. Leave the matter in my hands, good woman, and all will be well. We will save the honour of your daughter, and preserve my son from falling into the ways of folly."

"But what shall we do?"

"To begin with," Alice replied, removing a small sachet from her breast, "make your daughter wear this, and on no condition remove it from her person. By this wise her virginity will remain intact, and no man will have the ability to break it."

◉

Alice was greatly relieved to know that her son was now barred from the orchard of Miss Jane Kress. She saw him go out daily, on the hunt for the young woman, and return at night, discouraged and depressed. She knew very well the signs of lust, and could see how, without proper outlet, this heated state was wasting him. He was like a phantom, stalking around the house at all hours, prowling after Jane, and always thrown off—not by that virgin's dislike, because she liked him very much, but by the power of the sachet, which she wore hanging around her neck, according to her mother's instructions—never suspecting that it prohibited Christopher from satisfying her own strongest desire.

VII.

"Good woman," said Alice to Dame Moore, "I am afraid I need to trouble you further."

"Go ahead and trouble me with more silver; it is the trouble I care to take."

"I am afraid I have a rather strange request."

"You are in strange company, so make it."

"I must make a virgin of a whore!"

The old woman chuckled, letting her tongue hang somewhat from her mouth. "Oh, it is not so strange as you think my dear. Many is the time I have had such requests."

"Then it can be done?"

"It can be done, and done well—it all depends on what nonsense you are willing to do; and of course what expense you are willing to go to."

"The expense matters not."

"Then you would like the treatment deluxe?"

"Me? What makes you think it is me? Do I look such a whore?"

Dame Moore shrugged her shoulders. "You look as you are," she said. "There is no fooling an old woman like me."

Alice kneeled before the midwife. "Then tell me what I must do?" she asked in a low voice.

"Well, the problems with the operation are two-fold: Firstly, the matrix of the virgin is far narrower than that of either mother or consummate whore. Secondly, there is the matter of bleeding."

"The obstacles seem almost insurmountable," Alice moaned. "For I am indeed so far from that state of innocence, that I cannot even remember the time before my corruption."

"It matters not what you remember," croaked the old woman. "The magic of nature will readily lend assistance to your cause, as she has for countless other whores for countless centuries before this."

So saying, the old woman rose from her seat and went to her cupboards, opening which, numerous bottles, phials and decanters were revealed, each one labelled and containing some odd chemical, spice or other rare ingredient.

She powder together dragon's blood, bole-armeniac, mastic, galls and the shells of pomegranates and, dumping the contents into a phial, handed it to Alice. "Take this mixture," said the old woman, "and boil it in sharp red wine. Into that liquid wet a wool cloth, and apply that cloth most diligently to the part. The result will be a very marked shrinking, which will indeed surprise you."

With an eager hand Alice took the phial. "But about the blood?" she asked.

"Fear not," said Dame Moore, "I have not forgotten."

She took burnt allome, mastick, a little vitriol and orpiment, and mixed them together into a fine powder. Admixing a little water from her cistern, she made numerous tiny and thin pills, pressing the putty in her fingers and letting the items dry by the fire.

"Apply these," she said, handing the pills to Alice, "to the mouth of your matrix, being sure to change them every six hours, for a period of four and twenty hours, always dousing the place with rain water or water from a cistern. These pills will thereby produce small bladders which, when touched, will bleed, and the man who causes this will not know you from a maid. If you wish the blood to flow more copiously, you need only apply to the spot one single leech and then remove it. The scab thus formed will provide blood enough to deceive the most practised libertine. If this does not appeal to you, you could try in its stead an application of the dried blood of a hare or pigeon. When this blood mixes with your natural juices, it will flow freely."

Alice kissed the woman's hand.

"My fee."

"A fee I very gladly pay."

VIII.

Alice smiled and took up the hand of Mrs. Kress.

"You need simply tell him to meet your daughter in the barn at the stroke of twelve."

"But she will not be there, will she?"

Alice smiled at the simple woman. "Of course not. I will have my chambermaid Catherine there in her place, who has promised to sell her virginity to me at a fair rate."

"Then Jane will be safe?"

"Am I not going to great lengths to save her honour?"

"Indeed you are ma'am," Mrs. Kress sighed, nodding her head gratefully. "I would be a fool of a woman indeed if I did not follow your instructions which have thus far kept my good daughter's honour intact."

○

There was a strong odour of hay.

"This the place of rendezvous assigned by the fresh girl's mother," Christopher murmured to himself, stepping uneasily into the dark barn. "Jane, are you here?" he whispered.

There was a low, languishing sigh. He moved forward, feeling his way through the barn. He could hear her breathing, and then of a sudden felt something soft and hot: pliable flesh that pulled him forward and down. Thinking indeed that he was in the virgin embrace of young Jane, he played his role with gallant gentleness, all the while never guessing the extent of experience the being beneath him had enjoyed. She did very much comply to the requisites of the virgin state—a state he was eager and active to dismantle.

It could be truly said that Christopher enjoyed very much the sport. He had expected to find a timid bedfellow, and instead discovered a kind of anaconda, to strangle his quivering body with knots of living meat, and seal his lips with stinging kisses that brought forth blood, gluing his mouth to hers. Never could he have gotten better by expending pocketfuls of gold at the battle lines of the brothel, and his vicious heart rejoiced inside the heaving casket where it was lodged.

Shortly before the hour of dawn, he struggled out of the barn, as pale and weak as a man might be just returned from Hades. But the nature of this pain was to him attractive, anything but repulsive. One visit of this sort was not nearly enough. Every night he crept back into that barn, and every night was greeted by wordless but active lust.

IX.

Now, after several months of the darkest enjoyment, Alice found herself in a condition she had in no way counted on. With her clientele she had always made sure that, though her fortifications might be breached, the town was not razed and plundered; in this latest case, certainly more dire than all those, she had let passion totally consume her, and had thereby forgotten caution completely.

She visited Dame Moore, who with great ease ascertained her state and said that it was an absolute certainty.

"You are many months gone my dear," she said, "and you will not long be able to hide it from the world."

"Is there any way to do away with the creature—this thing I find now lurking in my belly?"

"That there most certainly is, but unfortunately not without some slight risk to yourself, and a further chance of damaging those goods by which every woman of your fine appearance must put great store."

Alice left the cottage in a state of depression. She did not know what to do. After those many nights of burning proximity, she could not help but love young Christopher more than ever. Truth be told, he was the only man she had ever loved, felt tenderly and sickly devoted to. If she did nothing, the boy would think his mother a hussy; seeing her pregnant and not knowing. If she trusted her body to Dame Moore, she risked not only her health, but her female property. —And if she told Christopher . . .

She arrived at her house still turning over these important thoughts in her mind, and, upon crossing the threshold, saw Christopher seated before the window, his eyes glued to the Kress household next door.

"Christopher my child," she said with a quivering voice.

"What is it mother;" he asked, rising from his seat; "why is it you look so vexed?"

She swallowed hard and parted her lips. "Have you ever wondered about the history of your father?"

"Naturally."

"You are distracted?"

He blushed.

"Tell me what it is," she said. "Open your heart to me, Christopher."

His eyes flashed and his cheeks grew pink before he said, with a kind of audacious embarrassment: "I am in love!"

Her blood almost froze within her.

And then she spoke. She told. . . . Of the father, Walter Burroway. . . . The stinking swamp of their family history. . . . Even some of her own career. . . . And then her deception, the deception she had played upon her son, and that great sin she had done, and tricked him into as well.

When she had finished, she sat down heavily on a chair.

Christopher stood stone still in revelation. The blood had completely drained from his face, which was now serious, startled and, to Alice, more handsome than ever. She herself could barely breathe. Uncertain what the young man's actions would be, whether he would simply leave her in horror, or take the more hot-blooded course and kill her, she closed her eyes, awaiting judgement. . . . Alice felt, and opened her eyes. Her dress was shifted up, the lips of Christopher were pressed ravenously to her leg, he there, half-collapsed, kneeling.

"Oh, my love!" he cried passionately. "My beautiful love!"

X.

Many years later, in the town of Martham, Norfolk, a figure was seen stepping slowly by the church, and then into the graveyard. Its arms hung low, almost to its knees; in one hand was grasped a bouquet of flowers, strangely robust in the tiny white paw of its porter, who was exceedingly small and withered in frame. Though of only middle age, this creature possessed the body of the feeblest of old men.

With eyes set close together and mouth hanging loose, lips thin and glossy moist, the head bent down and peered at the stones. A thick, yellowish substance oozed from those two blinking pores on his face, as he saw:

> *Here Lies the Body of Christopher Burroway, who departed this life on the 18ᵗʰ day of October, Anno Domini 1730, aged 59 years. And next to me Lies Alice, who by her Life was my Sister, my Mistress, my Mother and my Wife. Died on the 12ᵗʰ Day of February, 1729, aged 76 years.*

The last of the Burroways laid down those flowers, made his offering to the shades of his parents. . . . And so might you, for that stone is there in Martham.

FLIT

The sun was up in mid-sky gleaming blade-like against that endless blue cosmic expanse and I had one hand on the wheel. I reached my head over and saw a piece of me in the mirror, a capable and seasoned man with black hair and beard, skin tight around the cheeks and eyes narrow and watchful, two pale green gems. And I knew that what those eyes had seen and what that mind knew other men were not fit to see and know, those great and far eternal secrets that she had unveiled, had whispered in my ears.

My truck now bumped along the dust-covered dirt of the road and to my right I could see the fresh green strip where the river was, so shaded down there by the tall old cottonwoods and I turned up and over the hill, passed the dump and then entered the dry land. It was warm and I pulled behind a tree where there was not only a shadow cast upon the earth but also the broken bottles of what had been, of drinking and possibly even love making, those things so necessary for us human creatures vomited onto this globe of uncertainty.

She had come to me that morning and taken me from my sleep with the sweet sound of her instruction. So comparatively small did she appear, but it was still I who orbited round her, amazed at the very lucidity even as I put on my jeans and walked from that room.

Now I opened the door of my truck and got out. I moved around to the back, opened up the tail-gate and dragged that one towards me, reading in his strange smooth face the final lines of the hymn.

"Easy now," I said. "You're going to be okay with me."

And then I pulled him off the tail-gate so that he came down on the dirt. I put my hand upon his head, almost the only part of him that was big.

"Tommy, she's smaller than you now," I said and unbuttoned his shirt so that I could see the very white of his stomach and chest. "Small, but you would not believe how vast."

Those spoils that he thought he could make away with in fact could never leave. And the taste that was on his tongue and the images upon his mind needed to be consigned back to her hub.

I took my pocketknife out from my pocket and sound came from his throat but could not find exit through his mouth so filled as it was with the soft cotton of bandanna. Unclasping the blade, I saw his thoughts written across the sky of how this very blade could cut the binds that bound him, probably him scarcely daring to guess at the holy office for which it was emissary. He saw before him this easy-moving, lean-hipped, quiet-faced man and then started to wriggle like an eel as he felt the knife do what it had been born, destined from beginningless time to do, looking within as the flower bloomed upon the white surface of his waters.

A single crow flew overhead and I flayed the offering and then, squatting on my heels, built a fire from twigs and small brush and laid wood in order upon the fire as the shadow of the tree grew shorter and the beauty of the sun made golden the infertile hill of earth, her tabernacle. And in a short while she was there with me just like she had said, now followed by her sisters, all together humming their mystical tune.

I took away the two kidneys together with their fat and the caul above the liver and set these in the flames, a sweet savour for her and I looked across the land with my two pale green eyes. From my shirt pocket I took a cigarette and lit it with a flaming piece of brush, the blue tobacco smoke then blending serenely with the black smoke of the offering. She was there, so translucent-winged, and her musical voice together with the crackle of small fire and sizzle of juices interrupting the parched silence of the day.

My truck bumped back along the road, only this time I went down to the fresh green strip of the river and crossed over the bridge and saw the cottonwoods on either side. I pulled over and left the motor running as I moved down the bank to that enchanted place where water-cress grew as did the Russian olive trees. My hands I rinsed in the cool running water and then stooped and took a sip of the same. When I stood up, I knew that I was ready for my first beer of the day and so went back up to the truck and then drove along the road, which was now smooth tarmac. I pulled over at the tavern, that tavern where the sign read 'Joe the Wop's' and the only car out front was Joe's.

I sat at the counter and ordered a beer and saw the ghost of my own self in the fine sheen of the wood and looking up saw him again, that man with his competent face, black hair and beard, skin tight around the cheeks and two precious eyes. The cool liquid tasted good and Joe and I spoke.

It was not much later that Peter entered and I nodded at him and he asked me where Tommy was. I told him that I did not know.

"Edward said he saw him get into your truck this morning over on the frontage road."

I did not answer.

"He was hitch-hiking and you gave him a ride, right?"

"I didn't give him a ride, Peter."

"He didn't come home last night. I guess he was out drinking. But this morning we had things to do and I expected him back."

"He's probably off with some woman," Joe said. "Women are supposed to like the wicked ways of those little guys."

"Edward saw him get into Douglas's truck this morning."

"Peter, I don't know where your brother is," I said.

"You gave him a ride."

I did not answer, but simply finished my beer and watched the fat circle of Peter's head and sensed her, there with me and so eloquent, without blemish in her every word, and recalled her as she had been, that form with its divine bestiality, large of bust and so very able to banish this man's loneliness as I flew high on the wings of her lips. Her hair of gold I thought of, and then Tommy and the services he had rendered, those which each dwarf is expert in because they must forage as they are able, find what provender is within their reach.

"I know you gave him a ride because Edward Goldring saw you pick him up and there are not two men around here who drive a salmon-coloured Ford F-150. Now where did you drop him off and why are you lying to me?"

"I am not lying," I said.

Then we all heard it, the sound of another vehicle tearing up in front and the car door slam, then the steps of feet moving quickly and the door pushed open. All this for the moment muffling out her delicious voice and the distance between things seemed great and this man, this 'I', somewhere far out in the upper pools of the galaxy while still sitting on the stool, my senses absolutely keen.

Edward Goldring ran in, a tall and insubstantial man, his features painted with fear and him gasping out his words.

"God damn it, Peter. Tommy is butchered, Peter. Someone has butchered your God damn brother, Peter."

"Edward, what the hell are you talking about?"

"I was taking a load to the dump and saw smoke off the side of the road and pulled over and he was there all butchered up."

I saw her mounted on the lip of my glass.

"I'm calling the police," Joe said.

"Douglas," Peter said.

I slid off my stool, took out my wallet and told Joe that I wanted to pay for my beer, but he just repeated what he had already said and put his hand to the receiver of the telephone.

"I would like to pay for my beer first if you don't mind."

"Edward, Joe, it's Douglas."

"Douglas?"

"Edward, it was Douglas who killed my brother."

"Call the cops," Edward said.

"I'm going to," said Joe.

"Douglas," said Peter. "Douglas, you sick son of a bitch, I am going to kill you."

And then things occurred with both heat and rapidity. First, with perfect and crystalline clarity, I saw her fly from the rim of my glass to Joe, thus marking him out for the sacrifice. His profane and irritable hand brushed her aside while with the other he picked up the receiver. I moved like a hunter up and over the counter in a single swift motion, the abrupt and profound justice of the goddess guiding and making me a holy instrument. My right hand was on his throat and my left foot against his kneecap, which, like wax beneath the sun, melted under the decisive pressure of the heel of my boot, his cry suppressed by the five sacred rods of my fingers.

"He's killing Joe!" Edward cried.

Then Peter said: "Watch him Edward while I get the rifle out of my truck."

Leaving Joe to himself for the time being, I turned and leaped back over the bar without even needing to calculate where my feet would fall because I was guided.

"I'm going to have to get real with you," I told Edward, knowing that the man's only hope lay in flight but that flight was impossible because the mistress of our actions had already composed things through to the end.

"Let's get real," I said and took out my pocket knife, unclasped the blade and stalked towards Edward.

"What—what the hell," Edward stuttered, his tall and lean body frozen stiff by the eternity he saw in the philosophical pools of my eyes.

The blade plunged into his body for the first time just as Peter entered with the rifle and plunged for the second time just as Peter fired the rifle. I simultaneously heard three things: the gunshot, my own heartbeat, and the will of the knife accepting the invitation of the meat of Edward's throat. In that glorious instant I remembered how she would dry her hair in the sun, shoulders bare and a towel wrapped around that well-built temple of her body, which was more grand than any domed cathedral or even Indian Taj Mahal, and how she had made me help her in its transmutation, its physical reduction, while giving her soul power over every star's bright lantern and every mark of shade and light in the whirl of this Milky Way and so far beyond. And I was there, that seasoned man with black hair and beard, not floored by the shot to my leg, but contrariwise I was a being sucked forward. I delivered a teeth-shattering left to his mouth and his lower lip burst open and he just dropped, fell back and it was all so real, just like she had made me get real with herself to show those bright blooms of her flowers. She had made me get real with her to scatter to the winds the sacrilege of little Tommy's tongue and hands, preferring as she did the scarlet of his warm liquid in which she could dip her most lovely proboscis, that sacrifice back there behind the dump.

The barrel of the rifle was in my hands and the stalk moved up and down with great ease, like I was splitting wood. And then I found myself there fighting for breath. I dropped the rifle and stepped back a little, still steadfast in my covenant and actually feeling like a poor man made rich.

I worked my knife out of Edward's throat, wiped the blade on his shirt and then, hearing distinctly a sound from behind the counter, went to investigate. Joe was there with the phone in his hand, thinking he could finally get in that call he had been wanting to make, and he looked up at me, showed me his traitor's face.

"You shouldn't have treated her like that," I said.

I cut the phone cord with my knife and then re-clasped the blade and put it back in my pocket.

"You busted my kneecap," Joe gasped.

"We need a smoke signal," I said.

The pain in my leg was just starting to become a true and acute actuality when I made my way out to my truck. I took the hose and gas can from behind the seat, undid the gas-cap, stuck in the hose and sucked. Presently I got a drink of that motor spirit hot in my mouth, spit it out, and let the hose run into the can, the sound of the liquid a recitation of affection and loneliness, of longing and hardship and the cure for these things and how to lodge and dwell in her glory. I had considered her ways and wisdom in my heart and so understood her secrets and limped back into Joe the Wop's, a solid man not in leg, but surely in spirit.

Joe had crawled out from behind the counter and was in the middle of the floor.

"Let me go," he said.

"We need to give her a smoke signal, Joe."

"Killing dwarves is bad luck, Douglas."

"You aren't a dwarf, Joe."

And then he started talking real fast and saying many things which my guarded ears would not recognise while I spiced the room over with gas from the can and then the fidgeting figure of Joe himself. She was over there on Peter's head and told me to just go so I left, making a nice tail of gas as I exited.

From my shirt pocket I took a cigarette and lit it and then lit the tail of gasoline, watching it run off in blue and yellow luxuriance straight through the door of Joe the Wop's where then, as if by magic, it almost instantly splashed out into a glorious symphony of destructive burning. I took a few more drags of my cigarette, tossed it away and then slipped through the fence out back and worked my way up the hill, around patches of cactus and weeds, my boots digging in for foothold in steep places and the pain in my right leg extreme and strangely pleasant, so much so that it was a joy to aggravate it. Gaining the summit, I moved on under that great blue expanse, moved with difficulty and then descended down the other side, the whole while thinking of exquisite her who had power over my nature.

There was a kind of gully lined with rock, a place hollowed out by water over thousands of years and it was there that I sat, sheltered by that endless sky touched now with a signal of smoke. I took out my knife and made a slit down the right leg of my jeans so I could see the hole and the red petals that ran over the skin, like those of a cherry tree and those of love, like those which she had given to me. I called out to her and shortly thereafter she came, riding on the sound of the not-too-distant sirens, once again whispering those eternal secrets in my ears. And I sat in the dust of the hot earth, her drinking the fluid of my leg and me wishing she would lay her eggs in there because we had slept together.

KULLULU

I stayed there, in the interval waiting, thirsty and licking at the walls, gnawing at the door handle. Wondering *when will I taste poke the taste and them lash*. And at the window I pressed, seeing without, seeing the old one go and come; her round, overfed self balancing along the sidewalk on those two weak, so easily breakable legs.

The people down below I could hear, and on the staircase the whole of them I sensed. Me believing *time and then will come seek out their sting make a supper of blood the gore and fell satisfaction*. Then he came, thinking the place a bargain, his face a testament to naïveté and his apertures ripe for my cleaving to.

"It is smaller than I expected."

"It's a studio."

"But it has a nice view."

"I should say so."

"The atmosphere though. . . . It's cramped."

"Do you want it? Another man is supposed to come in an hour, and I'll have to let him know if it's still available."

(Lying; visibly lying.)

"Yes, yes: I'll take it. It's cheap and the location is good."

(Me laughing that *the rational are never the wise*.)

And then he and his comrades came, bringing mattress, chairs and table, drinking of xanthic liquid as they worked, not smelling me because they were together, not knowing or guessing me *lying in the cracks and spying need to make filthy and see hands with rose*. They noised and laughed and I too laughed as they drank, impatiently waiting my turn.

He, my new roommate, was quite young. His cheeks were indrawn, and that I liked. He was thin, but not without strength. He would do.

His friends were two: One stout, and obviously possessed of low instincts. The other was black of hair and had twisted, sarcastic lips.

They lay up my fellow's possessions: clothing, novels, kitchen utensils, with spatula and knife. The latter he cut cheese with, which they ate with smoked meat and unleavened bread, me counting xvij crackers slip upon his own tongue, many more upon the others' movable organs, muscles of the mouth (used in talking tasting licking). And boisterous drinking, and me believing, knowing them dull.

"It does have a strange feeling."

"Hell no! It's the perfect place to bring a——" (Discussing the female of the species in terms jointly crude and candid.)

"You talk," the twisted lips said, "but I never see you with any women."

The stout one turned a fine shade of carmine and let his tongue spew out a few words of filth, by way of defence.

My own dear man, thin and of indrawn cheeks, laughed and swallowed at his yellow liquid.

Then the friends left, hearts faux-full, heads genuinely empty, and I watched him prowl alone about the room, visibly uneasy.

Do you smell me (I thought, or felt) *who will use make you fill indiscretion and suffering and never glad [instead like gutted fish] will you know their twinge their twinge and always to leak those veins leak out hot springs of rose.*

Lights out and then on the mattress he lay full dressed; a fool.

You, young men, strutting around on a ball of mud and fire balanced in space; you are usually fools.

Me: I thirsted and sucked at his heels, turned, rushed and gnawed at wood. Knowing *I will taste poke and them lash; I will taste poke and them lash.* Rushing, rushing. Knowing *I will taste poke and them lash.* Over the floor, across and pressed against one wall. Twisting down, across, again to the table. Gnawing at wood and mounting up, atop.

The knife was there together with its odour of cheese. I licked and tasted. I sensed its blade sharp, thinking *of nursing it through bloody meat.* Moving upon the table, I wound rustling through the food stuffs and then back, dripping down its leg.

Across the floor, up upon the mattress, over leg and chest. I sat on his lips and circled one of his nostrils. I climbed in and tasted.

Murderous, he felt it, me stoking his brain, blowing on it my stinking hot breath. Giving him a dream of the middle night, an orgasm of rage; we sat up together as one. He, we rose, me clasping his blood and riding him, tickling up in his ribs and stirring his guts.

And then: *together going through the door down the steps onto the dark street under the open black sky and glittering cast of stars; stalking down the way to the mask of trees; hustling, scrambling through bushes (as wild pig); me pet the soles his feet; sighting two of them chaps joined to hand; I want to eat; I stir, I blow on his brain; we go, leap upon (smelling his salt manhood, animal fear) pierce roughly iv times; the other scared out of his high pitched wits does take to his heels, scuttles; we, after iij more slices rise, and hunt; run in glory, track and hurdle; stick him to leak those veins leak out hot springs of rose, xix times nursing entrails with the sharp the sharp fun flecked fun.*

We returned, gorged with sweets and slept: Him, putting the blade beneath the mattress; me filtering out through the round nostril, oozing into my cracks, him prone, replete on his bed.

(My friend, how strong you were in the action; how burning, how burning glad.)

The next day he awoke early, rubbed his head, splashed water on his face and left, as if he did not like the new home. He returned mid-day, sat on his unmade bed and looked dull.

There was a knock at the door. It was his friend, him of the black hair and twisted, sarcastic lips.

"So, how do you like your place?"

"Fine, I suppose."

"You suppose?"

"Well, I had terrible dreams last night—really awful."

"That always happens when you move into a new apartment."

"Really?"

"Yes. It always happens. When I first moved into my apartment I dreamed that my left arm was being eaten by rats."

"So it's normal?"

"Sure. You're not as original as you think."

They paused and each, to my amusement, sniffed the room.

"Did you leave this cheese out all night?"

"Ah, I thought I smelled something!"

"Idiot. Put it away and let's go for a beer."

He put away the cheese and they both left, him of the sarcastic lips saying as they walked out the door:

"Did you hear about those guys in the park last night?"

I sensed the door close, went storming, licked at all four walls, and then pressed, gnawed at the door handle. Oh, that first taste made me long for more, another sortie, a further raid on that vital energy. Me knowing *more is sweeter than less seek out their sting breaking fast with blood the gore supper of flies and pain.* I sensed and pressed at the window, seeing again the old one opposite, carrying a bag of food stuffs in her arms; overfed, tottering and displaying a right gashable back.

I waited; patiently I waited.

When he returned it was after dark, but a distance yet from the middle night. He was alone. He was apprehensive, though obviously seeing through a film of mild intoxication. I blew, foul reek. He inhaled, pouted and sat, then lay upon his mattress. He closed his eyes, and presently he dozed.

Me: Rushing, rushing. Twisting hungrily forward. On his lips I licked their parting, wishing to pry, and then, winding up to the cave again, climbed in and tasted. We sat up together as one, felt beneath for the caressing knife, and rose, me clasping and riding him, tickling and stirring his guts.

And then: *together going through the door down the steps onto the dark street under the open black sky and glittering cast of stars, her, the old one there for my glee; me riding him—us stalking across the way (her fidgeting with the trash cans, looking up defiantly); together tasting poking seek out and sting, seek out seek out and sting; make a supper, stick in your hand, of it fell gore; and trim her, frozen, shocked soundless; iij thrusts; again; nursing again until it was ix; it widening at our feet, that blooming rose.*

It swelled there on the ground and a scream sounded, from a nearby doorway. A woman, young and unattractive, stood there giving vent to her seasonable fright. With hands pressed to her head and tongue stretched from mouth, her bark bragged of its powers. She screamed, cried in stuttering panic of our slaying. Windows and doors opened. Eyes and untested flesh peered and glowed. We, still intoxicated high with the feed, turned and broke: flying across to the place, entering and then mounting the steps three at a time.

We turned the handle. He threw himself on the floor. I cried out of him, greatly tore out of him and left him gasping, swollen with alarm.

There were shouts without, of indistinguishable stupidity, the industry of justice;—distress signals and sirens. They, men of heavy heels, noised up the staircase, and burst in, hot with vengeful rage. Seething, they pointed at my apprentice.

His lips curdled and he looked down at his hands, wet with rose, one grasping the tool.

I licked and tasted. I sensed its friendly blade, recalling *nursing it through bloody meat.*

SIRENS

I.

Quite humid; for Julian the air was delicious to breathe; that atmosphere of the hothouse he had become obsessively accustomed to, and he could hardly manage without spending at least a few hours of the day: shifting through black soil, running his hands through delicate verdure; and the beauty that met his eyes, the beauty and gentility of flowers.

"But you shouldn't spend quite all your time in here," Phyllis said, somewhat wistfully. She was a tall woman, taller than Julian, sharp of nose and without much chest. Maybe forty, maybe forty-five years old; maybe a year or two older than him.

"Oh, well—it is my hobby," he replied.

"It seems like more than a hobby to me, Julian."

"And it possibly is, Phyllis, it possibly is. The flowers you see—they are quite good to me. For me, I mean."

"But coming to the museum today would also be good for you. The Impressionists are very uplifting. Particularly Renoir."

Julian, a frail and proper little man, bit his bottom lip and ran a finger over his well trimmed moustache. "But you see, the thing is," he said. "The thing is that I have just got these lovely Neoglaziovias—look at them, aren't they charming? —I have just got them and to leave them untended to, in these awful little pots, would be a crime."

"But it also would be a crime to miss the exhibition," Phyllis said energetically. "The paper says that it is the biggest showing of Impressionists ever to be in England!"

Julian glanced from Phyllis to the Neoglaziovias, and then back to Phyllis. "I am sorry, I can't," he said. "But come into the house. We will have a tea before you go."

Phyllis sighed. She pursed her thin lips; supposed that a tea was better than nothing. But didn't the little man see, didn't he see that she was intensely in love with him? It was true that she was not the freshest bloom, but she was, after all, living and breathing flesh.

☉

In less than an hour he was back with his plants; the Neoglaziovias he gazed at, relished their hermaphrodite, silica bodies, and distichous bracts, so conspicuous, so brightly coloured. —Yes, he liked Phyllis very much. She had always been good to him, but her company did not really compare to that of these silent organisms, which were certainly as alive as any animal, or even woman; these brilliant, colour-bearing spirits, whose company was a mystical indulgence.

He stepped to the door of the greenhouse, opened it and, standing in the opening, looking up at the mellow afternoon sky, proceeded to smoke a cigarette.

Quickly he turned around.

"What was that?"

There was nothing. Just his pets, that beautiful Tillandsia Punctulata, the Mexican Black Torch, and the Aechmea Fasciata, the Urn Plant, with its numerous light blue flowers borne in a dense pink spike.

"Oh, I should know better," he said to himself. "They don't like the smoke."

So saying, he stepped outside and closed the door behind him. His mind drifted, he daydreamed of floral nectaries, beguiling whorls: the Puya Raimondii, that rare Bolivian herb, which blooms once in one hundred and fifty years—that inflorescence, those clustering flowers on a floral axis, reaching eight feet in width and thirty-five high. Even to think of it was a titillation.

"The Royal Botanical Gardens," he murmured, "Kew. —She should have offered to take me there."

II.

He moved slowly through with his watering can, sprinkling here and there, as required; now he would pinch away a discoloured leaf, now examine a rosette, and then the gorgeous, star-like bud of the Wittrockia, veritably scintillating. —He stroked its leaves, tenderly. —In one corner was his Blooming Box plant, a bizarre giant from Madagascar that stretched right up to the greenhouse ceiling, almost berserk with fleshy, succulent leaves, and the terminal inflorescence of vivid yellow flowers which issued from dangling four-sided box-like bracts. He presented two cans of water, an offering, to the base of this queen.

Lunch had been eaten an hour before, lunch with a little wine, and he was mellow, content. Then the watering can was set aside and a seat taken, the soft light stealing in, over him, warmth contacting his slightly moist skin. He leaned his elbow against the little work table; then head propped in hand. Flitting. One here, another over by the door; and more, appearances, as little birds; he detected the almost divine presence of Quesnelia. And Hohenbergiopsis, her thick, golden buds; of a luxurious mistress.

III.

She wore a pair of grey linen trousers, rather wrinkled and frowsy looking. Julian could not help but compare them disadvantageously to the soft and mellow petals of his friends.

"I am having a little supper at my place this Friday evening,—a very casual affair,—certainly no more than half a dozen people. —Well, will you come? It would mean very much to me."

229

Julian was busy watching her reflection on the convexity of the tea kettle, which sat on the stove between them, and was just beginning to murmur: her head cone-shaped and eyes stupid dull little seeds, shoulders stretched enormously broad, the whole a grotesque caricature.

"On Friday you say?"

"Yes, and not too late. Say sevenish if that is alright with you?"

"Sevenish. Well . . ."

The kettle screamed. He lifted it from the stove, his hand in a baking mitt.

"Oh, Julian," she said in a hurt, slightly quivering voice, "please don't try to get out of it. No matter what you say—to be amongst people would do you so much good."

"It is not like I don't *ever* see people." He was preparing tea. "There is the Bromeliad Society and——"

"Oh, come," Phyllis cried in exasperation. "The Bromeliad Society and the society of your plants is just not enough! Not enough for a human life. Don't be a hermit, and *do* come to my supper."

He pondered for a moment. "Fine," he said presently, with an uneasy smile, "I will come to your supper. Thank you very much for your interest in me."

"And I am, I am *so* interested in you," she said, laying her hand on his arm, nostrils expanding to the fragrance of Earl Grey.

IV.

Of course the dinner was a failure. Phyllis, herself no social adept, had a difficult time attracting either interesting or lively people to her sphere. There was a heavy figured young French woman, much too shy to open her own mouth. And then a middle-aged couple, a selfish husband without manners named Kevin and his wife, a great lover of wine. And an old woman, chipper enough.

Julian arrived late, talked little during dinner, and left early. He appeared distracted and had a strange gloss to his eyes.

"Odd friend you have there," Kevin said when Julian had left.

"He seemed a very philosophical type," the old woman ventured.

"I suppose he is a nice enough little man," Kevin said rudely. "But not very interesting; pretty dreary."

"No, he is not dreary," Phyllis replied with some warmth, "he is just not used to company. He spends much time in—in study. I assure you, he is most interesting."

"He is a philosopher." The old woman smiled at Phyllis.

Kevin shrugged his shoulders. Phyllis compressed her lips.

V.

"I am sorry," he said. "I am sorry, but I had to go. Her feelings, Phyllis's, they would have been very hurt."

He stood still in the silence. The attitude of the leaves aloof, sulky. These plants, the Acanthostachys, the Neoglaziovias, the Mexican Black Torch, were really very egotistical—but this made timid Julian like them all the more.

"Come now, she—she is a nice woman. . . . And. . . . What?"

A trembling, so very faint, mellow—whisper—impassively superior.

"No," Julian murmured. "No; I hope not. She can't hate you. Who could—Who could hate you? —So—precious."

He exhaled his words; touched his moustache with his bottom lip. Through misty eyes looked, at those greenish-grey leaves formed into a crater-shaped rosette where the spiked inflorescence, with tiny lilac flowers on its margins, sprouted from the centre. It grew from a piece of wood hung from the ceiling. . . . And then the Spanish Moss, covered by a thick layer of hair-like trichomes, like slight sighs, to capture the humidity of the air.

A gaunt, brownish shape floated past one side of the hothouse, a blur through the opaque glass. There was a knock, and then she came in, Phyllis.

"Oh, are you alone? I thought I heard you talking to someone."

"No, just me," he said nervously.

"No friend, a woman maybe?"

"No, Phyllis."

"You were talking to someone though."

"Just the flowers."

"Julian!"

"And listening—I was listening to them also."

"You were listening to them, were you?" Phyllis asked in an emotional, sympathetic voice.

"Flowers preach to us if we will hear."

"Oh, Julian!" She was almost crying now. "You are too far away."

He was silent. His moustache quivered. She looked at him with pleading eyes; her pale, unattractive face blotched with purple.

"Phyllis," he said presently, "I think you should go now."

"Why—you don't want to see me anymore?"

"They won't allow it, Phyllis."

A few tears sprung from her eyes and she turned, left.

VI.

Fascination, it grew, and their fragrant spirits sang victorious, pastel tunes, unfolding new petals, turquoise, mauve, dashing reds and luxurious yellows; leaf-like divisions like wings and the atmosphere thick with those flutters, colourful flickers; aromatic songs. The airy epiphytics, no longer whispers, but screeches; saxicolous species, growing on rocks and howling; Bromelia Karatas, that semi-xerophilous dazzler, the fruit of which was edible, like its cousin the luscious pineapple, but the sexy beast now squealed, acted like a pig of a plant. The Indian Voodoo Lily, with the white and firm, minaret like stigma appearing from its speckled bloom, an ecstatic cry of spice. Bleeding Heart and Million Hearts, Bridal's Veil; cinnamon, ambergris, intoxicating myrrh. String of Stars, White Ghost. And presently the delicious xanthic and scarlet nodules of Acanthostachys piped as might the pitch of an angry flute; the ever graceful Vanilla Planifolia begat a seductive, slightly insolent laugh, and he was as a man being ridden by a naked woman and whipped with a switch of birch.

He sat on the floor and shook with tears, his lips stretched into an awful smile. The ecstasy of the slave; the final orgasm pre-anhedonia.

Sandkalossie Bergnaetjie, with her drooping tube flowers, bright pink, ruby red, garnet spots on pale yellow, seemed to almost bellow with heinous mirth. The absinthe-coloured Brassavola Digbyana gave its own satisfied sibilation.

VII.

She thought of Kevin's words, and wondered if Julian really were nothing more than a 'dreary little man.' And if he were, would that mean that she should love him the less, had a choice to love him the less? Her heart, that of a woman of forty, or forty-five years old, once fastened on a man, could not so easily let go—even if savagely repulsed.

Phyllis had a packet of chicken breasts in her basket, milk, bread and asparagus; the food of a single, lonely woman. She walked down the refrigerated aisle and picked out a container of toffee ice-cream, and then made her way towards the check-out stand. He was before her, in front of the bottled water, looking very tired, his moustache untended, much too bushy.

"Julian!"

He looked up. "Phyllis. Hello." There was really no enthusiasm in either his look or speech.

"Shopping?"

"Distilled water. For my sundews."

"I am just finishing here. Would you care for a cup of coffee next-door? It has been so very long since we have seen each other."

He bit his bottom lip. His moustache seemed to grow larger, overrunning his features. His eyes were shallow, glassy.

"No," he said in a low voice. "I need to go to the nursery. They need things."

"*They* need things!" She said this somewhat angrily.

"I need to attend to my plants, Phyllis. I—I can't see you. Goodbye."

He kneeled down and began examining a water jug.

"Julian," her voice was passionate, trembling. But he appeared to be in another zone, totally apart, without even ordinary social grace. She was mortified. Her long thin legs carried her away, to the check-out stand, to pay for her meaningless bits of food—the toffee ice-cream she did not even want. Then outside, climbing into her car:

"*They* want things; what about *me*—doesn't it matter that *I* want things!"

She was speeding away, into the country, flying past hedges, her eyes intent, her long, thin face with its sharp nose like the beak of a bird of prey. The car rolled past the familiar tracts of farmland and then through the little patch of those almost grand perennials, with their self-supporting trunks of wood and mellow shade; the vehicle turned, tires revolved up, into the drive.

The greenhouse door was not locked; it had no lock; and she threw it open so the panes of glass rattled. There was a hushed whisper, similar to a soft wind brushing through treetops. A hoe was by the door; she grabbed it and stalked in. The signal red flowers of the Oiseau de Feu truly were like flames ready to launch out and burn her; exotic blossoms gaped, as if they were insolent, open mouths; Miltonia Spectabilis, with its two pink petals, reminiscent of the genitals of woman brazenly flaunted.

"Whores," Phyllis hissed.

She swung the implement which was grasped in her hands, dashed it through the long, slender stalk, decapitated the prettiness. There was a slight cry, and she herself, the tall, gaunt woman, screamed in beastly rage. She spied the pot containing Spiranthes Cernua, Nodding Ladies' Tresses, of yellowish-white, spiking, spiral-shaped blossom, and this she frantically pulled down, sent tumbling to the floor. The air was filled with its odour, like vanilla or jasmine, potent as the hair of a freshly scalped courtesan. Then the whirlwind came. The woman spun through the room; uprooting exquisite rarities; she slashed madly with her weapon; swept aside the Neoglaziovias; attacked, hacked at the Blooming Box plant, scattered those vivid yellow flowers; fenced with the sword-shaped leaves of the Apostle's Iris, thrashed it until it was nude, stripped of every blue and white petal. From plant to plant, flower to flower she went, in unmethodical frenzy, clawing with the fury of a fighting cat, now and again letting loose some vulgar, un-lady-like phrase. Verdure, and the soft, colourful tissue of flowers flew through the air. The Natal Plum she killed, and stomped on the fragrant leaves of the Tropical Lilac. —She stood panting, dazed, the hoe still grasped loosely in her hands. All around was devastation; the floor strewn with their mangled corpses, broken pottery shards, disturbed soil; petals, countless patches of blood, gobbets of flesh.

There was an outlying sound; a car. And then he was there, standing in the doorway, a bag of vermiculite in one arm, the jug of water clenched in the opposite hand.

Both items dropped to the ground.

"You bitch!" he cried, his face twisted into hideous knots. "Bitch!"

Phyllis's awkward figure swayed slightly. There was a small amount of moisture in her defiant eyes.

"Call me what you wish, Julian," she said in an almost steady voice. "But if you will not be mine, you will certainly not be theirs."

THE

UNICORN

He had been an ugly child. The girls liked horses, but not him. As a young man, lacking in hygiene, awkward, his powers of repulsion were exemplary.

A shabby beard soon covered the misdemeanour of his face. His eyes, the colour of chestnuts, had a certain degree of soft warmth and, were a woman to find them, lying in a park, detached from that brutish face, she might very well have leaned over out of curiosity to examine, poked them with her heels.

But as it was, those skirted creatures, those Venuses in rayon, Aphrodites in exaggerated heels, were in no way curious about him and, in fact, avoided him as one might a wad of spit or lump of faeces on the sidewalk.

His name was Vladimiro.

He worked with motors, was constantly up to his armpits in grease, sniffing around beneath autos and shoving his head under hoods. The men he worked with despised him. There was a poster of a naked woman on the wall of the restroom as well as graffiti, petroglyphic, crude—symbolic indeed of the intellectual level of his surroundings and his brain, insomniac, often dreamed of fleshy stars into which he could sink his hands and pink lakes which babbled warm hendecasyllables.

In springtime, the sunshine would lay itself out on the sidewalk out front of the garage. At some distance, in the meadows outside the city, flowers would bloom and he, Vladimiro, would become agitated, haunted by an indefinable feeling that agitated his groins, made his head swim.

There was a woman who worked at the garage, a secretary, a Nadia. Closer to fifty than forty, her underdeveloped cranium was concealed beneath a mass of false-blonde hair; overdeveloped udders seemed up for sale like two chickens on their expiration date. A bit rough around the edges, as is always the case with women habituated to working around the lurid odour of men, an orgy of feminine traits still squirmed, occasionally squealed, in her person.

There was a plush unicorn on her desk, white mane, little lavender ribbon around neck.

"Nadia," Vladimiro asked, "would you care to join me for a cup of hot chocolate after work?"

"*Vaffanculo.*"

That evening, staying past his normal working hours, he fired up the torch, took up an old piston, welded it to a very large grade C all steel lock nut, through several internal-external lock washers.

Morning.

An envelope lay on her desk with the words *To Princess Nadia, First Dawn on a Flower* written on it.

She opened it and read the following note:

Dearest One,

Prepare for your Unicorn to wrap his lips around your throat like a choker, ride roughshod into your valleys. With his third eye he wishes to love you and stare deep into your sex.

Though the nuances of this missive might have been lost on her, the purport was not. She had not received a written declaration of love for some thirty years, since the Ordovician period of her sex life, when conchate virginity was still intact.

That day she was dreamy.

Vladimiro did not arrive for work and curses bloomed amidst the banging of wrenches and whine of electric drills.

She got off work at half-past five in the evening and went back to her apartment, was met in the living room by the man.

A large metal horn jutted from his bleeding forehead. It was helped to stay in place by a very large hex slotted screw hose clamp, a sort of vicious bandeau wrapped around his forehead.

Words came tumbling out of his beard while his thick fingers wiggled forward, ten muscular worms.

A splash of red.

The making of a therianthrope.

Nights fecundated by screams and street corners caressed by hustling footsteps.

"What woman would not care to know me," he said from the depths of a bush, "since I am that magical creature which, though it wallows in mud and slime, carries on its head the magical formula for carneous truth."

VIRGIN HEARTS

I.

The castles which loomed over the city were gripped by cold; and the merry-making of carnival had just been swept away. Those fortifications, residue of feudal times, were not the only things hewn out of stone. Chisel inside the breast of man, woman: living quarry sentiments of onyx dripping wet granite lilacs.

Austere walls. Pretty villas. Forests of chestnut trees like forests of twisting traumatized arms.

II.

A painting on the wall by Canaletto depicting a south-eastern view of the Piazza San Marco in Venice. A Louis XVI clock in blond oak adorned with carved ribbons, bows, torcheres and urns. A 19th century, Austrian, Biedermeier vitrine inside of which rested an Italian, Majolica, ovoid apothecary jar, one side decorated with the head of a woman in Venetian style, the other a penitent clergyman kneeling before a cross. A plaque by Giovanni della Robbia. A pair of French faience cache pots, and other pieces of costly bric-a-brac.

"When will you ask the assessor to come?"

"We had better wait. Uncle still has a bit of life left in him, and if we scare him off . . ."

"I am tired of waiting."

"Only a little longer my love," Jakob said, clumsily wrapping his arms around the contourless body of his wife. He planted a kiss on her ear, which was like the flesh of a cold shellfish brought up from the sea. "When this place is ours, you can have my child."

245

She bit her slender bottom lip.

She, Armanda, wished to see all the old furnishings gotten rid of, turned into cash, exchanged for vulgar manufactured goods. Like an infant, she was attracted by bright-coloured plastic. She had a taste for the inferior things in life. Her soul was like a sad and dried-up oak leaf quivering on the tip of a branch in fall.

III.

Behind closed green shutters. Memories beat their wings, hurled themselves about like panicking trapped birds. Everything would be fine if he could organize, calm them for a few moments.

He looked remarkably like an earth worm. His skin hung limp around his thin joints, frail bones.

"In the drawer," he murmured.

"This?" Jakob, the man's nephew, asked, lifting up a jar filled with a hazy liquid within which floated a small, maroon-coloured lump.

Gèvrey nodded his head. "There. Fill . . . my glass."

Jakob unscrewed the top of the jar and poured its contents into the tall glass which always sat by the side of Mr. Gèvrey's chair.

"What is it?"

With two trembling hands the man lifted the glass to his lips. "Heart . . . of . . . fourteen . . ."

"Fourteen?"

"Heart . . . of . . . fourteen . . . year virgin."

A few drops of the liquid slid down his chin. The organ disappeared between his lips, descended down his narrow throat.

"Maniac," the younger man thought.

IV.

They found in the hallway a skin, not unlike that shed by a snake—a repulsive and ghostlike tissue.

Armanda was frightened; Jakob bemused.

When Gèvrey's broth was brought to him that evening, he pushed it aside. He demanded horseflesh—a piece of horsemeat grilled with onions. A drop of old brandy was poured into a very large glass. Golden-orange tongues squirmed in the fireplace.

In the middle of the night a wild boar could be heard grunting in the near-by woods. Dogs barked. In the villa floorboards creaked. It was as if people were walking through the empty halls.

Then morning.

The shutters were opened and light slid into the rooms.

V.

The perfume of old suits not worn for thirty years withdrawn from trunks, saturated with memories of gay laughter and the lingering scent of antiquated cigars. Then stylish ties, such as are unknown to the young men of today, for whom the word 'tailor' is as deserted as syllables of ancient Greek.

Acetate red and silver patterned bright bold swing necktie with large circles with red and yellow flowers.

He stood in front of the mirror and tied an elaborate knot, a Christensen, with a dimple in the centre of the tie just below the joint, forcing it to billow, creating the fullness that is the secret to its proper draping.

"It is his last gasp," Armanda said. There was a note of desperation in her voice.

VI.

Jakob was a tall, big-boned fellow with bad posture and brooding eyes. He was of low intelligence and stubborn. He slept badly. He suffered from a mild form of obsessive compulsive disorder, his behaviour controlled to some degree by stereotyped ruminations of a vengeful godhead (punisher).

Armanda was his wife.

Her hair was as straight and dull as a sermon, bundled up on the back of her head, looking like a musty ball of thread. She dressed herself in garments that did not fit, kept her small, flagging breasts pinned down in rigid pointy bras and her feet in flat-soled shoes that squeaked.

Narrow-minded, she blamed the woes of the world on the influence of dissolute foreigners; feared integrated marriages, homosexuals, and science; respected money and the Church.

The two were linked by one of those bizarre and miasmic connections which keep the world well-supplied with oafs.

Jakob was unattractive. Without friends, he lavished all his fanatical attention upon his wife. He was addicted to this woman's presence like an insomniac to sleeping tablets—her love being equivalent to some highly overcooked piece of poultry, for which he had acquired a taste like a hyena for carrion. He dreamed of crawling into her womb and resting there. He longed for this woman to have his baby—a little piece of living tissue which would help shackle her to him through the uncertain passages of eternity.

VII.

With black night stooping overhead, Mr. Robert Gèvrey walked along, leaving his footprints in the snow-clothed streets.

He waved his hand in the air as he entered the bar and people—rough looking men hunched over glasses of wine, antiquated jades, skulls crowned with yellow wigs, mouths exhaling celery-scented reddish smoke—gaped. The man was like a hallucination, a monstrous insect attracted by light.

"A curaçao and cassis," he said to the bartender.

This latter fumbled with bottles, prepared the beverage with unsteady hands, then placed it before his client as a devotee of some wrathful god would an offering on the bloody altar.

A glass rises to thin lips, waters a dry tongue, unlocks the vault of a brain out of which tumble the corpses of dead loves, desiccated screams, the bones of a thousand whores and the frozen handshakes of a hundred broken friendships.

"It is a cold evening."

"Not for those who know how to drink."

"And may I buy you . . . ?"

"Certainly!"

"And the lady?"

"Oh, well, if you are buying I will have a martini." A hag's lips stretched themselves out like two scrawny vipers. The acute corners of her mouth lunged towards her ears.

Mr. Gèvrey ran his hand through the dry wigs of those elderly Cyprians, slapped their flagging rears, winked at the men as he treated them to another round. The faces of the thin became extraordinarily pale, those of the fat suffused with blood.

"*Salute!*" a man growled, lifting up a tall and slender glass of uric beer.

A sound filled the room like that of geese being chased by a dog.

Eleven o'clock. The door of the bar opened.

Enter: young man and young woman. Him: tall, lanky. Her: sugar crystal clothed in silk. ·

For a moment they stood stunned, struck by the stink of the place. Then they approached the bar, ordered two digestifs. Gèvrey inserted himself between them, his right eye winking at the young woman while, to his left, his mouth told the young man heroic tales of bygone ages. The woman felt his thin fingers crawl down her spine; and her body tingled with pleasure.

A ballet of words danced off Gèvrey's tongue, sarcastic words which twirled on tip-toe, mocking the virility of the younger generation.

The grins of the habitués hung behind him in a mist of fumes of schnapps, a fog of stupidity and tobacco smoke.

At two in the morning a figure could be seen, staggering through the frozen streets—climbing up the steep, cobbled pathway—a strange gurgling laughter coming from his throat, to be swept away by icy gusts of wind.

VIII.

In springtime he expanded like a sponge, soaking in the sun like the green plants that burst from the earth. A strange, crinkly moustache sprouted from beneath the sharp thorn of his nose, and this squadron of dissolute hairs he dyed a rich coal-coloured hue, brushed and waxed, dividing them into two dangerous blades.

Mr. Gèvrey beat his fingers against the keys of the piano, played an old score by Sammy Cahn.

The music glided out the window, dangled in the air, settled itself on the blossoming branches of an apple tree, before sinking to the ground, each note like an egg fallen from a nest—an aborted epiphany, prone to wrench out tears from the satin eyes of virgins, make short-necked butchers pause thoughtfully while they sharpened their meat cleavers.

Greedy for intoxicated laughter, for girls wrapped in ivy and drenched in wine, whose lips hang, waiting to be crushed like the glossy flesh of pomegranates, Mr. Gèvrey would have been content to live one thousand lives—corrupting both age and youth—spending freely of money gained long ago, by enterprising and rapacious ancestors who had torn gold from the bowels of the earth as ancient priests had the entrails of their victims, and gleaned silver from men's hides as an inquisitor would the frantic screams of a shin-viced heretic.

IX.

Jakob strode about the villa gloomily.

The place was filled with the cheer of late night suppers—the constant tinkle of glasses, never full, never empty, contacting in toasts—the whinnying laughter of fat women whose enormous breasts heaved, plunged forward over plates shiny with the grease of cooked meat, diacritically indicated by stripped chicken bones.

Old wines were dragged out of the cellar, bottles Jakob had earmarked for his lifelong retirement, to be drunk in romantic postures on bearskin rugs next to the lingeried caresses of his blade-like spouse.

On a certain Saturday night: the large oak table in the dining room piled high with pâté, oysters, glossy roe of sturgeon . . .

The doorbell rang. Silence fell over the company.

It was the young woman from the bar, Luisa by name.

She blushed.

"Oh, you are busy. You have company . . ."

A roar of playful indignation; and she was forced into a seat, a half-dozen oysters poured down her throat, which was white as the host and being lashed by the eyes of the men.

Midnight was marked by the popping of champagne corks and the last vestiges of modesty being trampled underfoot like the wriggling halves of severed worms.

A woman named Alessandra, whose formidable buttocks were stuffed into a pair of pre-faded jeans, mounted the table, began to dance wildly. Forks and plates and glasses rattled in their places; throats roared out laughter, belched forth hot, excited words.

At dawn the villa spilled out the survivors of the orgy, pale-faced, shaky-legged.

And later, just as the hollow sound of matins bells floated through the air, another figure seeped out: tearstained cheeks balanced on a smile of depraved joy.

X.

The nephew and his wife went to church regularly on Sundays, to the Collegiata dei Santi Pietro e Stefano. Jakob listened, with vague and clumsy reverence, to the droning voice of the priest, which flung itself around the lugubrious baroque interior. It seemed to oil Jakob's spirit, lubricate it so it would slip the easier into heaven.

Afterwards he would take Armanda's rough little hand in his and they would ascend the path to the house, forgetting their absurdity in words mumbled at random, which crawled off their tongues in the manner of grub from a rotten log.

XI.

Luisa was as a flower about to be blighted by frost, her morbid fascination for Gèvrey like a high-pitched scream ringing out from a night-black cemetery. Carrying the seeds of corruption in her from some past life, she easily adapted herself to the man's whims. She gobbled up the grubs he offered her, dipped her beak in his repertoire of cocktails.

"It is disgusting," Armanda would say mantrically.

"We need to be patient," was Jakob's comment. "He can't last long going on like this."

"But he is stronger than ever!"

And indeed, partaking of Luisa's tonic flesh, he was. He fed her on a strict diet of desserts, and like a hummingbird, extracted the nectar from her oozing flower; in dramatic rays of animal sensuality shredded maiden episodes calling her into dark wells swine of whimpering half-notes capped by cannon balls of brutal hilarity.

XII.

"What is that on your lips?"

"My lips?"

"Yes—you have something on your lips!"

"You boob! It is lipstick! Haven't you ever seen lipstick?"

"But . . ."

"Listen here. Your unemployment benefits run out next month. If you aren't going to look after me I am going to have to look after myself."

Jakob frowned.

"Amongst man and wife . . ." he began to murmur.

But Armanda left the room.

Left alone, he gazed around himself like an ox. Slow, oily thoughts flopped through his brain.

XIII.

Armanda painted herself, flashed her putrid smile at Gèvrey, infiltrated her talk with bold insinuation. She reminded him of a certain prostitute he had once slept with while touring Corsica; a woman whose passion appeared like a switchblade, sudden and exquisitely sharp.

His nephew's wife followed him around like a cur.

As they tied their limbs together, as she coiled around him, they could hear Jakob, in the adjacent chamber, weeping, a series of stupid sobs, and this added an acute piquancy to the event.

XIV.

A brief, ugly scene. Luisa a guppy flung in the mud. A tossed away empty bottle. She floated away on her own tears, downstream, into the gutter.

Armanda was delighted. She swore to Gèvrey that she would be his all. She fixed him highballs and curled up at his naked feet, scalding them with her kisses.

She had her hair cut short like a boy's, smeared her thin lips with bright paint and martyred her narrow hips in a pair of obscenely tight-fitting leather trousers. Hurling herself into her new persona, she wrenched passion from her guts and served it up, gurgling and oozing like a stinking sulphur hot spring.

XV.

The blind hear quite well, the deaf see quite well. Fish live but men die in the water. Forced to swallow the rancid oil of humiliation, Jakob's frowns were as long as other men's legs. He struggled like an insect skewered on a pin.

XVI.

Jakob stood in the library. One wall was covered with rows of leather-bound volumes, titles mainly in French, a few in Italian, some in German—titles evocative, of dancing sinners, faux-oriental lands inhabited by peach-skinned prostitutes and silk-robed demons, crepuscular unpleasantness decayed lilies bleeding screams of amphitheatrical vice. Several antique blades were ranged above a fireplace: a Turkish yataghan with a bone grip; an Armenian bichaq; an Abissynian shotel from the workshop of Asad Allah.

Jakob took an antique ivory-handled Mughal dagger down from the wall, sharpened it, concealed it on his person. He stalked around school yards, forehead beaded with sweat, and eyed drooping maidens. He was torn apart, by his desire to sin and his fear of retribution, eternal damnation. He followed two young women to the Castello Grande. They walked through the courtyard, across the grass and then, laughing, entered the tunnel which runs along the interior of the great wall. He watched them disappear into the dark. He fingered the dagger, trembled. Approaching the cavern, he smelled its slightly acid dankness. Mites swirled around him. He turned, walked away, then climbed the Black Tower. As the wind struck him in the face, he shed heavy tears which almost dragged him over the side, almost pitched him to his death.

XVII.

He took the dagger to an antique dealer in Lugano. The man stroked his beard, looked at it with admiration and handed him a pair of thousand franc notes.

Some 50km further south, in Italy, a city rose up out of the plains of Lombardy—a huge smoking mass which shrieked and panted beneath the summer sun.

In the city of Milan anything can be bought for a price.

"A heart?"

"Of a virgin."

"Yes . . . but it will cost you."

"How much?"

"Three thousand euros."

"But I only have half that!"

"Give me your money."

A sleazy man with thinning black hair and a pug nose, Gianfranco Carafa was a trafficker in human body parts. He had stalked skid row, dismembered homeless waifs and old drunkards, fed their organs, kidneys, livers and lungs, into the bodies of parliamentary members, wealthy Europeans and visiting African dictators.

"A heart, eh?" he murmured, as he poked through his stock. "All out of hearts. . . . Or . . . wait . . ."

A dusty, formaldehyde-filled jar. Of an aged prostitute, her body found on the docks of Genoa.

"Here it is."

". . . of a virgin?" Jakob asked in a quaking voice.

"Absolutely."

He took it home, swallowed it desperately, washing it down with a glass of apple juice.

XVIII.

He slept at the foot of their bed. Every morning he spit out a tooth. As they lounged about, half-naked, their skin wrapped in a single pair of silk pyjamas which smelt as if they had come from a barnyard—a pair shared between the two of them, her the top, him the bottom—Jakob served them breakfast: German coffee, croissants, and fruit which he peeled with his own trembling hands. The hair fell from, abandoned his scalp, like rats hurling themselves from a pestilential ship—and those few that remained, desperately clinging to the rim of his skull, became blighted as by frost.

Outside the birds ridiculed him with their song, and the sky, painted a miraculous blue, filled him with the profoundest of melancholy. He went to the church and prayed before the skeleton of San Fulgenzio, Martyr, who stood, in full armour and holding a sword, in a huge glass case.

He took the firearm down from the wall. When he had been a boy, his uncle had shown him how to load and shoot the thing.

He loaded it. Stuffed the barrel of the gun into his mouth. His eyes, exuding their shiny globules of sorrow, looked on as his cruel finger pulled the trigger; and with a whiff of powder, applauded by a bang, a ball hurled itself through his head.

XIX.

He was lying in a pool of black, coagulated blood with a piece of paper pinned to his chest. Gèvrey pulled it off, tried to read it, but it was so stained with the grim liquid that only a few words were decipherable—just enough to see that it was a list, a list of Jakob's grievances.

XX.

The sky bled with the glow of the setting sun. Armanda deposited a bouquet of plastic flowers on her husband's grave.

"Poor man," Gèvrey said dryly.

"He loved me."

"Yes." Mr. Gèvrey wrapped his thin arm around her waist.

"What are you doing?"

"Come now . . ."

"But . . ."

He pushed her down on the marble tombstone. She writhed, entwined herself around the satyr's caresses. Lather and pitch melody of panting slobber.

XXI.

One day they caught sight of Luisa. She had a baby in her arms. When she saw Gèvrey, she blushed crimson, grinned pathetically. Though she was still a very young woman, she did not look it—wrinkles limp cheeks body gone to hell.

"Poor bitch," he said.

As he walked away he thought he heard a muffled cry.

At home, while listening to an old LP, Christopher Eschenback playing *Werke von Béla Bartók*, he drank a bullshot #4[1]. He lounged about

---

1. Pour equal parts vodka and strong, cold beef bouillon into a cocktail shaker. Add 1 tsp lemon juice, 1 dash Tabasco sauce, 1 dash Worcestershire sauce, 1 dash celery salt and several ice cubes. Stir and then strain into a glass straight up. Garnish with a stick of celery and serve.

the polytonality, sniffed at the chromatically altered chords and dissonant thirds, mentally reviling those of the opposite sex and glorying in his own timelessness.

XXII.

Armanda woke up in the night screaming.

"He's come to demand his conjugal rights!"

"Who?"

"Jakob!"

Her husband, with a huge gaping red hole in his head, haunted her. Had Gèvrey and her, in the lubricious acts they had committed on his tombstone, called him back from the dead? From his cold grave was he coming to search out the uncertain warmth of her womb?

Transfix ethereal weep what coral mist involuntary petrified feeding stale vision of sulphur blotted stockings suspend nasty from ceiling.

Not an isolated occurrence.

His shade not only drifted through her sleep, but flavoured her waking hours as well. A twisted grimace subtle stench. She saw his face, like a gargoyle, mounted in high places: tree limbs, rooftops, summit of clouds.

Pitifully, she collapsed one day in the yard, grovelling in the grass, cried, while ants climbed up her ankles and the sun smiled.

Jakob wound himself around the night, sometimes wandered through the bowels of the earth—but, resisting the clamorous music of purgatory, always came back, attracted by the cheese-like odour of her flesh. Sometimes, making use of certain feeble cosmic powers at his disposal, he would manage to rattle some crockery, make a door creak, or let be heard an incorporeal groan. Without mind or body, he was moved by impulse alone, at night rooted about in their bed like a pig looking for truffles, suffered without being able to scream, existed in an immaterial paste of hate and desire untainted by thought.

Confronted with the possibility of a haunting, Mr. Gèvrey simply shrugged his shoulders. Ghosts are seldom afraid of ghosts and he was willing to let the entire spirit world witness his passion for Armanda (smothered in loathing).

XXIII.

Castles drip sweat hewn traumatized lilacs austere walls.

He saw her standing in the piazza, the finest of white meat. Her name was Strezena. A Russian beauty of only eighteen years. A long sheet of straight black hair fell over her shoulders. She was tall and slim, with a haughty mouth the colour of lamb's blood. Her teeth were like two rows of pearls, glistening with a charming wetness, her gums like salmon under gelatine. Her skin was pale and carried with it the elusivity of moonbeams, the richness of cream. The daughter of a Moscow banker, she was fabulously rich.

"Excuse me," he panted, "but I believe we know each other."

"We do not."

Her warm breath had the faint scent of violets, was as intoxicating as absinthe—when her lips closed they formed a poppy redolent of morphine.

She turned and walked away, evaporated like a drop of morning dew exposed to the candent sun.

That evening when he came home: In the kitchen there was an overturned chair. Armanda was hanging from the ceiling, her toes pointing towards the ground.

He shrugged his shoulder, prepared himself a dry Rob Roy[2].

He quivered as he drank; and little delicate blue flames danced before his eyes.

---

2. In a mixing glass half-filled with ice cubes combine 75ml Scotch whisky with 1½ tsp dry vermouth. Stir well. Strain into a cocktail glass. Garnish with a lemon twist and serve.

XXIV.

When a man such as Gèvrey gets struck with love, it is an all-consuming passion, of almost nuclear violence. A rotting Romeo, debauched in the extreme, he was as unreasonable as a force of nature—a hurricane, a blast of hail.

He sniffed out Strezena's scent like a hound; slithered after her, wound his way through the streets in her wake. She gazed at him with disdain, treated him like the lowest of lackeys.

He could not sleep. He did not eat and kept himself fuelled with hyper-potent cocktails. Dragging himself through his empty mansion, he recited verses of Pierre Quillard. He composed bizarre love letters in which the humble croaking of the toad was spliced with the ornate language of an erotomaniacal rhetorician, his frantic handwriting running across the paper in self-flagellating flurries dribbling

> *red is the colour of your pitch black hair*
> *red the colour of your white skin*
> *white the colour of your tongue*
> *hot*

his heart crackled like dry pine twigs cast into flames.

And he decorated the oozing wrinkles of his vices with garlands, doused them with Eau de Cologne.

XXV.

He sat on the piazza, drinking caffé correttos, waiting for her to appear. Around five in the afternoon, just as the day was beginning to cool, she did. She was dressed all in white, like an angel descended from heaven (pith of parched noise gypsum sand pith of flame).

He ran to her side. His lips stretched themselves into a sickening smile.

She walked along slowly, him buzzing around her like a fly around a lily. He belched out words of passion in half-whispers, bit at the air, grasped at her elbow, offered the reeking incense of his breath to the altar of her eyes.

Her innocent [sic] lips parted. "I could love you . . ." she said.

Gèvrey felt his mouth flood with saliva.

"I could love you," she continued, "if you were willing to adapt yourself to a whim of mine."

"I would murder a man, even for a taste of the shadow of your lips."

"I don't want you to murder anyone. I want a necklace."

"A necklace?"

"Yes. You see that woman over there. . . ." She pointed, straightened her index finger in the direction of a thick-bodied elderly woman dressed in blue around whose neck hung eight fiery opals set in gold. "You see that woman over there. . . . Well, I want her necklace."

Gèvrey's voice became as soft as the down feathers of an eider duck.

"A bauble," he murmured soothingly. "I will buy one just like it for you tomorrow!"

"No. I want that one. I want you to steal it—take it from her by force. I want you to be a public thief—humiliated scum, trembling in the dark vaults of a prison. . . . And when you are done, after you have committed your absurd little crime, my arms will be open for you, my sharp breasts yours. . . . Yes, I will love you!"

She smiled an invitation, intimate.

His lips quivered.

"Ah, you hesitate," she said icily.

"No . . ."

He felt like his veins were rivers of molten rhyolite, rocket fuel, his head a cloud of fire.

He approached the woman. Stretched forth his hands. She screamed. He smacked her.

"Give it here!"

He clawed at her face. Then ripped the necklace from her neck. She toppled. He turned and began to run as fast as his thin legs would carry him.

"Thief!"

"Thief!!!"

"!!!!"

A number of large men grabbed him, threw his frail body to the ground, lept on him. His face was pressed into the brick-paved lane.

In the background the woman whimpered. Blood oozed from the gashes in her powdered face. And she could not move.

XXVI.

Lawyer: "She will not be able to walk again!"

The judge, a middle-aged man with a very round face, prided himself on his impartiality. He would treat the prisoner as he saw fit. Maximum penalty of the law.

Condemned. Clink. Gèvrey was hauled off to prison clink walls system enforced sequential relations. His brain, which was like a warty pickle, was host to smoky libidinous dreams of woman worship gagged morose petals floating down his back cockroach flowers at midnight headless rooster pouty whimper iron cravat scum daiquiri.

When he got out, she would be there for him.

But could he wait?

Jellyfish.

WE SLEEP
ON A
THOUSAND
WAVES
BENEATH
THE STARS

I.

White, hot sand strewn over with shells and then a great sweep of green; an island rich in vegetation, investigation revealing all sorts of tropical fruits, some of which the crew was familiar with, while others none of them had ever seen before—in the shape of stars, swords and crescents. Large brightly-plumed parrots squawked in the trees and small brown-furred monkeys leapt from branch to branch and chattered while, from the depths of huge ferns, the height of a man, came the pleasant scent of land—welcome indeed to those who had been six continual weeks aboard a ship after being thrown off course by a storm.

It seemed like an ideal place to gather in supplies. There was a fresh-water lagoon in which fish swam and octopuses clung to the rocks. Dozens of giant land tortoises sat on the beach. There were groves of coconut trees.

Some men were sent to gather fresh water, some bread fruit. Six tortoises had been slaughtered for their afternoon meal and men sent into the interior to see what hunting could be done, while La Motte, ship cook, a short, round, balding man with sensual lips and lively eyes, prepared two giant fires, one for his cauldron, the other his weighty cast-iron skillet.

After bleeding the turtles, removing the entrails and assiduously trimming away the fat, he braised their flesh and then set it to simmer with a little claret, bay leaves and various spices.

With sweat pouring down his face he stood, legs somewhat apart, stomach stuck forward, going about his art as if he had been in some famous Paris kitchen cooking for lords and ladies instead of on an island, he knew not where, using his skills to feed thieves and cut-throats.

Late in the afternoon a number of shots could be heard in the distance.

"It sounds like they are having some luck with the game," Lagoverde, first mate, a quinquagenarian, an Italian, a man with a long, thin jaw, said.

La Motte: "It would be nice if they were to bring in an eater of ants or a few monkeys, for such a variety of cutlet would augment the meal nicely."

"For me, I am happy as the sun with a plate of simple seafood. And indeed, though I like flesh meat well enough, I am always happiest with haddocks, oyster pies or a plate of sweet periwinkles."

"Then you have chosen the correct career," the cook said, his words peppered with the vaguest hint of hauteur, "for in truth we have eaten little more than bream, cod and flour for the past fortnight."

"A sailor's life."

"One might as well call it the life of a madman. What I would not give to be able to press my lips against a white young lettuce every now and again!"

A figure could be seen making its way along the beach, towards the cook-site. Long strides. The sun to his back. His own shadow preceding him.

"Any luck, captain?"

"Indeed I have," the latter said, opening his sack. "I have captured a crabbe-criarde, which cries like a little cat, a hermit crab hosting a *Calliactis tricolor* and a few interesting echinoderms. The rocky shoals, at the far end of the beach, are rich with a diversity of life."

This individual, who was addressed as captain, and therefore we must assume was in a position adjudicative and determinative over others, merits a description. Extraordinarily tall and thin, his head was crowned by a thick, full-bottomed white wig, somewhat the worse for wear. His face, remarkably pale for someone who had spent a great deal of time sailing in tropical climates, was like the skull of a horse and his lips seemed to sit in a perpetual frown. He wore a collarless grey coat with deep cuffs and a long overcoat, both lined with grey, and black breeches, white stockings and shoes with large brass buckles. His name was Nikola Bruerovich.

The dish was just then beginning to let off a strong and pleasant aroma which stretched itself out on the air, journeyed to lagoon and jungle and tickled the nostrils of the crew and made those fellows agitate their legs in the direction of the little beach camp.

A mass of accent colours, blond beards and long wispy black moustaches, bright red sashes and brown jackboots; semi-aniline faces embossed with carefree grimaces, some men with willow legs, some with spruce, others with legs of oak, strong burly-knuckled fellows able to stand their ground against hurricanes or men. There was Bull-Milo, a fellow of little intelligence but great strength, Amraphel, who wore a beard long and sharp as a pike, and Martini, a small Italian remarkably skilled with a blade;—as well as a great diversity more, from the rough-finished to those with polished foreheads and sharp teeth.

Then, from out of the jungle, came the others, the hunting party, their faces eaten by grins, sabres waving in hands, muskets prodding five small beings. Hollering and laughing, these men walked forward with a group of natives between them—in palmetto skirts, long, oily hair brushed forward, so as to completely obscure their faces.

La Motte opened his eyes wide.

The captain frowned.

The men gathered round in interest, laughter and jests.

"Let's bake them like apples!"

"No, we'll have La Motte fricassee them!"

"The girl looks tasty enough to eat raw!"

And then:

"They have something on their bellies it seems," one individual said. "A tattoo or scar."

He pressed his finger to an old man's stomach and then let out a cry, for the thing had opened up, like the mouth of a shark, showed two rows of jagged teeth, bit off the tip of the finger—a splash of orange and then the wounded pirate, frenzied, cutlassed the native and blood excited the desire for more blood, crewmen joining in to slaughter, exterminate those with the long, oily hair—sound of pistols, thrust of blades, till, in just minutes all but one lay wasted bleeding on the sand.

"Stop!" the captain cried. "You men who spend your lives searching for treasure—do you not see that what we have before us is a treasure in itself? I want this interesting specimen kept alive, for I believe it is worthy of study."

A small female sat quivering in the sand, in the midst of the corpses of her people.

II.

One might ask how it was that so many rough men were obedient to this rather decayed looking gentleman. The answer was quite simple: he was both cruel and generous.

He never took a larger share of loot than his men—having the said loot divided equally amongst all. In the same way, he never ate better food than the rest. Yet he was exacting in his demands for discipline. The slightest breach of conduct would have him blow out the brains of the offender.

It must also be said that he did not lack bravery. For, during assaults, he did his part, coolly and methodically killing men as if he had been gathering specimens from a tide pool. He had never been known to laugh, smile, cry or raise his voice in anger. If he raised his voice at all, it was only to be heard. He seemed a man totally devoid of emotions.

He had been born in the Republic of Ragusa, brought up watching the ships in the harbour, the water splash against the rocky shore. As a young man he had studied at the University of Padua, where he distinguished himself by writing a 4,970 Latin verse epic in dactilus hexameter on the lunar eclipse, a work of technical excellence, though dry in the extreme. He fought several duels and dabbled in invention, map-making and botany. Later, he had spent fourteen years sailing the known world, composing a work on tides which, when it was finished, was promptly condemned by the most Holy Roman Church for certain theories it set forth that were at odds with the idea of a single supreme creator and ruler of the universe.

Treated with sudden disdain by the higher ranks of society, met with silence by comrades in science, he swore off the world, procured a ship, gathered together a crew of desperate but for the most part intelligent men, and set out to make his fortune.

III.

Swimming amidst creeping ludwigia and undulated crypt, schools of dazzling fish gazed up at the jolly boat as it coasted from shore to ship and ship to shore, supplying; hold soon stocked with about fifty living land tortoises which could be kept alive and killed as needed, thus offering a steady supply of fresh meat. Also brought aboard were about four hundred coconuts, and numerous other fruits and a good supply of fresh water.

Then a fragrant breeze filled the sails of the Sparrow, a miraculous ship, a sloop, an incredibly fast vessel with pontoons of coconut shell fibre attached to its sides, making it almost impossible for it to sink even during the most raging of storms; and it skimmed over the ocean; behind it, a group of fins following for many a league.

IV.

The captain was working on a tract entitled *A Catologue of Sea Waters, Their Moods and Concomitants.*

"Come in," he said brusquely, not even lifting his head from the page he was vigorously covering with lines of fine handwriting.

The door opened and Lagoverde entered the small and crowded cabin;—on one wall was attached a table of trigonometry next to a huge thermometer. Shelves were stuffed with books and manuscript pages and scientific apparatus were stored on every side, versorium nestling against circumferentor, a nonius in one corner, in another stood a dusty, neglected looking glass.

"She has been cabined separately as you requested and, God willing, she will not lead the men to any kind of monstrous temptation."

"Anyone who attempts to violate her will be flogged to pudding."

"I'll let that be understood."

"And how is she behaving?"

"Well, she refuses to so much as touch her hammock, preferring instead to crouch in a corner on a pile of straw like a beast, her tongue hanging out over her stomach. She cries a great deal and spat out the cooked food offered her but became ravenous at the sight of raw tortoise entrails and seemed to relish a few fresh guavas that La Motte put before her."

"Have La Motte shave her head—and tell him to be quick about it, as I want to examine her cranium, which seems surprisingly healthy, this very evening."

V.

Later, Captain Bruerovich, as he had said, went to examine the creature. With her head now shaven, her already large eyes appeared even larger. He was surprised by the delicacy of her skin; touched her face and noticed that it excited the action of her larynx; touched her cranium, took note of all the surface peculiarities, letting his long thin fingers, nimble as wasps, travel from the ethmoid bone to the mandible, and then back to the sphenoid.

Around the lofty heights of his mind, thoughts gathered, dispersed, gathered again, like drifting clouds. Infamy slaughtered by fame. The discovery caged, displayed throughout the capitals of Europe, astonishing princes and princes-elect, loosening their purse strings while making the women of court squeal like mice.

The captain spent the following days in assiduous study of the creature. The desk in his cabin was strewn with notes, measurements, diagrams.

"Nature, hereditary, has fitted her with a most unusual structure—and I must ask myself why."

Gauge her jaw, assess her limbs; try and determine, along Anaximanderrian lines, by what transmutation she had come into being; if there was any possibility of a common progenitor.

VI.

"A ship to larboard, captain."

"What variety of ship?"

"A galleon."

"Nationality?"

"She's flying a Portuguese flag."

The captain finished the sentence he was writing, placed his grey goose quill pen back in its holder, rose from his seat and made his way on deck.

"What do you think?" he asked Lagoverde.

"It is a large vessel."

"Indeed. And undoubtedly holds booty to match its size."

"But it is clearly a risky enterprise. There must be three men to every one of ours aboard her."

"True enough, but our men are restless. If we pursue the prize, they will fight hard, if we forgo it, they might turn morose."

"Yes, they are thirsty for blood."

"First we must cripple this oversized bastard," the captain said. And then to his chief gunner: "Jacques, cut away its masts."

The Sparrow was armed with nine bronze cannons, a few of these ornately decorated with scrolls and escutcheons. The gunners worked off a guidance table that the captain had written up, using chain-shot to take down the rigging of the ship, after which they fired carcasses, incendiary ammunition, in excess of forty rounds per gun until they were no longer safe to load.

It was then that they boarded; faced the odds of over two hundred to their seventy; the deck a veritable hell.

The captain calmly ran his cutlass through one man, exploded his pistol at another.

Fire danced on all sides to a chorus of screams and curses. Heads tumbled from shoulders and limbs, in bursts of blood, went flying from trunks. Faces distended in horror, some men were thrown overboard to be swallowed by the waves, others butchered on the spot.

A Portuguese grimaced so that his gums could be seen. Bull-Milo, wielding a large axe, lopped off his left arm while, nearby, one of the crew of the Sparrow felt a projectile take off one of his ears—a far better fate than that of the first mate of the galleon who, moments later, had a bullet shatter his skull.

Captain Nikola Bruerovich nodded his head in approval, looked to his left, saw: Mademoiselle Savage standing before him, a huge knife in her hand, her arms flecked with blood.

Their eyes met for a moment. Then our hero turned and continued his methodical work of exterminating all resistance aboard the ship; after which, the deck having been made slippery with gore, the hold was inspected: good quantities of minted silver and cochineal, as well as other items of value.

That night, while the men were celebrating their victory and mourning the death of their shipmates—both functions requiring the playing at reverse Diogenese (barrel in stomach rather than stomach in barrel)—the captain stayed sequestered in his cabin. The next day, the crew were cheerful, singing and joking while they went about their tasks, for the voyage was now turning profitable, but the captain seemed downcast, his frown longer than usual, his manners more clipped. His soup that day he barely touched; of claret he took two cups.

VII.

Lagoverde was presented with a sight that surprised him. The looking glass, long neglected, was now hung, its surface polished, prominently on one wall where the table of trigonometry had once been. The captain himself had no time for talk, for he was busy—washing his wig!

The first mate scratched his long chin, made his way to the kitchen.

La Motte sat with a length of light blue silk on his lap, a needle in hand.

"What are you doing?" the Italian asked.

"Making a set of female garments."

"Eh! And who, pray tell, are they for?"

"Well, the only femme on board obviously. Captain's orders. It seems her grass skirt has gone out of fashion."

Lagoverde went on deck.

"Who would have believed it," he murmured to himself, gazing out at the bloody sun as it descended beneath the waves.

VIII.

As bizarre as their romance might have seemed, it was fitting—for no normal woman could have ever thawed the rigid ice of Bruerovich's heart—the task being reserved for something else—a specimen; a dark cave full of slime and spiders for the first time flooded with light. And a strange but true fact: the most violent passions are often between beings who share no common language.

The crew did not laugh or joke over the matter. For they knew well enough how lonely the life of a sailor was and there was a certain pathetic element in this high-seas romance which made them silent on the subject; their lips sealed by a mixture of awe and pity—maybe even fear.

And it is often difficult to say why one being is attracted to another and why it is that every man, at some point in his life, will fall in love. There was not a great outward change in the captain's behaviour. He was still as rigid as ever, his lips still as unsmiling, but behind the closed door of his cabin, those slender strips of flesh became tender.

It was during this period that, casting their fishing nets, the pirates pulled up from the sea a strange creature—a serpent with a head that closely resembled that of a human child. La Motte diced it into sections and served it, batter-fried, for lunch.

IX.

The weeks that followed were prosperous, full of butchery, fire and shrieks. The ship flew past cone-shaped islands, glided along the rippling scales of the sea, skimming over white horses and dying them red with foaming blood, the crew happily indulging in despicable behaviour. They attacked no less than seven ships—two Dutch, a Spanish, a French, two English and another Portuguese—divesting them of gold and silver, cochineal and indigo.

It seemed that the native girl had brought them good luck.

The captain had taught her to use pistols, had given her a brace of them, and these were stuffed into a sash of bright blue silk, which was wrapped below her mouth, around her thighs. She wore a pair of loose-fitting, brightly-coloured trousers; a brocade vest, parrot-green in colour; and a tasselled hat, shaped like the roof of a pavilion.

And she, in these adventures, would always become excited, homicidal—a terror to those poor souls attacked—for to them it seemed truly as if they were being confronted by maniacs and monsters, a band come from hell.

She found a certain ecstasy in extreme violence. During one assault, she jumped on a man, straddled his neck and choked him to death with her thighs. On another occasion she was caught gnawing on a human foot, but this in no way disgusted the captain—possibly he even found it charming, as lovers often do the foibles of their beloved.

And on those days when the fighting was the most ferocious, the native girl's appetite for love was most keen, and Bruerovich, trembling, pressed his lips to those hands, beneath the nails of which might have been found deposits of human flesh.

X.

Dark grey. Steady, light precipitation. She leaned against the gunwale, her eyes gazed off, dreamy, letting her body absorb the drizzle, which ran over her face, made her clothes cling tightly to her lithe form.

When it rained she was always like that, lost to the world, absorbed in nature; and the captain kept his distance, being to some degree awed; and later, glancing in her eyes, he thought he could make out far away vistas, palm fronds, mysterious sun-drenched beaches on which beings swirled together in worship of the waves—an enigma his analytical mind refused to confront; for Mademoiselle Savage was an odd mixture of boldness and shyness, brutal enthusiasm and sadness. She could scratch and bite but also hug tenderly. She carried with her some primordial inscrutability, was a path which led back to those days of formless void; waters under heaven and boiling rock when the world was born.

"What do you make of her?" La Motte one day discreetly asked the first mate.

"She is an animal picked up from the islands."

"Which means?"

"Just that."

XI.

A dead calm. Evening. The captain stood on deck, gazing out at a purplish sunset, Lagoverde by his side.

"I think this will be my last voyage."

"Indeed?"

"Indeed."

"You are retiring then?"

"I have always thought Greece would be a nice place to go . . . to live peacefully, to study the marine life there while walking over the land once inhabited by Pythagoras and Sophocles."

It was at this point that their discourse was cut short by the approach of Martini.

"Pierre, the powder monkey, is ill," the latter said.

"It is probably simply a bilious complaint caused by some bad piece of fish La Motte served," was Bruerovich's comment.

"That is not the kind of sickness the boy has. He has a fever."

The captain and his first mate went to investigate, saw the boy lying in his hammock, face glistening with sweat. He was wracked with pain and coughed violently.

"How long have you been feeling ill?" the captain asked.

"I haven't been quite myself for the past few days," the patient murmured. "If you have something that would make me feel better . . ."

Nikola Bruerovich examined his body, saw the rash on his chest.

"It is typhus."

"This is bad," Lagoverde said.

"Yes, it is. I want the entire ship to be cleaned, from top to bottom—throw the bedding overboard, swab the cabins with vinegar. And by no means let any man near my cabin."

The next day the boy died and they wrapped his body in sheets and threw it overboard.

"It's never nice to throw a colleague to the fish," sharp-bearded Amraphel said, "but it does mean more grain for the rest of us."

XII.

The captain's orders were followed to the letter and the problem seemed to be under control, as, for three days there was no sign of the pest. But then, on the fourth, Bull-Milo was found unable to rise from his hammock and, eight hours later, he died.

That same evening two more members of the crew came down with the sickness. The next day another two. The day after a full seven.

These men, who regularly faced death in the form of battle with smiles on their faces, trembled before this invisible, virulent enemy. Some stained their throats with rum. Others remembered prayers of their childhood. But strong and weak, drunk and sober alike were ravaged.

Men writhed in their hammocks; a few lay on deck, hollow eyes staring up at the blue sky. One, hallucinating, saw the ship enveloped in the flesh of a giant sea snail. Another, singing, said he was having a musical competition with demons.

While some recovered, others did not. Within a week a half-dozen crew members had been cast to the waves.

XIII.

On a certain morning Lagoverde knocked on the door of the captain's cabin.

"Do not come in," was heard from within.

A moment later the captain showed himself.

"She has got the pest," he said.

Lagoverde did not reply. There was nothing he could say and truly this world is as fleeting as a flash of lightning.

She became delirious and Bruerovich found it difficult to keep her in bed.

He tried, in that brief period of time, to squeeze some answers from nature, to unweave its very fibre. He frantically studied his books, consulted his mind, ground together powders; made the girl drink water infused with sulphur, smeared her body with tar diluted with spirits, filled the cabin with vapours and smoke.

Dozing off briefly, he imagined that thousands of hands were crawling towards him, pushing themselves against his lips, demanding their pressure; a frightful obscenity that transferred itself to inanimate objects when he awoke—glasses, table, grey goose quill pen all begging him for his affection.

XIV.

Her breathing was very weak; her face appeared to be melting like a candle. Stomach exposed, the mouth thereon wore an awful grin. Her large eyes stared at the captain, the pupils endowed with a bronze immobility. Then she turned her head away.

He got up and left the cabin. His heels clicked against the boards; his steps steady. The few on deck went about their business in silence. The gentle splash of water against the hull.

A bubble.

A drop of dew.

He stood on the bridge of the ship and gazed out over the water—an endless meadow, a vast blue-green carpet. The ship floated on the lonely sea, in the distance a mass of dark clouds rested on the horizon and his lips were set firm.

XV.

When he re-entered his cabin, he was surprised to find that she was not beneath her bedding, but rather sat on the floor, completely naked, in an odd position; ankles locked behind neck; body covered by a thin, slimy film.

"You need to get back to bed," Bruerovich said, approaching.

The jaws on her stomach opened; she snapped at him, would not let him near her; and so he stood back, watched as she began to shiver violently, writhe; jaws now protruding from belly, stretching themselves forth; and eyes migrating.

Around her he noticed gobbets of flesh, toes, terminal members of the hand.

"What transformation is this!"

Gasping, she began to flop around the cabin; gills quivering, a deposit of sticky yellowish gelatine left on the floorboards in her wake.

The captain's right hand agitated, as if it had a volition of its own, wished to seek out a quill and take notes, but the convulsive situation before him made him see necessity and so he called in the aid of a few men and, together, they cast a net around her, dragged her on deck, a swirl of tempestuous movement.

"It wants water," Lagoverde said.

Captain Nikola Bruerovich was silent for a moment, and then gave the order, watched as the load was hoisted to the gunwale and, a moment later, with a splash, the object fell into the blue; a glistening flash and she was gone, lost in that expanse which might be called the largest of teardrops.

But there was no time to recite poems, no time to sing deep ballads of passion for freedom or dolorous life.

"Ship to port, Captain. A frigate."

"Flag?"

"English."

"How many are we?"

"Forty-seven."

The captain turned to Lagoverde. "Do you think we can take her?" he asked.

"I do not know, but I would not mind killing a few Englishmen."

"And you shall."